She Scoops to Conquer

A Mystery by Robin Brandeis

NEW VICTORIA PUBLISHERS

Published by New Victoria Publishers Inc., PO Box 27
Norwich, VT 05055
A Feminist Literary and Cultural Organization founded in 1976.

Cover design Claudia McKay

Printed and bound in Canada
1   2   3   4   2005   2004   2003   2002

This is a total work of fiction. Any resemblance to persons living
or dead is purely coincidental.

Library of Congress Cataloging-in-Publication Data

Brandeis, Robin, 1961-
  She scoops to conquer : a mystery / by Robin Brandeis.
      p. cm.
  ISBN 1-892281-17-1
  1. Women journalists--Fiction. 2. Lesbians--Fiction. I. Title.
PS3602.R35 S47 2002
813'.6--dc21

                                        2002006879

To Valerie—
For Always

Thanks to the staff of New Victoria Publishers for all your suggestions and patience. Special thanks to my Louisville Writers Group: Mina, Jesse, Kathy, and Chris, for giving me great advice and keeping me on track! And to Valerie and Leslie — each of you were always there, in your own way, to encourage me and show that you believed in me. I love you both!

Chapter One

I was so sound asleep when the telephone rang, it didn't wake me. It resurrected me. When my fingers finally found the receiver and dragged it to my face, Terry from the paper was on the other end.

"Lane, sorry to bother you and all, but Rosemary said if you didn't answer to just let it keep ringing until you did."

"Rosemary," I moaned. "How did she know I was at home?" I was being sarcastic. It had to be at least three a.m. I had finally crawled into bed at eight after having endured a grueling day that had begun at four the previous morning.

"You know Rosemary. She doesn't believe you really put in eight hour days."

"I sell more papers for her than any other reporter on the staff, and she's telling garbage like that about me behind my back—"

Terry interrupted. "It's not personal, Lane. You can't take her seriously. Rosemary just talks off the top of her head. She's always been suspicious of the investigative reporters because they're out of the office so much. She just rattles off stuff like, 'They say they're working weeks and weeks on a story, but they're really just going to matinees.'"

"Really? She ought to assign someone to investigate it."

"Lane…"

"Tell her I'll take it. I can do my research at the cinemas. Kill two birds with one stone. Get the big story and still catch all my movies. Why did you call me?"

"There's been a hit and run in Butchertown. It may be a DOA. Dale is sick in bed with the flu or I'd have called him."

"It's been a long time since I've covered car accidents."

"Take your camera."

"Sure. What time is it?"

"Quarter to ten."

"Quarter to ten? Quarter to ten?! I thought I'd been asleep for hours!"

"The police are still at the scene. You can make it if you hurry."

"Gotcha." I was pulling on the clothes nearest to me on the floor—dress jeans and a summer blazer. "I'll have to write it at the scene and phone it in."

"That'll be fine. And Lane," Terry was still trying to appease me, "Don't let Rosemary get to you. The rest of us know what all you do."

I hopped on one foot to the kitchen for some caffeine because I was trying to tie my running shoes at the same time. In my fridge there was a six-pack of soft drinks and leftovers from a restaurant meal I had meant to throw out last week. I live in one of four apartments in a converted Victorian home in the Highlands neighborhood, which is a few miles east of downtown Louisville. The Highlands neighborhood is full of these grand old homes standing shoulder to shoulder to each other, and all about a hundred years old. What my apartment lacks in the way of modern amenities, however—such as water pressure—it makes up for in character. I have polished wood floors, ten-foot ceilings, and large, tall windows in every room overlooking mature trees. A couple of blocks from me is Bardstown Road, which is a crowded thoroughfare into the wee hours of almost any morning. Bardstown Road has the largest concentration of restaurants of any place in Louisville—fifty restaurants within three miles, most of them one-of-a-kind, and any two of them in a year the hottest new place to eat in Louisville. Which is most fortunate for me. I never cook.

Grabbing my keys, I skipped down the stairs and went out back to the parking area behind my building. I own an old green Jaguar. I like to think of it as an antique, but really it's just old. I bought it five years ago, used, with just over a hundred thousand miles on it. Although I have been religious about oil changes and other maintenance, the guy who owned it before me wasn't, and his sins are unjustly haunting me. It now has over two hundred thousand miles on it, and its days are numbered, but I continue forking over the occasional couple hundred bucks to my mechanic simply because I dread shopping for another used car. I started the Jag with a little trouble, made a right and then another right onto Bardstown Road, and headed toward Broadway.

On the drive there, to wake myself, I made a mental list of things I needed to do. I was wrapping up one project at work and now was the time to squeeze in some housekeeping before I got started on another. I had some dry-cleaning to take in. I was running low on detergent. I needed to check in on my grandmother to see if she was running low on groceries.

Inwardly I winced. If I talked to my grandmother, she would ask if

I had called my parents. Why should I? I would want to ask her. They never call me.

From Broadway, I made a right, and the character of the neighborhood began to change within the block. Metropolitan Louisville can give the impression of being not so much a city as a patchwork of very diverse neighborhoods or small towns all pushed up against one another. Downtown has a completely different ambiance from Butchertown, which is unlike upscale St. Matthews or historical Crescent Hill. There you won't find a neighborhood bar like you will in Germantown or a coffeehouse like you will in the Highlands neighborhood.

Nevertheless, we all share the small, skyscraper-lined city of Louisville, which sits on the edge of the Ohio River and gleams like a small lavender jewel on a clear summer night. Except for two minutes each year, during the world-famous Kentucky Derby horse race in May, the rest of the world doesn't notice us much.

I made a left in Butchertown where the old stockyards used to stand, which gave this particular community its name. Located at the edge of Louisville's city limits, Butchertown is a patchy mix of businesses and low-income housing which spills down from Market Street into the muddy shore of the Ohio. The humidity of the warm summer night made the air heavy and gave it a fog-like quality in the darkness, which increased the closer I drove to the river. I could see the lights of the police cars and an ambulance long before I arrived. The watery air gave them halos the colors of steel blue and blood red. I parked and walked a block to the scene.

Yellow police tape cordoned off the area. As I approached the tape, I caught sight of the victim and stopped short. I hadn't expected it to be a child. He was African-American, maybe fifteen years old, dressed in a blue University of Kentucky T-shirt, khaki shorts with buckled pockets, and new white tennis shoes. He lay in the street on his back in an awkward pose, the only visible blood on his chest, which I thought strange for a hit and run. He was dead; no one stood near except for a police photographer who was busy taking photos.

I made a half circle around the body, staying behind the tape and make my way toward an officer further off who stood guard against possible spectators. Glancing back casually at the body, I stopped again. The boy was facing my direction. He looked like a child asleep—a child who slept like a child, easily with nothing to fear. A pang of grief gripped me unexpectedly. Perhaps his parents had seen him looking just like that last night, asleep on the sofa in front of the television or in his bed. I lowered my camera. I would cover the story without pictures of the body.

Glancing around, I wondered where his parents were. There was only a handful of police and a few reporters across the street. No one was crying. I circled the tape, then took a few photos of the police officer who was standing guard and a few more of the detectives, just to have something to take back to the paper.

One of the police officers approached, so I showed him my press ID. He was polite and answered a couple of my questions, telling me that an older woman had called the police station to report a hit and run, but once the police arrived and took a closer look, they discovered what appeared to be bullet wounds in the chest. The boy did not appear to have been hit by a vehicle. The officer then asked me to move away to wait for more information.

Several yards to my right a few other members of the media had gathered, also waiting for interviews. I headed in their direction. As I stepped to the curb, the roar of an engine took me by surprise. The small media crowd tensed as a car came screaming around our corner. The brakes locked up and the car skidded to a stop, inches from the police tape. The driver, a photographer, leaped out and began taking photos of the dead youth. I looked at the car. Printed on the side was *The Metropolitan Inquirer,* "Your Eye on Louisville." I wasn't too surprised at the photographer's behavior. The *Metropolitan*—that other newspaper in town—follows the philosophy, "If it bleeds, it leads."

A few other reporters with me began a low grumbling. This was your typical, brash *Metropolitan* reporting style. Arrive at the scene, get the bloodiest photos, then splash it all in neon color on the front page the next day, along with only the most sensational part of the information.

"Depth" and "insight" were not words you often heard applied to the *Metropolitan.* Local reporters, in radio and television as well as on my paper, were merciless in making fun of the paper, often comparing Louisville's *Metropolitan Inquirer* to the gossip rags in grocery aisles. I, however, sometimes wondered if everyone's sarcasm toward the paper—mine included—didn't mask more than a little bit of envy.

The *Metropolitan,* despite having an editorial policy inches from that of a Hollywood tabloid (or maybe because of it) was wildly—and I mean wildly—successful. Privately, I was certain that there wasn't one grumbling reporter standing in this crowd that didn't eye the circulation numbers of the *Metropolitan,* or the paychecks of their staff—with a little awe.

The same police officer who had approached me approached the

Metropolitan photographer, and a mild argument ensued. The photographer threw a few curse words at the police officer, and the officer threatened to arrest him. After that, the photographer got back in his car, slammed the door, and drove away.

"He told him!" someone in the crowd muttered. A titter of stifled laughter rose from the group. I could feel the tension ease somewhat.

A man stood in the bright light of a television camera interviewing a white-haired African American woman, probably the woman who had called the police. I edged over to where they were and waited my turn. Out of the corner of my eye I could see a blond man with the boyish good looks of a young Robert Redford approaching me. It was Dirk Rutgers. Dirk was a television reporter for one of the local stations. He was a nice guy but, unfortunately, he was single and had a little crush on me. Conversation with Dirk was always pleasant, but at the end usually left me exhausted from the date dodging. However, he was good at what he did and we sometimes shared information.

"Hey, Lane!" Dirk smiled. Self-consciously, he straightened his tie.

"Hi, Dirk," I turned to him, smiling warmly. I always try to be kind to him. After all, he is a nice guy and it isn't his fault that no matter how badly he wants to date me, he's still a man. I indicated the woman being interviewed. "How was she involved?"

"She's the one who reported the hit and run that wasn't a hit and run."

"What do you think about the shooting?"

Dirk shook his head. "I don't know. Could be gang related. Could have been a drive-by. It took awhile for Louisville to get gangs, but now we've got 'em like everyone else."

"I wonder why she reported it as a hit and run?"

"Ask her! No one else has." He glanced at me approvingly. "Congratulations on the investigative story you broke about the mayor's office last week. That was brilliant! All the TV stations followed you on that one, did you notice? They all gave your paper credit for the story, but in case you didn't notice, our station named you personally."

I grinned at him. Publicity like that was invaluable to anyone's career. "That wouldn't have been because of a suggestion on your part, would it?"

Dirk looked shy. "I just say, give credit where credit is due. How long had that guy been skimming money from the city budget, anyway?"

"Not long. He'd gotten away with less than thirty thousand. I think that's why the mayor's office is falling all over me about this. It wasn't enough money to be that big of an embarrassment to them yet, so they're just grateful that someone caught him."

"Well, once again, you scored another ace for the *Louisville Daily*. I bet that story sold a few papers, huh? Did that help you guys pick up circulation a bit?"

I sighed. "Well, Dirk, let's just say that we'll be able to pay the light bill another month. You know how it is at the *Daily*."

Dirk looked away, frowning. "Well, you guys hang in there, you hear? You folks are the only real paper in town, you know that? Not like the *Metropolitan*. You guys have class. And journalistic integrity. And—"

"—bills." I concluded for him. "And debt. Yeah, we've got lots of debt! Oh…and tiny little paychecks."

He laughed. "Hey, when we've finished here, and as soon as we get our stories in, how about a late supper? My treat."

"Dirk, I'm sorry. I just can't. The hours I've been putting in on the mayor's story have exhausted me; I'm still doing final follow-ups. I'm hitting the sack tonight after this."

"Sure." He smiled, but I could tell he was disappointed. Dirk has always had too much pride to ask why I never go out with him; otherwise I would have told him by now. Perhaps it is the Southerner in me, but I consider my sexual orientation a personal matter. My friends know, many of my work acquaintances know, and I am often involved in gay and lesbian causes. But, here at the top of the buckle of the Bible Belt, people tend to have twisted perceptions of gays and lesbians. I want to be sure I'm close enough to the people I tell that I can overcome their stereotypes before their stereotypes overcame me.

Dirk nudged me. "Looks like you're on!"

"Thanks! See you, Dirk!" I gave his arm a friendly squeeze, then stepped in quickly to speak to the woman who had called the police. She shook hands with the television reporter who had taped the interview, then turned to me. She looked tired, but agreed to talk.

Her name was Mildred Wilcox. She was a retired nurse, she said, sixty-three years old. Since none of the other reporters had asked her about the hit and run call, I asked Mrs. Wilcox why she had called it in that way. She wrapped her arms around herself as if she were cold. She was clearly not impressed with being the woman of the hour.

"I was driving home after visiting with my daughter and my two grandchildren. My daughter and her husband are both attorneys and live out in the East End. I had turned the corner a couple of blocks away when I was nearly run off the road by a pickup truck. I had only driven

10

another block when I saw something in the road, and I got frightened because it looked like a person. As I got closer it became more clear, and all I could think was, 'That idiot in the truck ran over a child!' I picked up my cell phone and called 911, stopped my car and ran over to help—but he was already dead, poor thing. So I just watched over him until the police and the ambulance arrived."

"What did the truck look like?" I asked.

"Oh, he wasn't hit by the truck. Don't report that. He was shot. I only thought he was hit by the truck because I passed that crazy driver a little way back."

"Yes, I know. I just thought the speeding truck might somehow be related."

"Well, it was one of those little ones, red, with a white topper on the back," she replied.

"Did you catch the make or model?"

She raised an eyebrow at me. "No. I'm afraid I was much more occupied with keeping my car on the road. But if my husband had been with me, he could have answered that for you. He can tell you what kind of car it is even at night, just by looking at the headlights and grill. This one was missing a headlight, though, on its left side—like it had lost it in an accident or something.

"Out of curiosity, what's your hunch? Do you think the killer was the one driving the truck?"

She shrugged. "How would I know? He was certainly driving like he wanted to get out of there fast. But maybe he didn't have a cell phone like I do and was racing to phone the police himself. I don't know."

"The driver of the truck was a man?"

"Oh, I don't know," she corrected herself. "I didn't see the driver. But the point is, the truck passed me two blocks back. It may not have had anything to do with the murder."

"Do you live down here, Mrs. Wilcox?" I asked.

"Not exactly. I live about a mile from here."

"Did you recognize the deceased? Was he someone you'd seen in Butchertown before?"

"I'd never seen him before, but I don't pay that much attention to the teenagers. My crowd's a little older." She smiled weakly at her joke.

"How do you feel about living around here? Do you feel like it's a pretty safe neighborhood, or is there a lot of crime?"

She sighed and glanced around. "Until tonight, I've felt pretty comfortable. This shook me a bit, as you might imagine. My daughter keeps nagging her father and me to move out closer to her because she doesn't think it's safe for a couple of old folks like us, but I've lived here most of my life, you know? And moving seems like such a big job when you're my age."

I thanked Mrs. Wilcox as another television reporter stepped in and began asking her similar questions. I finished writing notes to myself, then found a seat on the curb to think and wait.

A half hour later, the police came over to give us their report and take questions. I had just one. Had anyone else called 911?

At three twenty-three the next afternoon, I stormed into Rosemary's office, the afternoon edition in hand. She glanced at her watch, took off her glasses and looked up at me from behind her desk.

"Good afternoon, Lane. Just get up? I hope you didn't skip breakfast just to rush in on our account."

Even Rosemary's wiry red hair seemed to glow sarcasm. I waved the paper in front of her face. "What's the meaning of this?"

She ignored my question and looked at my clothes. I was wearing jeans, a T-shirt and running shoes, and my skin was glistening with perspiration. "Is this how you dress for work?" she snapped at me. "Is this how you represent us to the public? Who's going to give you a serious interview with you looking like that!"

"I was following someone."

She looked up at me. "I don't think he came in here."

I glared at her. "I was following someone for a companion article to that story I broke last week about the mayor's office. Don't respond to that, I don't expect you to understand. If you want to know more, talk to Harry. I want to talk to you about this." I threw the paper on her desk.

"All right, Miss Hot-Shot Investigative Reporter. What's the matter with it?"

"You buried my story."

"What story?"

"The kid who got shot last night in Butchertown! You buried it in the obituaries!"

"Well, he died, didn't he?"

I didn't answer. I was busy trying to burn holes through her head with my eyes.

"Look, Lane, if this is what you're worried about." she opened a drawer and pulled out a copy of the *Metropolitan Inquirer*. "The *Metropolitan* buried it, too. See?" She turned to the page and pointed

12

to the article. "And they didn't get any good photos, either. So, relax! Nobody scooped you."

"That's not the point," I growled. Of course I had seen the *Metropolitan* that morning. I had breathed a sigh of relief when I saw their photos hadn't been included—not because I had chosen not to take any photos of the body, but out of respect for the young man who had been murdered. Apparently—and this took me by surprise—the *Metropolitan* had at least one person on their staff with a measure of human sensitivity. "This isn't about the *Metropolitan*," I said firmly. "This is about us—the *Daily*."

"No. I think this is about you—and your ego."

"What?!"

"This may come as tough news to you, Miss Montgomery. You may be our best investigative reporter, but not every word that drips from your Midas fingers is front page gold. Some stories are just obituary page articles, no matter who wrote the copy!"

"But he was murdered!"

"Yes. He was murdered," she said coldly.

"And you left out all the information about the truck!"

"Oh, yes, the truck." she rolled her eyes. "What was that, anyway? You went on and on about the truck, but it wasn't even a hit and run!"

"The truck may have been involved! I was the only reporter who got that information!"

"Lane, face it—the story wasn't worth the number of words you gave it!" Rosemary grimaced.

"What does that mean?"

"The incident just wasn't that important of a story!"

"I disagree."

Rosemary straightened her thin body in her chair. "Lane, you know there is an element of censorship involved in the news media simply because we can't report everything. It's just not possible. So you know the paper is going to lean toward reporting the stories that sell papers—"

"And most people in the city—" I interrupted, "African-Americans, for the most part—can't afford the little luxury of a subscription to the paper?" I was nearly growling.

"Don't change the subject. I told you his murder just wasn't that interesting."

"Why? Because he was from the city?"

She eyed me. "You know there are more killings in the city than out in the suburbs. It's not especially unusual to see murders in the city.

13

At least it's not front page stuff."

"But this was a kid."

"Yes. And my hunch is that by keeping it on the back pages we're just saving the family some pain."

I couldn't believe her reasoning. As clearly as I could think at this point, I was trying to decide whether if I strangled her now would it be first degree murder, or second? In all honesty I would have to admit under oath that I had been thinking of it for at least five minutes. But did five minutes constitute pre-meditation? And what of our rather frequent and sordid run-ins in the past? I would be hanged on circumstantial evidence, if nothing else.

"That statement has no basis in fact," I retorted. "You are making a prejudicial assumption that because this child was poor and living in the city that he was a bad kid—not to mention that you're also implying that he was somehow responsible for his own murder! That sounds vaguely familiar, Rosemary, like the opinion that a rape victim asked for it!"

"Whoa—I didn't say that!" I'd gotten to her with that one. Her pink skin was becoming blotched. "I've been at this job long enough to have a feel for certain things, Lane. Answer this for me—why was that kid wandering around three miles from home when he was killed?"

"I don't know. You tell me."

"And what was he doing so far from home after dark?"

"I don't know."

"Where are his parents? Why is his grandmother raising him?"

I shrugged. "I didn't have time to collect all that, Rosemary. I had an hour before the late deadline. That was just enough time to visit the murder scene. I didn't have time for background interviews."

"Why didn't his grandmother know where he was? Did she ever know where he was?"

"I don't know. I don't know! Why do you assume she didn't ever know where he was?"

Rosemary didn't answer. She just looked at me as if she'd made her point.

Pressing my fingers together and leaning over her desk, I spoke as calmly as I could. "Rosemary, as I tried to state at the beginning of this conversation, this is really not about you or me or our opinions, but about our paper—the *Daily*."

She inhaled loudly as if she was going to interrupt, but I kept talking. "Three years ago a white teenager from the East End went to a party at a friend's house downtown and later that night was mugged

14

and stabbed to death on the way back to his car. Do you remember that?"

"Yes, of course I remember that. What of it?"

"That was front-page news. That was not only front-page news the next day, it was front-page news every day until the police had a suspect. Then the trial—do you remember the trial?—the trial led the news every day until the convicted killer was behind bars."

"So?"

"So..." I took a deep breath—this was like teaching table manners to the Three Stooges. "A white teenager gets murdered downtown and it leads the news for months. A black teenager gets murdered downtown and we bury it on the obituary page. It smacks of racism. It more than smacks of it. This is a heavyweight championship wallop you can hear all the way across town, courtesy of our very own Muhammad Ali."

I seemed to lose her with this last metaphor. She struggled with it for a moment. Then all at once a light went on behind her eyes—a dim light, the yellow porch bulb that you use to keep bugs away kind of light—but, nevertheless, a light. I was stunned. I had gotten through to her. I had actually gotten through to her.

Mortified, she said, "You mean we're going to get letters."

"What?"

"Letters! We're going to get letters! Don't you get it? People are going to think this is a racist thing!"

I smacked my forehead, but answered calmly, "Yeah. People are going to think this is a racist thing."

"You've got to get us a good profile piece on this kid."

"I do?"

"Yes, you do. You're the one who got us into this mess."

"I did what?"

"A basic second day follow-up will be fine, something about his background, with attribution. I'll need it by ten. I'll slug it for the front page, late edition. I bet we're getting phone calls already. I hate stories like this."

"Rosemary, do I really have to do this? I was only called in because Dale was out sick with the flu. Maybe he could pick up where I left off? I'm very heavy into another story right now."

"Dale is still out sick with the flu."

"I can't do it by tonight. I need more time."

"You can do it by ten. That gives you six hours."

"Rosemary! This is a biographical piece, not a five-alarm fire! It can wait a day! Besides, I need time to do interviews! I have no guarantee I can catch anybody who can tell me anything about him at this late hour!"

"So, you'll do it?"

I hate when she corners me like that. "I've been working eighteen hours a day on this mayor's office piece and I was going to get a full night's sleep tonight for the first time in a week! Don't you have anyone else?" I stopped cold. Looking Rosemary right in the eye, horrified, I asked, "What time is it?"

"What?"

"What time is it?"

She looked down at her watch. "Twenty-five till four."

I gasped. "I...I've got to go..." I stuttered. "I've got an appointment! What am I doing here? I'm late." I started out of the room, then ran back in. "Is my camera in here? Did I bring my camera in here?" I glanced around, then remembered. "No. I brought the paper in here. My camera is in my office. 'Bye, Rosemary." I dashed out.

On my way out the door the second time Rosemary yelled, "Three o'clock tomorrow! I want that bio piece on my desk by three o'clock for the early edition, you understand?! I want plenty of time to do any rewrite! Do you hear me? Montgomery? Montgomery!"

Chapter Two

Fourteen stories below me, concrete and traffic writhed like a nest of snakes. I glanced at the clock tower across the street and six stories down. Three fifty-seven. Just looking at it ignited an electrical storm in my stomach.

Instinctively, I took a step back. I was standing—or rather, swaying gently in the breeze—on the fire escape of the ancient Fourth Street Dental Office Tower. The fire escape was narrow and doddering, and the landing beneath my feet was nothing but rusty metal slats spaced widely apart. If I'd been any skinnier, I would have fallen through.

I gripped the slender railing. Why did I get myself into these things? As an investigative reporter, I usually prepare my spying strategies carefully in advance. But for this little adventure, I had decided to improvise. Now I wondered if I hadn't gotten myself in over my head. I'm not usually squeamish about heights, but something about the way this structure whined when I breathed bothered me.

I'd learned about the access to this fire escape from a conversation I had overheard last winter during my semiannual dental checkup, one floor down. The medical complex had just implemented a new no-smoking policy, and a teenage girl who was working as my dentist's receptionist was bragging to the hygienist that she had found a way to beat it. There was this broken emergency exit door on the top floor, she said, which led out to the building's original fire escape. So she sneaked out onto that old fire escape landing on her breaks to grab a smoke. I don't know why, but that comment had filed itself away in my mind. Funny, the things that stick in your head.

As I wrapped my fingers tighter around the metal rail, I was gaining an unusual admiration for the lengths that teenager would go to continue her nicotine habit. Unfortunately, though, I had a four p.m. appointment on the roof, and four o'clock was just three minutes away. I resigned myself to the fact that I was going to have to loosen my grip and actually move up one more story.

Securing my camera-case strap around my neck, I edged my way to the right, putting my hand on the final ladder of the fire escape. This last long ladder, held by a few bolts to the brick wall of the building, reached from the platform on which I was standing to the roof. As I put my hand on it, it squeaked and shifted almost imperceptibly to the left. I stared at it a minute, wondering if I was idiotic enough to climb this piece of junk.

I was. I turned to face the ladder. "Well, Lane," I mumbled to myself, "if you fall, just choose carefully where you fall and you'll land on the fire escape landing. If you miss, you're going to feel really stupid for about seven seconds."

I put my right foot on the first rung, gripping the handrails with both hands. The thought occurred to me that maybe investigative reporters carry some kind of gene that makes us take unwarranted risks. That was about the only explanation I could come up with to explain my behavior half the time. It was either that or admit I was succumbing to one of those stupid, macho impulses that we lesbians walk around pretending we're above having. Holding my breath, I hoisted myself up, putting my full weight on the ladder. I hesitated, then bounced once, testing the bolts that held it to the brick while I was still close to the landing. Okay so far.

I put my left foot on the next rung and pulled myself up. Still good. I stepped up two more rungs.

A horn sounded belligerently below me, followed by the screech of screaming tires. I glanced down into the traffic, where a cab had narrowly missed a young girl crossing in the middle of the block. My head swayed, pulling me toward the pavement. Grabbing at the metal handrails, I closed my eyes and panicked.

Not smart. Why had I looked down? Adrenaline shooting through my veins, I hugged the ladder for a full minute before opening my eyes to concentrate on the rust-colored brick just six inches from my face. Just me and the brick, me and the brick; don't think about how far away the ground is. But the heavy, pungent smell of the city buses reached even to this height, and the traffic rang with a hollow sound, as if I was scaling the side of a giant barrel in which cars were driving round and round.

I was running out of time. I had to keep moving. I closed my eyes and stepped up another two rungs. All at once a high-pitched note rang out, followed by a slow, strange give in the ladder. Then, suddenly, the ladder jolted downward, hard.

Metal screeched against metal. My eyes opened in shock and I threw my arms around the rung in front of me. For a moment the ladder hesitated, and then I felt that sort of weightlessness that happens when one's center of gravity begins to shift and my stomach crept to my throat.

The ladder was tilting backwards.

My heart pounded thunder in my ears as I felt myself falling away from the building. I held one rung in a death-grip with my left hand and with my right I was grabbing frantically at the brick wall in front of me. Desperately, I tried to wedge my fingers between the bricks to hold just one brick to pull myself back. But no matter how hard I tried, I couldn't grab it. I couldn't get a grip on it. It just couldn't be done. It was not meant for gripping.

Suddenly, and for the first time in my life, I wanted long fingernails. Long, beautiful nails like they advertise in magazines and beauty salons. Long, beautiful nails like my mother was always telling me I should have. She knew this kind of thing could happen. But it was too late. The ladder tilted beyond arm's reach of the wall.

Then, silently, it paused. In mid-tilt, as if it had forgotten what came next.

I froze, waiting. Stupid. Stupid to risk my life like this. My left hand had turned to concrete around the ladder rung, and my right arm was still extended in supplication to the brick wall. Somehow, my feet were still planted on the rungs beneath me. Afraid to breathe, I decided to scout out the situation.

Trying not to move as much as a face muscle, I looked up. A couple of bolts had slipped out at the top, allowing the ladder to tilt backwards, but the rest of the ladder below me was still connected to the building. Cautiously, cautiously, I climbed the rest of the way up. Then, leaning over the top of the ladder, I pulled it back to the edge and climbed onto the roof.

The roof was black and the temperature up there was about as hot as the Big Bang. I peered through the gauzy atmosphere to look for something to hide behind. An air-conditioning unit was the only candidate. I ran for it, hoping I wouldn't be spotted by office workers in the building across the street. From behind the air-conditioning unit, I peered at the spot where I needed to be—behind the walled ledge opposite the offices of Barnes Property Management, which were located across the street. A quick glance around convinced me that the only way to get there unseen was on my hands and knees.

I got down on all fours and began crawling. The roof was so hot I could barely stand to put my hand or knee down before I jerked it away with an "ow!" so I was making pretty good time. Tar from the roof and about ten thousand tiny sharp pebbles were sticking in my palms and the knees of my jeans. My new jeans. Why hadn't I changed? I'd just assumed I'd have more cover and would be able to walk like a normal person, that's why. That's what I get for assuming. I made it to the ledge, which had a three foot wall to give me some nice cover from the opposite building, and sat down in the tar. Careful to keep my head down, I pulled the camera bag strap over my head and set the case at my feet. It was time to risk a look.

I raised myself up and peeked over the edge. I'd done a great job. I was lined up with a view of the penthouse office of the president of Barnes Property Management. What was even more perfect was that the offices were housed in one of those glass-walled buildings where you can see everything that goes on inside whenever the light is right, and the light was right. Sliding glass doors opened onto a small terrace which was decorated with potted trees and flowers. The sun was behind their building, which put me in danger of being exposed, but they wouldn't be looking. It was perfect. I congratulated myself.

Squinting, I examined the office. Located in a skyscraper that boasted high security and high rent, it was expensively decorated. As they were in the rest of the building, security cameras were mounted on the ceilings of Barnes' offices, watching over what appeared to be original oil paintings and oriental rugs. Various certificates adorned the walls, and there were plenty of healthy plants.

To the right, next to the window, was a large polished cherry desk with a black-leather chair in which was seated a big man. Apparently I had made it in time. He was still alone.

At just that moment, the man stood. I followed his glance across the room, catching my breath. At the door of his office appeared a woman of stunning beauty. She was slender, elegant, with an expression that carried just a hint of savoir faire. She wore a slim-fitting black dress with high heels and a simple chain around her neck. She paused, crossing her arms and leaning her graceful frame against the doorway, and smiled a smile that would melt ice.

Reluctantly, I looked back to the man as he walked toward her. The president of Barnes Property Management had a fat, puffy red face and chubby fat hands that he was now placing on the woman's bare shoulders, left uncovered by her dress. He took her hand and led her out onto the terrace to enjoy the view.

I couldn't help the smile that was now teasing at the corners of my mouth. I reached into my camera bag, attached the telephoto lens to my 35mm camera, then raised it to the ledge. This was going very well. I could get perfect shots from here.

Gerald Barnes led the woman to the rail and began pointing out various landmarks. She seemed to enjoy this very much, taking it all in. Then, impulsively, he leaned over and kissed her on the cheek. Just what I needed. Pictures of the two of them looking naughty together. Good. Snap.

Mr. Barnes then took her hand and led her to a patio table, seating her in one of its swivel chairs. Then he bent down and kissed her on the top of her head, which she seemed to enjoy very much. Both of their faces would be clearly identifiable in the photo. Excellent. Snap.

Barnes swiveled the chair so that the woman was now turned so she could look toward the river. He stepped to the side of the chair and caressed her neck while he talked. Snap. Then he stepped away from her chair and walked toward the back of the terrace, still perfectly visible to my lens. He continued talking, and I suppose she was still listening, but she continued to listen with her chair turned out, almost as if she was posing for me.

I zoomed in for a headshot of the woman—the raven-black hair with a cut that lay in waves just touching her shoulders. Bright green eyes with long dark lashes. Full lips, of which my camera, even at this distance, could catch the gloss. The high cheekbones. The long neck. Snap.

I brought it back a little. Now I could see the line of her neck and shoulders, the modest neckline of her dress, which just exposed the swell of her breasts. She turned in her chair just enough at that moment to give me a beautiful three-quarter profile. Snap. Snap. Snap.

She turned back toward me again and then slowly away, swiveling in her chair as she listened to Barnes gab on and on. She paused and tilted her head back in a perfect body profile. My eye traced the line from her chin down her neck, over her breasts and down her flat stomach, across her leg and over her knee, down to the black hemline which ended halfway down her calf, and then on down her black stockings to the toe of her high heeled shoe. Snap. Snap. Snap. Then Barnes must have said something that she was supposed to find funny, because she turned in my direction and laughed, but I couldn't tell from her expression whether she was laughing with him or at him. Beautiful. Snap.

She said something in reply to Barnes, rising from her chair at an angle to me and walking to the rail, where she looked out over the city at the horizon. She reached out and touched the handrail in front of her. I could see the arch of her back and the curve of her hips. Snap.

She spoke again and turned her back to me. The dress was backless. I swallowed hard. She clasped her hands behind her, and I could see the full curve of her figure from behind—the long V to her narrow waist, the rounding out of her hips, the soft flow of the skirt of her dress. Snap. Snap. Snap. Snap.

I shook myself hard. What was I doing?! I was supposed to be getting shots of the two of them together, not just of her! How many shots had I wasted? Kicking myself, I ducked behind the ledge. Why did this woman always have this effect on me?

Perhaps I should explain. You see, this wasn't business. This was personal. I wasn't working on an assignment for the paper. I was on a little assignment for myself. Self protection, you might call it. Self-protection works something like blackmail in reverse. You don't use the photos unless you have to. It's like insurance. She gets one up on you, you show you've got one up on her.

You see, this wasn't just any woman with Gerald Barnes. This was Ann Alexander. Ann Alexander to most of the world—but I call her My Deceitful, Guileful, Cunning, Calculating, Underhanded Arch-Enemy-Number-One, for short.

In other words, my competition. Ann is my counterpart at the *Metropolitan Inquirer*. We have a lot in common. Like me, Ann is a lesbian. And an investigative reporter. In fact, like me, she's also her paper's best. And right now, she was just doing a little investigative reporting. In a very compromising manner, I might add. That's where I come in.

I had heard, through hushed reporter gossip, that Ann was onto a story about Barnes Property Management company. By making some phone calls and piecing together a few facts, I was able to determine that Ann had an appointment with Barnes at his office today. I had no idea what kind of story Ann was after with Gerald Barnes, but I had a hunch about how she would go about getting it—and I figured I could make good use of that. Ann was here to get information to use against Gerald Barnes, but I was here to get information to use against Ann.

I have to do anything I can to slow Ann down whenever I can. If anyone can scoop me on a story, she can. If anyone can find a source before I can, Ann can. Ann is smart, and talented and capable of penning insights so sharp you can cut your finger on them. That's why I can't stand her. The only disconcerting thing about all of this is that she's…well…drop-dead gorgeous.

I was breathing hard—from anger, I think—so I turned and sat back down in the tar behind the ledge and checked the camera. I still had eight shots left. I didn't want to use more than a roll on this little expedition.

Still breathing hard, I eased myself back up and repositioned the camera. Through the lens I could see that they were both standing now, facing each other. With his slicked-back black hair and gold medallion, Barnes reminded me of someone impersonating Elvis Presley. The fat Elvis. His suit fit surprisingly well for such a fat man, however. I had to give him that. Barnes stepped closer to Ann to say something, raising his fat hand and taking her necklace in his palm, delicately brushing across her breast with his chubby fingers as he did the old, "Oh-what-a-beautiful-necklace" ploy. I should have taken the shot, but suddenly everything looked blurry. My hands were shaking. "Forget this," I mumbled out loud, angrily. I had enough shots.

I spun around and sat down hard behind the ledge wall, stuffing my camera and the telephoto lens back into the camera bag. I zipped it up and slung it over my shoulder and began the low fast crawl back to the air-conditioning unit. I was irritated and moving awkwardly, so my camera bag kept slipping around my body and banging against my right knee. My palms were scraped and bleeding now from the sharp little pebbles, and twice my jeans stuck to the roof with such a grip that I thought I was going to go down like the dinosaurs in the tar pits.

When I finally made it to the cover of the air-conditioning unit and stood up, I was drenched in sweat. It was a miracle I wasn't simmering. I glanced down at the mess that had been my clothes; I looked like I had been tarred and pebbled.

I returned to the edge of the roof and attached the ladder to the building with a spare bungy cord from my camera case. Then, without looking at how far I could fall, I stepped backwards onto the rickety ladder. I climbed down to the fire escape landing, stepped back in the building through the broken emergency exit door, walked down the hall, and—ignoring the stares at my perspiration-soaked, tar-stained and pebble-covered body—took a crowded elevator to the ground floor.

The alternator is going on the Jag, so it dies if I run the air-conditioner unless I'm driving fast—like on the expressway—so most of the way back I sat in heavy traffic with my windows rolled down, raising the carbon-monoxide level in my blood. As I made my way through the city, elbowing my way from this lane to that one looking for a ramp so

I could turn on my air-conditioning, I fantasized ways I could use the photos of a smiling Ann with Gerald Barnes' pudgy hands and lips all over her.

First, she would have to do something really nasty to me, like beat me to a source, blowing to pieces weeks of work for me. Nah, that was too typical. Maybe she would appear suddenly in a situation where I was working undercover and call me by name, putting my life in mortal danger. That had never happened, but it could. But why push it? Maybe she would just scoop me again. That was a good enough reason as far as I was concerned.

Then, I would blow the photos up to eight by tens, slip them into a manila envelope and mail them anonymously to her editor, with a note about the unethical practices of his reporters. Nah. He'd probably consider Ann's behavior an example of the best in the spirit of American journalism. No, I'd mail copies of them to Barnes' wife as an anonymous "friend" and tape Ann's address and phone number to the photos.

No. Not evil enough. No, I knew what I'd do. I'd make multiple copies of Ann, laughing and smiling with Gerald Barnes' hands all over her, and take them around and plaster them on the walls, bulletin boards and bathroom stalls of every lesbian dance bar, bookstore and coffeehouse Ann frequented in the city. That ought to improve her love life. The picture of Barnes' fat hands on those slender shoulders. The picture of his fat fingers caressing that long neck. The picture of his fat lips planting a wet kiss on the perfect skin of that perfect face...

My knuckles were white, I was gripping the steering wheel so tightly. I slammed on the brakes and my car skidded to a stop. I had driven past my own office.

I backed up and parallel parked. Grabbing the camera from the passenger seat beside me, I unstuck myself from where the tar on my jeans had glued me to my car seat and climbed the three flights of stairs to my office. There's no elevator, of course. I'm not even sure elevators had been invented when this building was built.

The *Louisville Daily*'s offices look like the set from a newspaper movie of the 1940s. There's no carpet, just tile; the central air is so bad we still use the ceiling fans; and—I don't know this for a fact—but many of us have a sneaky suspicion that the furniture hasn't been replaced since World War II. All of this, combined with the computers and cell phones and other contemporary technology, tends to give you a feeling of disorientation as you walk in, as if you can't quite figure out what century you've just stepped into.

24

But at least the Daily was around during World War II. The *Louisville Daily*, founded at the beginning of the twentieth century, was Louisville's grand old newspaper. The golden years of the *Daily* were from World War II through the end of the Vietnam War. The economic slowdown of the seventies hit the paper hard, and then, in the late eighties, the *Metropolitan Inquirer* entered the scene.

The *Metropolitan* shouldn't have had a chance to become the news power that it did, but the *Daily* was, and still is, owned by a wealthy Louisville family who take an active part in running it. During the eighties, the patriarch of the family, who was also the managing editor, was in his late seventies. Personally unequipped to deal with the competition of the *Metropolitan*, he never took the threat of the new paper seriously.

The *Metropolitan* gained a foothold; where it couldn't compete with the *Daily*'s perceptiveness and breadth, it compensated for it with flash and quick information. The *Metropolitan* caught the attention of an ever-busier, time-starved public, and soon became a powerful competitor to the *Daily*. When the younger generation of the *Daily*'s owners—who understood what was at stake—finally took over in the late nineties, it was almost too late. The *Daily* made enormous changes and managed, barely, to hang on into the twenty-first century.

Personally, I credit the survival of the *Daily* to the character of the people of Louisville themselves. Although it is a metropolitan area with a population of about a million, if you include its surrounding counties, Louisville and its people retain a certain small-town atmosphere and sensibility. The fact is, the people of Louisville knew the *Daily*; they knew the family who owned the *Daily*; they had grown up with them. To Louisville, the *Daily* was one of "us." The *Daily* was a paper that had earned their loyalty.

The *Metropolitan*, however, was owned by a corporation based out of town and was therefore somehow suspicious. The people of Louisville would be willing to be convinced, but by golly it was going to take more than a couple of decades for the *Metropolitan* to prove its trustworthiness. Nevertheless, the *Daily*'s existence had become a month-to-month struggle. This was the reality that we, the staff of The *Louisville Daily*, lived with every day.

I said hello to a couple of folks, unlocked my office door, pushed it open, and was met with a gust of hot air. That was one of the nicer perks about having a third floor office. Did I mention the aerobic benefits?

My office is very small, but it is an office. That is one of the nice things about working in an old newspaper building. At a modern newspaper I'd get my very own pressboard cubicle. A couple of steps into the office is the chair in which any visitors to my office sit. Facing this are my desk and desk chair, with its back to the windows. Along the walls to the right and left are filing cabinets. A computer, a coffeemaker and mug that sit on top of one of the filing cabinets, even though I have given up coffee in this office for the summer, as you might have guessed. I have an air-conditioning window unit to the left of my desk chair, and balanced on the top of the air-conditioner is a plant. I always keep a plant there until it dies, and on the same day I throw it out, I drive down to the grocery and buy a new one. I think they die of heat in the summer and cold in the winter.

I walked over to the front of my desk, took the camera out of the bag and it hummed as I rewound the film. I planned to develop the pictures right away. It was as hot as an oven in the office, so I set the camera down on the corner of the desk and walked over to the air-conditioner to turn it on. I flipped the switch but nothing happened, so I smacked it on the side. It started up with a whine.

The office was too dark, so I decided to raise the blind on the window over the air-conditioner. This blind always gives me a hassle, so it took me about a minute of struggle to get it to stay up. When I finally turned back around, I nearly fell on the floor. Ann Alexander was standing in my office.

"Hello, Lane," she said, low. It made me want to step closer, but I knew better.

"Hello, Ann," I replied. We stood there just looking at one another. We hadn't seen each other for months—not counting my afternoon on the roof, of course.

"Well," she said, taking off her sunglasses, which she slipped into her purse. She gave me a sort of smile.

For a moment, I couldn't think of anything to say. My brain sometimes goes into pause when Ann is near me, especially when she looks like she looks today. It's some kind of hormonal thing. Why was she here? And *where* did she get that dress?

"So," she smiled warmly. "What have you been up to lately?"

"Not much," I lied. I crossed my arms and shifted my weight, and with that, several tiny pebbles unstuck themselves from my jeans and struck the floor with soft pings. I had completely forgotten what I looked like. I set my jaw and firmly restrained myself from glancing down at the puddle of pebbles forming at my feet.

Ann scanned my clothes with her eyes and pretended not to notice anything unusual. Normally, I would consider that polite of her. Today, however, it only confirmed my suspicions about this coincidental visit.

She spoke again. "I hate to sound like an old movie, but aren't you going to ask me to sit down?"

"Of course. Have a seat. What's been going on with you?" I offered. I still had to figure out what game Ann was playing.

"Oh, nothing much, just work." she replied, blowing off my question the same way I had blown off hers. Ann walked around to the guest chair and sat down, crossing her long legs. Every movement was as smooth as silk. Even the air around her seemed to shimmer.

Of course, it could have just been the heat. It was at least ninety-five degrees in my office, but Ann looked as cool as an evening in October. And this was after she had walked up three flights of steps.

"So, Ann," I said curtly. "How have you been? Have you been working on any big fat stories lately?"

She eyed me for a moment. "No. Just the usual. I'm wrapping up a story this afternoon about the owner of a property management company. He's ripping off his building owners and their tenants and anyone else who crosses his path."

"Yeah, yeah, I know the type," I said. "Probably just kissing up to all the right people."

She raised an eyebrow ever so slightly, then glanced casually around my office. "Sure is hot today."

She was killing time. But why? I knew she was up to something, and because I couldn't figure out what, I got angry. "All right, Ann," I walked around to the front of my desk to take the offensive. "I'm sure you didn't stop by to chat about the weather. What do you want?"

"What?" she asked, looking vaguely confused.

"You know what I mean," I retorted.

She didn't look offended. I think she understood well enough what I was talking about. "I was just in the neighborhood and thought I'd drop in to see you," she said.

Right. She hadn't been anywhere near here.

"It's been a long time since we've seen each other," she added.

It was my turn to lie. "Yeah, what's it been, about six months?" I asked, leaning back on my desk.

"Eight," she almost whispered. "We haven't seen each other since the beginning of January."

New Year's Day, she meant. Of course, I knew exactly—the morning after one of the most passionate nights of my life. But I was sur-

27

prised she had any memory of it.

She was squinting at me because the sun from the window behind me was now shining directly in her eyes. She smiled and leaned back in her chair a little, shading her eyes with her hand. "Sweetie," she laughed, "would you mind dropping that blind? I can't see a thing with all this light in my eyes."

I sighed. Her whole conversation with me had been one distraction followed by another. I wondered when she was going to get to the point. "Sure," I said, the slightest exasperation revealing itself in my voice. "I'll get it." I turned around and began fighting with the window blind again. It was as difficult and to bring down as it was to put up. After about thirty seconds, the whole left end of it dropped suddenly, hitting me on the shoulder.

"Darn!" I blurted out.

"Darn?" Ann said from the chair behind me. "That was mild."

I lifted the blind again with a jerk and started wrestling with the right end.

"But then, of course, you never were one for strong language," she murmured. "Although you do take the Lord's name in vain. Under certain circumstances."

I felt the flush start at my ears. This is the greatest curse of being blonde, even worse than the mindset so many people have that blonde women are stupid. In my line of work, I could use the dumb-blonde assumptions to my advantage, but blushing always gives me away. I pretended to be very involved in the mechanics of the right side of my window blind until I felt my face cool down. When I believed my cheeks were back to their original color, I managed to level the blind and lower it so that it stayed.

"There," I turned and faced Ann. The light from the window was out of her eyes now. I came around to the front of my desk again and confronted her. "So, I believe we were discussing why you're here? Is it some 'weighty' matter?"

This time she completely ignored me. She finished touching up her lipstick, then snapped her compact shut and put them both in her purse. "There's something I want to ask you, Lane."

"Good. Fine. Ask me." I leaned back and glanced over my desk. Something struck me as wrong.

"Lane?"

I looked back at Ann. Her clear green eyes met mine searchingly. "I want your opinion on something. I trust your hunches." She paused a moment, looking at me. "But I'll have to ask you about it later. I have an appointment." She picked up her purse and stood up.

"What?" I was completely thrown. What was she pulling?

"I know, I know. I'm sorry," she said, going to the door. "Maybe I shouldn't have brought it up at all, but if I don't go now, I'll miss my deadline." She paused to look at me from my office doorway, her eyes narrow, serious. "I'll call you later, Lane, all right?" and she was gone.

I followed her to the door, unable to keep myself from watching her bare shoulders and back in that black dress as she weaved between the desks in the main room, then disappeared down the stairwell. As she passed their desks, men stopped typing to stare. Call me later. Sure. Weird. She was completely weird.

I walked back toward my desk. What was she doing? What was going on?

This was irritating. She wanted to talk to me about something. No, she wanted to talk to me about something later. No, actually she drove twenty minutes out of her way to climb three flights of stairs in searing heat to tell me she wanted to talk to me about something later. This did not add up.

It was then that I realized what had been teasing at my brain a minute before, when I had glanced across my desktop while talking to Ann. My camera, which I had placed on the corner of my desk when I was alone, had, almost imperceptibly, changed its angle. I leaped at it, grabbing it and ripping open the film compartment door. It was empty, except for a folded piece of paper that fluttered out onto my desk. She had stolen my film.

I sat the camera down on the desk and unfolded the piece of paper. In a feminine hand it read, "I'm not nearsighted, darling."

Throwing the note down, I bolted out of my office and across the news room to the stairwell, but Ann was already out of sight. Running back to my office, I opened the slats of my blinds and looked down to the street below. Ann was slipping calmly into her white T-top. I struggled to open my window but, as usual, it was sticking. Ann signaled, pulled out slowly, and then drove off too fast. Smooth. Always so smooth. I turned around and kicked at my chair.

I had been an idiot. I knew Ann wouldn't show up without a reason, and yet I had turned my back on her. Defeated, I sat down at my desk.

All at once, I remembered the pictures I had taken on that roll. Shot after sensual shot of Ann—and now she had the film. Groaning out loud, I leaned face-down on the desk and prayed that she would throw out the film without developing it.

29

Chapter Three

I lay in bed the next morning with the covers pulled over my head and calculated. If I never ever left my apartment again, how long would I live? The food I had in my refrigerator and cupboard combined would last me about four days, tops. Since I hate to cook, I never keep anything except cereal, coffee, and an occasional package of cookies in the apartment. However, I had an endless supply of water coming through the tap. I read once that a person can live up to two months on water alone. So—two months and four days. I could survive that long without having to venture out of my apartment and risk running into Ann Alexander. After that, everyone would probably assume I was dead anyway, and I could move to another city and start my life over again under an alias.

This whole situation with Ann was untenable. We were both reporters working for competing papers. Any relationship between us bordered on a breach of ethics. Time and time again, however, we found ourselves crossing that line. Then, inevitably, something in our jobs would tear it all apart again.

New Year's Day, Ann had whispered to me in my office yesterday. New Year's Day. Of course I remembered.

For a few perfect hours that day, following an incredible erotic night of passion with her, it had seemed to me that this time we were going to be able to make it work. We spent the morning in bed, then went downtown to the old Brown Hotel on Broadway for an extravagant midday brunch together.

Ann had insisted we order Hot Browns—a baked Southern dish with turkey, bacon, bread and a cheese sauce—since the Brown Hotel was where the Hot Brown had originated in 1923. It was Ann's way of ringing out the old. Afterward, I insisted that we hold hands as we took a frosty walk along Riverfront Park. It was my way of ringing in the new. We were in heaven—until our cell phones rang almost simultaneously.

The calls were from our respective papers. A passenger plane had made an emergency landing at Louisville International Airport after the cabin and cockpit had filled with smoke. Under difficult circumstances, the pilots brought the plane down, but it had skidded off the icy runway. There had been an emergency evacuation and some injuries, but the astonishing information was that the pilot was nowhere to be found. The co-pilot and all the flight attendants were there and accounted for, but it was as if the pilot had simply disappeared off the face of the earth. No one had seen him leave. He was just gone.

Seconds always count on a breaking story. Ann pretended to be patient, but my call lasted longer than hers, and I knew she wished we were on our way. Then, because I had driven to brunch, I had to drive Ann back to her car. There was no way in high heaven as competing reporters we could show up on the scene of a story in the same car. It slowed both of us down.

But what happened next cinched it. Ann's faster car beat me and everyone else to the airport, giving her just enough time to manipulate the situation. Ann quickly rounded up the passengers with the most harrowing stories, then convinced the airline representative in charge that she and her little group of passengers should be rushed to a private room in the terminal. They needed quiet in order to phone their loved ones right away, she argued. The young, nervous airline representative agreed. Ann accompanied the group to a conference room and while some phoned their families, Ann got dramatic, private interviews with the rest.

I arrived perhaps ten minutes behind Ann, but by the time I got there, all I or any of the other media could do was wander around wondering where all the good stories had gone. The passengers Ann had left for the rest of us either answered our questions with a yes or a no or described their experience as "I don't know; my eyes were closed." Ann was nowhere in sight, so I had a suspicion who was behind the mystery of the missing articulate passengers, but I still didn't know how to find them.

Most of the media that day finally slumped away in defeat, taking back to work less than compelling stories. I, however, was determined to take a different tack. The next day, Ann pounded the competition—including the television news—with a fantastic spread in the *Metropolitan*. Complete with spectacular interviews, the articles illustrated the horror of knowing something has gone wrong with your plane from a vivid, first-person perspective.

I, however, had an interview with the missing pilot.

It seems the pilot had taken a little bump on the head himself. He evacuated the plane, and then, disoriented, wandered away without anyone noticing him in all the confusion. I discovered him a block away from the airport at a run-down little bar in the Highview neighborhood, downing a scotch.

I had gotten the real scoop, after all. But instead of feeling elated, as I should have, I thought about Ann.

I hesitated to call her. It might sound like I was gloating. I waited for her to call, but she didn't. After two days, I wondered if she was going to call. After two weeks, resigned, I started giving myself a good talking to.

I started with the usual reasons. There was no way we could make it work. Any relationship we might have would have to be kept secret because of our jobs. We would find it impossible to pursue our stories without cluing the other in to what we were researching. We would drag each other down; we would lose our competitive edge. All the same things I told myself every time we got together, after it inevitably fell apart.

Of course I hadn't felt sorry for Ann that I scooped her that day. On the contrary—why should I? She had never felt sorry for me. The time we were together before, the relationship fell apart after she tracked down a source with whom I had an appointment and purposely gave him wrong directions. But then, of course, there was the time she missed a deadline because I let a little air out of one of her tires. She completely overreacted on that one.

She'd scooped me twice since New Year's. But I hadn't seen or heard from her again until yesterday. Now I was just going to have to push her out of my head and keep her out. But that was nearly impossible. Working in the same field, for competing papers, meant eventually we were going to cross paths.

I had to go to work on the Ricky Simms profile, so I got realistic, faced the fact that I couldn't spend the rest of my life hiding in my apartment, and dragged myself out of bed. After all, in the newspaper business, every day is a new game. Plus, if I didn't have the piece on Rosemary's desk by three so that she had her opportunity to hack at it before the six o'clock deadline, she was going to kill me, or worse, get the moral upper hand. So I took a couple of antacid tablets and headed to Ricky's house.

Identification of Ricky had been quick because his name had been written on the soles of his shoes with a magic marker—the kind of thing kids do. His only surviving relative was his grandmother, with whom he had lived. Her address was three miles from where his body had been found, in a duplex in the city close to where I had photographed Ann the day before.

I pulled up in front of the duplex, which was a simple old brick building that looked like the kind built in the early twentieth century. It probably had no more than four rooms to an apartment and was in sore need of a new roof. A chicken-wire fence enclosed what there was of a front yard. I swung open the door, entered the foyer, walked up a flight of stairs and knocked on the door of Apt. 2. I could hear a television set inside, but no one answered. I knocked again. This time the television volume went down, but still no one came to the door. I was about to give up when the door opened. It caught on a security chain, and the face of a woman about sixty years old—probably that of Ricky's grandmother—appeared in the space which the chain allowed.

"Yes?" The woman was hoarse. She didn't appear to be in good health.

"Mrs. Watterston?" I asked. She nodded. "I'm Lane Montgomery. I'm from the *Louisville Daily*. I wanted to talk to you about doing an article on your grandson, Ricky Simms, for the paper. Would you mind talking to me?"

The woman choked back tears. "He was a sweet boy. I can't talk about this. I'm sure people want to understand why this happened, but I don't know either. I wish you reporters would go away right now. It's too soon. I'm sorry." She made a motion with her hand through the door as if to wave me off. As she began to close the door, I interrupted.

"Mrs. Watterston, I understand. It's okay. Could you give me the name of someone else I could talk to? A friend or someone?"

She closed the door in my face, and I took that to mean the interview was over. But then the chain moved against the door, and she opened it again. She stepped into the hall, wearing a thin, worn housedress and house slippers. Her skin was a deep black and contrasted with the light gray in her hair.

"He didn't have friends," she said. "He kept to himself. He was a loner. And he didn't have any relatives 'cept for me. His daddy left when Ricky was just a baby. He couldn't get work and he was ashamed. His mother was killed in a car accident when he was two. She was my daughter. Now this. It's not right that one little boy should have so much go wrong in his short life."

Nor is it right that you have had to lose first a daughter and then a

33

grandson, I thought. I've done a lot of interviews with grieving relatives, but they are never easy. They're difficult for the relatives and awkward for the reporters—because despite what the public suspects, many of us do still have emotions. A heaviness descended over my body as I observed Ricky's grandmother. I thought of his face again, last night, the boy in sleep.

"Mrs. Watterston, I'd like to write a nice article about Ricky, let everyone know something of what he was like. I'd like to put a picture with it. Do you have any photos of Ricky I could borrow?"

Although her face was gaunt, she seemed encouraged by the thought of an article in the newspaper that would memorialize her grandson. "I have his school picture from last year. It's big. It's a eight by ten. Will that be okay for you to use?"

"That would be perfect."

"I'll be right back." She disappeared into the apartment and returned a moment later, pulling a photo from a frame that held two eight by tens. She started to hand it over to me, then hesitated. "You'll bring this back to me, won't you?"

"Yes, ma'am. Just like you gave it to me."

"I don't have another one like it."

I indicated the photo that had been next to Ricky's. It was a wedding photo of a young couple standing on the front steps of a church. "Were these Ricky's parents?" I asked. "They look so happy."

She nodded. "Things just happen to young people sometimes, to tear them apart. He couldn't get any permanent work. They started to fight. One day he just left. I don't know why men don't understand that it's better for them to be around their children even if they can't get work. I guess it's just a man's pride."

"What do you do for a living, Mrs. Watterston? Do you work or are you retired?"

"I work at a drugstore in the South End."

"That's quite a way from here."

"I take the bus. Forty-five minutes each way. But I like the people I work with. I retire next year."

"What would you like people to know about Ricky?" She was talking comfortably so I began to steer the conversation.

She took a breath and thought a moment. "He always went to church with me. He was good about walking me there, making sure I got there safe." I began taking notes. "Oh, and when he was younger, before his voice started to change, he had the sweetest singing voice you ever heard. He sang in the children's choir at church. The music director always had Ricky sing the solo part. He sounded like a little angel, that boy." All at once an expression of grief passed across her face at the imagery she had just used. "I suppose the angels will have the pleasure of hearing him now."

She trembled and covered her face with one hand. "I should have made him stay home. It's dangerous for young people to be out late at night. The world's gone crazy. Why would anyone want to kill a fifteen-year-old boy? Tell me that. Why? Probably someone who was drinking or high on drugs. That's what the world's come to. They took me down to see the body last night, to tell them for sure it was him. You know, they wouldn't even let me see his body to identify him? Because he'd been murdered, they said, it was like his body was evidence. They just showed me a picture of him on a computer. It was horrible what they did to him. How could someone do that to a child?"

"I'm sorry."

She nodded. "I'll be okay." Her voice caught in her throat, but she looked at me as if to indicate her willingness to continue.

"Ricky was quite a way from here last night. Do you know why?"

She shook her head. "No. He'd be out to all hours. Kids these days do what they want."

"Maybe he was out riding his bike?"

"I couldn't afford to buy him a bike. He knew how to get around on his own. He took buses. Maybe he went to see a friend, but he never mentioned having a friend out that way. He never mentioned having any friends at all, poor thing. I was always afraid he was lonely. But he wasn't here when I got home from work, so I don't know what he was doing."

"Mrs. Watterston, are you Ricky's sole provider?"

"Yes," she answered. "Ever since he was two. His mother didn't leave any money."

"Then you bought him the new shoes he was wearing.?"

The question confused her, for good reason. What kind of an interview was this? What did shoes have to do with memorializing her grandson? But I ask these questions when something doesn't connect for me. I just slip the question into the middle of the interview, and people usually answer it. In fact, if you're brazen enough to ask the question—no matter how rude or personal or just ridiculous—I've learned that most people will answer it. It may not be good manners, but it's good journalism.

"Yes. I'm sure I did. I don't know exactly which shoes he was wearing last night, but I buy all his clothes," she answered politely. "But they weren't new shoes, even if they looked new. I got them at the consignment shop right up here on the corner. That's where I get all his clothes."

"You've never purchased anything for him anywhere else?"

Her brows furrowed and she shook her head. "No. I can't afford much on my income. But he never did without. He might not have had the best, but he never did without." That sounded like a bit of a lecture to me.

"Where did he go to school, Mrs. Watterston?"

I veered the conversation away from the shoes, only to learn she really knew nothing of her grandson's education beyond the name of his school. She looked drained. I could tell she needed to escape back to the solace of her apartment.

I wrapped up the interview and thanked her for her time. She reciprocated by thanking me for writing something about her grandson, then went back inside her apartment, shutting the door behind her and locking it. I hesitated a moment, hoping against hope that this woman was not facing her grief without someone—a friend, a neighbor—someone who would be coming later to be with her. Impulsively, I pulled out one of my business cards with my office number on it, turned it over, and wrote on the back, "If there's anything I can do, please call me." Then I wedged it under the metal apartment number screwed to her door.

Gently, I clipped the eight by ten photo of Ricky to the top of my clipboard and turned, skipping back down the flight of stairs. I reached for the door to go back to my car and flung it open, but when I stepped through it the ground seemed to dissolve beneath my feet. Instead of emerging into sunlight, I was slipping downward into damp darkness. In total confusion I flailed out and gripped a rail with my hand, catching myself and skidding to a stop.

From a twisted, unnatural angle, I looked up and realized I had gone through a different door. I was lying on stairs that descended to a cellar. My heart pounding, I sat up on a step to check for broken bones.

The only light in the cellar came through the open door above me and from one or two small dirty windows built into an exterior wall. Cellars in these old buildings were often like rustic basements. This one covered the area of roughly half the size of the building. As my eyes adjusted, I could dimly make out a string or two hanging from bare, dark bulbs and a hard packed dirt floor. Cobwebs hung from beams that ran the length of the ceiling above me.

Beside that, there were two rusting water heaters—one for each of the apartments—and one of those ancient ugly furnaces with large, bloated tentacles that seem to be descended from octopi. Nothing was stored down here, because no one would ever want a reason to come down here.

Something shuffled, like a whisper, and I froze. It shuffled again, and my eyes searched the darkness. A mouse. Something clanged, then whooshed. I looked up. The gas jets of a water heater had gone into action. This was the kind of cellar that scared children. It was time to go.

I raised my bruised body and climbed the stairs out of the cellar, shutting the door solidly behind me. I turned to the identical door on the other side and opened it. Ah sunlight, warmth, color! This was more like it. I felt like Dorothy entering Oz. Happily, I got into my car.

I pulled out of my parking space, drove half a block, passed the consignment shop, slowed, decided to keep driving, drove another half block, made a U-turn and parked back in front of the consignment shop. I don't know why, but when things bother me, I just can't let them go.

The shop was so packed with merchandise that I couldn't squeeze myself between the racks without dragging clothes off the hangers. I hate that. I spotted a woman in a blue jacket who looked like she ran the place, so I headed in her direction. With great effort I moved my body through the racks toward her, at one point considering that if I had a machete I'd make better progress. She looked up at me cheerfully when I reached her.

"May I help you?" she asked over her bifocals.

"Well, yes," I replied. "I was just talking to someone who bought a nice pair of shoes here for her grandson, and I was wondering if you had any more like them."

"I'll show you what we have." She led the way to the shoes, weaving her way among the racks with little effort. She had learned just when to twist and dodge. I eventually caught up with her, shopped the shoes a little, then shook my head.

"No. None of these are quite the same."

"Well, honey, you know we just sell what other people bring in."

I frowned. "I wonder; could you look up those shoes in your records and see if the family who brought them in brings clothes to your shop on a regular basis? They might bring in another pair if they do."

She nodded. "Sure. But that'll take awhile. Can I call you?"

"That'll be fine." I gave her my phone number and an exact description of the shoes Ricky was wearing the night he was killed.

Using my city map I found my way to Ricky's middle school. Classes weren't supposed to start for another month. I parked in the back parking lot and walked around the building, pulling at doors until I found one open. From there, it was just a short distance down the hall to the front office. When I walked in, the secretary—a plump, middle-aged woman with glasses—greeted me pleasantly. As I approached the counter she saw Ricky's eight by ten on my clipboard. "Is that Ricky Simms?" she asked.

"Yes," I answered. I wasn't sure what to say. I didn't know if she had heard the news yet.

"Is he in trouble?" she asked, watching my face.

I hate it when I'm the person bringing the bad news—at least when I'm doing it in person and it's not in print. "No," I began, "You see, he—"

"Well, Alice, do we have a guest?" A strikingly handsome, tall blond man appeared in the hallway on the secretary's side of the counter, wearing a mauve suit and matching tie. The secretary's attention was immediately drawn away from me and to him. Unconsciously, her hand went to fix a stray lock of hair on her forehead. I suspected that despite the age difference, she had a bit of a crush on him. Something about his style reminded me of a cologne ad in a magazine. He paused, then walked toward us.

"I'm Jack Tinsley, the Assistant Principal. Has Alice been able to help you?"

I shook his hand. "Actually, Mr. Tinsley, we just met. I hadn't gotten to the 'help' part yet. My name is Lane Montgomery. I'm a reporter for the *Louisville Daily*. I was wondering if I could talk to you or the head principal, whoever could spare a few minutes?"

"Dr. Lever isn't in right now. She had an afternoon appointment. I'd be glad to talk to you. Why don't you step back to my office?"

Tinsley led the way. The hallway, like the rest of the school office area, was plastered with posters. They all had captions like, "Hang in there, it's almost Friday" and "Don't worry, be happy," written under photos of babies and fuzzy animals. The posters imposed a forced cheeriness on the rooms. It was all very friendly and not a bit welcoming.

We turned into his office and he sat in the big upholstered chair behind his desk, indicating for me to sit across from him. I took a seat and fought the vague sense that I had been caught in the hall without a pass. I noticed that his desk was perfectly neat. Not being a neat person myself, I have always sustained a certain suspicion that people with neat desks don't really work.

I initiated the interview. "I don't know if you've heard this in the news, Mr. Tinsley, so I hope I'm not taking you by surprise, but one of your students, Ricky Simms, was murdered the night before last."

He paused for a moment without saying anything. "No, I'm afraid I hadn't heard. We don't usually have a radio on in the office and I didn't catch it in the paper last night."

I briefly explained the circumstances of Ricky's murder, and he listened intently. "Sad, very sad," he commented, "to lose one of our students to such meaningless violence." I saw him glance to see if I was wearing a wedding ring. He wasn't wearing one.

"I was wondering if you could tell me a little about Ricky. I would like to do a biographical piece about him. I think our readers are always interested when our community loses someone so young."

"Yes, the young are our future. Many people don't consider that. Unfortunately, most politicians don't take the rising violence among our young people seriously enough."

"Do you see a lot of violence among your students?"

"Oh, I didn't mean here, specifically. But it's always sad to see one of your own students become another statistic."

All I was getting from this guy was cliches—and not even good ones. "But about Ricky," I tried again.

"I'm surprised you actually drove all the way over here for an interview," he commented, smiling at me. "Why didn't you just phone?"

I was a little surprised at the turn in the conversation, considering the circumstances, but I went with the flow. "I suppose it's a matter of style," I replied. "I've found that I learn more face to face with a person than I do over the phone."

"How interesting! I'm sure that's true!" He responded with an enthusiasm I felt was somewhat magnified given my comment. "I've always found journalism fascinating," he said, leaning toward me from his side of the desk. "I'd love to be able to write. I was never very good at that, though. Just good enough to get through the research papers for school. My major was Physical Education. P.E. seemed the only logical major for a basketball player. But I suppose you guessed I played basketball, didn't you, from my height?"

I hated to disappoint him in that I hadn't really given him or his height that much thought, so I nodded and smiled. Unfortunately, he seemed encouraged by this and continued.

"It turned out to be a fortuitous choice, however," he grinned, "because I quickly learned just how much I love kids." He paused.

I looked at him expectantly, then realized he was waiting on some sort of response from me. "That's wonderful," I said. "I love children, too."

He waited for me to say more, but when I didn't, he pushed the children thing further. "I don't understand the lack of involvement so many fathers have with their children. You know, I feel as if every one of these kids at this school is my own." He shook his head slowly. "This thing with Ricky, well, that hits hard."

Ah, yes; I recognized this game now. Silently inside, I groaned. He was flirting with me—watching my expression, attempting to determine what impressed me. Normally I could use this situation to my advantage to get someone to talk, but I couldn't get this guy on topic. Ricky's murder was just an opportunity to bring up the subject of himself.

I politely reiterated the purpose of my visit. "Mr. Tinsley, I would like to do a follow-up article about the murder. Something biographical about Ricky."

"I see," he said.

"I was hoping you could give me an idea about who Ricky was—something that would help me explain to our readership what he was like. I want to portray him as a real person to our readers, not just another statistic."

"Oh, sure." Confusion was creeping over his face. Something was missing in my response to him, but he couldn't name it. It wasn't that I didn't seem interested in what he was saying, or that I wasn't being gracious, or that I just didn't like him. Something else was missing—the thing he couldn't name—and all his button-pushing was not triggering it in me. He was knocked a little off balance by this, but I would have to ignore it. I waited. When he didn't offer anything, I asked more pointedly.

"I was wondering what kind of student Ricky was? What clubs was he involved in? What was he like?"

"If you'll excuse me a moment," he said, smiling, "I'll go get his file." He left the office and returned minutes later, reading from a manila folder. "He was an average student. He wasn't involved in any clubs, but we don't have that many clubs at the middle school level. Most clubs begin at the high school level."

He was so stiff on these simple questions about Ricky that I decided to open it up a little. "Why do you think it happened, Mr. Tinsley?

40

Do you have any idea who would have wanted to kill Ricky?"

I thought it a provocative question, but for a moment, Tinsley looked threatened. "Jack, please. Call me Jack," he said. "I don't know. Some of our kids come from rougher parts of town. I suppose it could have been a gang thing."

"Ricky was in a gang?"

"Oh, no; I didn't mean that. I don't know. I meant maybe he ran into the wrong element out in his neighborhood, that's all. It's tough for kids who grow up economically deprived. That's why we try to encourage them to finish high school, get good jobs. I tell them, 'Look at me. You could do what I do, if you just work hard.'" He was watching my face again. "Principals make a pretty good living, you know. It's not like teaching."

He was giving it one last try. The fact that he had played on a college basketball team hadn't gotten the response he was looking for, his love of children hadn't, and now he was trying the good bread-winner tactic. Nothing was working. He couldn't figure me out. I was doing all the right things. I was being polite and smiling warmly and listening with interest. So why did he feel rejected? He stopped talking, not knowing how to go on.

I knew what was missing. It was simple. It was the thing that happens between two people—usually expected between members of the opposite sex—even when they're just sitting around having coffee, or passing one another in the grocery aisle, or sitting in the principal's office conducting a newspaper interview. It's that little bit of electricity in the air—that *je ne sais quois*—that happens between two people who are attracted to each other, whether or not they intend to act on it. And since he was good-looking enough to fall in love with his mirror, I'm sure this was unfamiliar to him. He was used to women responding to him, and it wasn't happening with me. It couldn't. I didn't have the...what? The neurology for it?

"What about his home life?" I asked.

"He lived with his maternal grandmother. She was his sole guardian. She's in her sixties, I think." He checked the file again. "Yes. That's right."

"Could you tell me about her? I was wondering if Ricky was happy at home."

Mr. Tinsley moved uncomfortably and then leaned against the front of his desk, holding the file in his lap. He hadn't quite recovered his bearing yet.

I was amused. Obviously, he was accustomed to having a certain

41

power over women, and now that power was missing. At some level, he seemed to sense that because he wasn't holding the power in the room, I must be. The resulting vulnerability he was experiencing was foreign to him.

"I've never met her. Unfortunately, many of our parents, or guardians, as the case may be, are rather uninvolved in their children's education. I'm afraid it's a national trend."

"Yes, I've heard," I replied simply. Good grief. Of course I knew that. I work for the paper. "All right, what about Ricky's friends, then? What kind of group did he hang with?"

He sighed heavily. "Ms. Montgomery, this is very embarrassing, but to tell you the truth…" He looked down at his hands, and then back up at me. "…I can't tell you very much about Ricky. I can give you the basics. But I have eight hundred students in this school. I can't know all of them. The ones I do get to know I know because they spend a lot of time in this office—it's the discipline problems that are sent to me."

"I see," I nodded. The comment disturbed me, however, especially from a man who "felt as if every one of these kids" was his own.

"School starts in a few weeks. I'd be glad to let you talk to his teachers when they return. Perhaps they could give you information about Ricky's friends, what he was like as a student, whatever you want to know." He smiled.

"Thanks, but that will be a little late for me."

"What if I call some of his former teachers? I could set up some appointments for you to meet them. Some of them will be in early for in-service."

"How about some phone numbers, so that I could call them at home? I have to hand this story in to my editor at three a.m."

"I'll do what I can," he offered. "Most of our teachers have unlisted numbers; I'd have to ask their permission."

This whole interview was turning out to be not at all helpful to me, and I was getting the distinct impression that Mr. Tinsley really did not want me to be here writing an article about Ricky Simms. All at once he seemed to sense what I was thinking. He hesitated a moment, then walked to the bookshelves that lined the wall of his office, selected a tall, thin hardcover bound book and handed it to me. "I'm sorry that I can't be of any more help. But please take this. This is last year's school yearbook. You might find something in it that could be of use to you."

I stood and thanked him. In the doorway, I stopped for one more question. "Mr. Tinsley," I began, "you implied that Ricky was a well-behaved student—otherwise you would have known him better." His face flushed slightly, then he nodded. "So would you say that Ricky was a good kid? From what you know about him?"

He looked me in the eye. "Oh, yes," he said. "He was a good kid." Mr. Tinsley held my gaze steadily without glancing away, which might have appeared shifty. He was lying.

"Thank you." I slipped the yearbook under my arm and left him in his office. As I walked past the secretary's desk, I stopped. "Excuse me, Alice?" She looked up at me. "When I came in I think I saw a red pick-up truck with its lights on. Do you know anyone who drives a red pick-up? One of the headlights was missing."

What can I say? These ideas just get in my head. For all I knew, the little red truck with the white topper that had been seen so close to the murder scene might be a regular vehicle in the school parking lot. At least I could ask. Alice stared straight ahead, giving the question serious thought. "No. That doesn't ring a bell with me."

"Okay. I won't worry about it then. And Alice…" She looked up at me again. "Thank you. You've been very helpful."

I left Alice looking very pleased with herself, even if she wasn't sure just what it was she had done.

Back at the paper I called the Department of Public Information at the LPD and then Homicide to get the latest information about the murder. Ricky had been killed with a .32 at close range by someone who had unloaded five bullets in his chest. Shots from such a small caliber weapon would not necessarily be lethal except that one of the bullets clipped an artery. I asked if the fact that it was at close range indicated that he was killed by someone he knew, and got the answer, "possibly." I asked if they had any suspects and was told, "We are pursuing all leads at this time."

I can always count on the Louisville Police Department for thought-provoking information and stimulating quotes. I tried to reach Beverly Holloway, a homicide detective I have sometimes used as a source, but she was out of the office. I was going to have to go with what I had.

At one o'clock, Harry wandered into my office. Harry is big, barrel-chested, mustached, has a good size paunch on him, and I love him. He's my boss but he thinks he's my mentor, my buddy, and sometimes my father. I was looking over my article one last time before I sent it down. Harry started reading over my shoulder.

"Harry, that's rude," I complained.

"Quiet. I'm reading," he grumbled.

He finished my profile on Ricky and stepped back. "Hmm," was all he said. That irritated me.

"What?" I challenged him.

"It's fine," he said.

"What do you mean, 'fine'?"

"It's nice. I'm sure it's just what Rosemary wanted."

"What's that supposed to mean?!"

"It's very nice. Honestly. Nice. How his grandmother said he sang like an angel. The quote from the assistant principal saying that he was a good kid and what a tragedy it was."

"That isn't what you really want to say."

"No, it is. It's a nice memorial for that kid. It's just not very interesting, that's all."

I snapped. "Oh, don't you give me that, too."

"What are you talking about?"

"First Rosemary; now you."

"What?!"

"That's just how Rosemary was talking about my first story on Simms. I had to fight her to get this follow-up piece."

"What are you talking about?"

"What you were just saying! What Rosemary was saying this morning! That Ricky's murder wasn't a 'story'—that it wasn't interesting enough to make the front page!"

"What are you getting all heated up over?" he said defensively. "What did I do?"

"Rosemary implied that it wasn't an important story because he was just another black kid dying in the city. Now you're saying it's not interesting because Ricky was a good kid. So when he gets murdered it gets two inches on the obituary page. Nobody except his relatives, if he had any, reads that. Yet if he had robbed a bank you can bet it would've landed on the front page!"

"Yeah, I guess so." He sat down. "'Ninth-Grader Knocks Over Downtown Bank.' So, what's your point?"

"It's just that the media trumpets stories about whites who are victimized, and ignores victimized African-Americans unless it's a class action suit or something. I guarantee you, if Ricky had been the killer and not the victim, and the person he had killed had been white, then Ricky's face would have been all over our front page. But because Ricky was African-American and came to a violent end, we shrug our shoulders and act like that's acceptable. I don't think that's acceptable at all."

"I know it's not right, Lane. Newspapers have never given the African-American community the same coverage they give white America. You know that."

"Yes. But lately I've been thinking about how that distorts white America's understanding of who African-Americans are. What is white America supposed to think, when we wave banners under their noses of the crimes committed by African-Americans, but bury the stories about the average, hardworking, upstanding African-Americans, all in the name of a good 'story'?"

"You're absolutely right. But, a little off the topic…" He leaned in toward me. "What happened? You've seen this kind of prejudice in the news for years. Something woke you up to this. Want to tell me about it?"

I nodded and looked down at my hands. "Sorry I snapped at you. Yeah, I guess you could say something woke me up to it. Once it happens to you, you start noticing how it happens all around you."

"All right." He waited patiently.

"Last month Rosemary asked that intern, Tiffany, to cover the local Gay Pride march. Did you read Tiffany's article?"

"Can't say I remember it."

"You didn't miss much. There were about a hundred people in the march, mostly average folks who straight people would never be able to pick out as gay if we had been in a shopping mall instead of in a Gay Pride march. But to read Tiffany's article, you would've thought the circus had come to town."

He smiled. "What do you mean?"

"Out of a hundred people, all she wrote about was the three drag queens who were there, the two women who marched bare-breasted, and the woman who rode the unicycle that pulled the wagon with her little two-year-old holding a sign that said, 'Condoms Belong in the Schools.'"

Harry started to laugh.

"Don't laugh, Harry! Now, don't get me wrong. I'm happy to count among the gay population drag queens and bare-breasted women and unicyclists. That's fine. It's just not necessarily representative of the entire gay population. The article was deliberately slanted to invite the ridicule of people who don't understand our diversity."

"Tiffany's just an intern, you've got to understand." He was still suppressing laughter.

"It's not just that. The exact same thing happened with the newspaper coverage at our last March on Washington. I saw six drag queens and about forty bare breasts all day out of hundreds of thousands of people at that march. But guess what I read about in the newspapers the next day?"

"Ah, yes. The 'local color' story. But would the press have even bothered to show up if the parade hadn't had drag queens and bare breasts?"

"Exactly. They came to report a show. It's a double-edged sword. We owe it to the drag queens and the bare breasted women for getting attention drawn to our concerns, but then the press doesn't cover the rest of it—just the part that middle America is going to find too odd to be acceptable."

Harry was grinning again. "And why don't they cover homosexuals like you? Because from their frame of reference, you're not gay enough!"

I looked at him. "And what's that supposed to mean?"

"You don't fit the stereotype that they have built for themselves. A reporter would never interview you. You wear make-up, you own dresses, you have hair—and lots of it!" His humor was contagious. "And I don't mean on your legs or under your arms, either. You're not always found in sensible shoes. You might even be described as—gasp—feminine! Face it, Lane. You have to tell someone three times to their face that you're a lesbian before anyone believes it. You're just not a good story."

I was laughing now. "For the record, though, Harry, I want to state that I don't consider that a compliment. People just have very narrow definitions about what being gay means."

"Your point, exactly."

"Also my point about Ricky."

"I know." He stood and patted me on the shoulder. "Your story is fine. Send it on down."

"I will. I want to give it one last look."

Harry left, and I contemplated my article. I knew the story wasn't interesting, but it wasn't because Ricky was a good kid and therefore dull. It was because I hadn't found the real Ricky yet. Part of that was the fault of my time limitation. You can't find the essence of a person in a few hours.

But part of it was my own fault. I hadn't looked any closer because I hadn't wanted to report the Ricky I had begun to suspect I would uncover if I kept looking. In only two interviews, I had gathered enough

46

clues to indicate that Ricky wasn't exactly the person described in the article I was about to send to Rosemary.

Mr. Tinsley, the assistant principal, had lied to me twice. He had said that he didn't know Ricky very well, and that Ricky was a good kid. But Alice, who all misbehaving students had to pass first, had identified Ricky immediately from the photo on my clipboard. And her first question to me had been, "Is he in trouble?" so I don't think she remembered him from the last honor society meeting.

Why had Tinsley lied to me? For the sake of the article and Ricky's family? Or to protect his career? Then there was the question of Ricky's shoes, awaiting confirmation.

But it didn't really matter. It was just an article that would hit the paper tomorrow, make his grandmother happy, and then be forgotten. I punched the keys on my computer and sent the profile on Ricky to Rosemary's desk, an hour and a half ahead of Rosemary's deadline.

Chapter Four

"You sure feel strong about how your paper is handling that Ricky Simms story."

My grandmother was pouring sweet tea into two tall glasses filled with ice. I had taken off to the country after work, and was now seated next to her at the kitchen table in her farmhouse outside Louisville. It wasn't a long drive. Rural countryside was a stone's throw from any skyscraper in Louisville.

"Like I just said, it's because of that intern, Tiffany, and that awful article she wrote about the Gay Pride march. It just made me look at things in a different way." I reached past the fried apples for another homemade biscuit and buttered it. The butter dissolved into the flaky bread.

"I reckon that's part of it." Grandmother set the glass of tea next to my plate and eased herself into her chair with her cane. "And that poor boy seemed so abandoned, from what you said. His helpless body laying out there in the dark, and nobody around except a few police and reporters just doin' a job—nobody there for him who had ever loved him."

"Yeah," I mumbled, trying to push that image from my mind.

"Have you talked to your parents lately?"

I looked up and met my grandmother's eyes—lavender eyes now recessed within a face of many crevices, but eyes which had in their day been compared to the lavender eyes of a younger Elizabeth Taylor. I hadn't missed her point. "The telephone rings both ways, Grandmother. They haven't called me."

"That doesn't mean that you can't call them."

Something like a cold fist clenched inside my chest. This was the conversation I didn't want to have. "They're the ones who are abandoning me, Grandmom. I embarrass them! They don't know how to explain me to their fundamentalist friends whose daughters are all getting married, having babies, and selling cosmetics part-time."

Grandmother sat back in her chair and frowned. "Your daddy loves you, Lane. So does your mother. She just cares too much about what other people think. I'm old. I got over that a long time ago. Now, I love your mother, but she hasn't learned yet that a daughter's love is worth a whole lot more than other people's opinions."

I felt my throat tighten. I dealt with the chasm between my parents and me by staying angry at them. That way, thoughts of my parents could intrude in my daily life and I could go on mostly unaffected. The reason these conversations with my grandmother were always so difficult was that she invariably got me to face the fact that I loved my parents, too.

"So why don't you call them?"

"Because I can't stand it that the most I get from them is politeness."

Grandmother leaned forward and dipped more warm garlic mashed potatoes onto my plate. "Well, maybe if you talk to them, you can get past all that. But you don't have to call them tonight. Call them when you're ready. Here, your supper's getting cold. You finish this up and then I'm going to take you outside and show you how pretty my garden is!" She stood and walked to the sink.

Grandmother had made her point, and now she was letting me off the hook for the rest of the evening. She knew she had come too close to bringing me to tears, and wouldn't have dared embarrass me like that. I ate quietly for the next few minutes while she busied herself cleaning the kitchen counter, giving me time to collect myself.

As usual, sitting in this warm little kitchen on a summer evening, I was flooded with memories. When I was a child and my grandfather was still alive, this time of year meant that my family was out in the tobacco field, helping to house the tobacco. My father and grandfather would carry machetes into the fields and cut the sticky, large stalks by hand, impaling several stalks on a single tobacco stick, standing it upright in the field, then going on to the next.

Next, it was my job to drive the yellow and orange tractor and tow the wagon slowly up and down the field. My legs were so short I had to stand with all my weight to depress the brake. My mother and grandmother stood on the wagon, while my father and grandfather handed the heavy sticks up to them. When we had a wagonload, I pulled it all to the barn, where we unloaded it.

My father and grandfather balanced between the lower tiers of the barn, one foot on the beam to the right and the other foot on the beam to the left. My mother would hand up a stick at a time, heavy with tobacco plants. Alternately, my father and grandfather would either set the stick across the tiers at their feet, or lift the heavy sticks up to the tiers above them. As a child, I didn't have the strength to lift the heavy tobacco sticks above my head, so I got the top tier.

Flattered by the responsibility, but terrified of being thirty feet above the ground balancing on beams spread three feet apart, I never had the nerve to let go with both hands, as I was expected to do. I clung for dear life with one hand, and with the other reached below my feet for the tobacco stick being handed to me, easing it onto the tiers one end at a time, mostly with the help of my grandfather.

At some point during this process, my grandmother would have slipped away. When she returned, we knew it was time for supper. This was the kitchen we returned to, for a meal of fried chicken, melon, fresh corn on the cob, green beans, lemonade, and always dessert and laughter and happy conversation. Afterward we'd shower off the sticky sweat and tobacco gum, then watch a little television until we went to bed, completely exhausted. It was always a good tired, the tired that comes from having pushed yourself to your physical limits, and not the kind of tired that comes from sitting in an office or working under deadlines all day.

That was the kind of picture-perfect childhood I had. It was also the happy, picture-perfect relationship I had with my parents—until I grew into a person who was a disappointment to them, a person my parents could only interpret as undermining all the things they valued. And all for the sole reason that I fell in love with women, not men.

I finished my tea, took a deep breath, and turned to my grandmother. "Let's go see that garden of yours!" I offered.

Giggling like she was ten, she took my arm and patted it as we headed to the porch door. "Wait till you see my green beans!" She bragged.

The next morning when I got to the paper, I stopped by Terry's desk to check for messages. He was fanning himself with the morning mail. At ten a.m., it was already an oven on the third floor. In my office, I picked up the phone and called a sporting goods store at the mall. As I was hanging up, I noticed the morning paper lying on my desk. I picked it up and scanned the front page. Irritated, I opened it and checked the next page looking for my piece on Ricky. It was nowhere to be found. As I turned the page again, Harry, my editor, walked into my office.

"Hey, have I got news for you!" He waved a fist in the air. "The mayor's office called. You're being considered for some kind of award!"

I was still focused on the paper. I had reached Dagwood and Blondie, and there was nothing at all about Ricky. "Is Rosemary in?" I asked him.

"They covered it on the morning news! I heard it on the radio on my way in. They gave your name and mentioned the *Daily* and—"

"Is Rosemary in?" I repeated.

"What?" he began, flustered.

"Have you seen Rosemary?"

He couldn't understand my mood, considering his news. "Yeah. I think I passed her in the hall about ten minutes ago."

"She didn't print my story about Ricky!"

Harry frowned at me. "Lane, forget that. Look at what you got!"

"Harry, this was important to me. I wanted to put a little crack in everybody's stereotype of inner-city teenagers this morning. I wanted every person in this city to wake up and read a story about a good, decent African-American kid."

He shook his head at me. "Don't you ever just write stories? Is every word you put to paper part of a greater ideological plan to bring truth and justice into the world?"

I exhaled loudly in exasperation, but Harry just laughed at me. I stormed out of the office, paper in hand, in search of Rosemary. She was seated at her desk in her office, just as she had been the day before yesterday when I last talked to her. I walked in without knocking, waving the paper in front of her face.

"Where's my story?" I demanded.

"All over the airwaves, last I heard," she answered, not looking up at me.

"Not that story. That's just city government easing their conscience after what I dug up on them. The story about Ricky."

"Ooooh!" She looked up and feigned a chill. "Deja vu!"

"What happened to it?" I asked again, ignoring her dramatics.

"Well, for your information, after we talked the other day I went into the editors' meeting and told them how it had occurred to me that burying that story about the murder of an African-American teenager might be interpreted as racist by our reading public—"

"Occurred to you?"

"Yes—you remember, during our talk—and I told them I was afraid that might generate some negative publicity for us so we should do a follow-up biographical piece."

My eyes narrowed but I held my composure.

"And they seemed to think it was a good idea. Then last night they mentioned to me that we hadn't gotten any calls or anything about it at all—nothing—so I said 'let's just drop it then,' but they looked at the article you'd written about Ricky and they really liked it."

"They liked it?"

"Yes. They said it was really—what was the word? Oh, yeah—nice. It was really nice. And sweet. Somebody called it sweet."

My stomach was turning over, but it was my own fault.

"So someone suggested giving you more time on this to do something in-depth. Give you three-thousand words or so, more if you want it. There's no great rush because no one's calling threatening to cancel their subscription or labeling us racists. Just get it in sometime in the next week. All right?"

I panicked. "I can't do this, Rosemary."

Her eyes widened. "Why?"

I had to think of something fast. "Well, my story about the mayor's office. You know I'm still generating a lot of follow-up material..."

"Well, sure, Lane. But I know how you work. Ha! You're a researcher! You've got enough material in those ratty notebooks of yours or sitting right up there in your head for three weeks of follow-up! You can't fool me. You just want to slack off for a few weeks."

I was shaking my head. "I can't, Rosemary. I just can't."

"Sure you can. Besides, it's already been decided. You're assigned to it. Now leave me alone. I've got work to do." She waved me off. I wandered out and back to my office.

An hour later Harry walked into my office, not realizing that I was in there until he was halfway to my desk.

"Oh. You're here."

"Yeah."

"I got a message for you. It's from a woman named Elaine who owns a consignment shop downtown."

I looked up hopefully. "What did she say?"

He threw the message on my desk. "She said that from her records she's never sold a pair of shoes like the ones you described. You must have the wrong shop."

I wiped my hand over my face. "Great. Just great. I was afraid of that."

"Then the Jefferson County Board of Education called."

"And?"

"The middle school you called about is considered a school in crisis. They recently replaced the head principal; they're hoping she can turn things around. Apparently the school is inches from the state coming in and taking over."

"Well, I guess that answers a question for me." I swiveled in my chair.

"What?"

"I had a very unsatisfactory interview with the assistant principal there—a Jack Tinsley. He was very evasive and extremely unquotable. I was suspicious of his motivations."

"Ha!" Harry burst out with laughter. "Smart guy, if you ask me. He's already got a school in crisis; the last thing he wants is his name to be mentioned in a possibly unflattering article—so he gives you nothing but boring quotes. I think that's brilliant!"

I grinned. "Well, you're right, it worked. I only quoted him once about what a tragedy Ricky's death was. Even that was too insipid to print, but I used it anyway."

"I'm sure he's sorry that you mentioned him at all."

"Oh, well—another disappointed reader."

"And there's one more," Harry held up the last message note. "From an Ann. It says, 'Congratulations.'"

"Congratulations?" I raised an eyebrow.

"For being nominated for the mayor's award, I'm sure."

"Oh, yeah."

Harry looked around. "Good grief. Why don't you turn on the lights?"

"It's cooler this way. And I'm thinking."

"Really? About what?"

"Rosemary wants the piece on Ricky. Only longer. More in-depth."

"All right!" He raised his hand to give me a high five, only I wasn't responding. "Hmm," he pondered, lowering his arm. "I thought that was a good thing. Isn't that good?"

"I don't want to do it, Harry."

Harry looked at me, dumbfounded. "Maybe I'm confused here, but isn't that why you charged into her office this morning—to demand an explanation for why your piece didn't get printed in the first place?"

"Yes, but that was to make a point. I didn't think she'd want me to write any more on it."

"And why don't you want that opportunity?"

I looked at him a long moment. I was going to have to confess. "Because I have a hunch that Ricky isn't the inner-city teenager I need to upset people's stereotypes. I think he's probably just going to confirm them."

"Funny," he frowned and sat down across from me. "The article I read over your shoulder yesterday didn't seem to imply that."

I squirmed. "Yeah, I know. But in my defense, I just had one day to collect information on a person's whole life."

Harry crossed his arms. "What gives you the idea that Ricky isn't the kid you need to dissolve everyone's stereotypes?"

I told him about my interview at the school. Then I went into the part about the shoes. "I called a store at the mall this morning. One hundred fifty dollars for a pair of basketball sneakers like that."

"Hey, this is Kentucky—basketball country. A pair of shoes like that gives a kid status. You suspect he stole them?"

"I don't have enough information to draw a conclusion. It's just weird, let's say, that he owned a pair of shoes his grandmother knows nothing about that would have cost her a week's income."

"You got yourself into this, you know." He laughed.

"Shut up. I know."

"You're a reporter. You should report. You shouldn't have an agenda."

"I know. I know. But the things Rosemary was saying! It was disguised, but it was racism. I wanted to confront her on it. I've been hurt by isms myself, you know."

"You shouldn't have used the story as your ammunition against Rosemary."

"Tell me about it. Now it's aimed at my own head." I pushed away from my desk. "I'm going to hate it if this story ends up being exactly what Rosemary said it was going to be—a story about another inner-city black teenager involved in some kind of criminal activity."

Harry pulled his chair closer to me, straddling it. He looked carefully at me. "That would be awful, wouldn't it, if Rosemary was right and you were wrong?" He wasn't smiling; he was watching my face. I looked down.

He continued. "The temptation must be pretty strong to put a little spin on this story, then—emphasize the good points about Ricky, de-emphasize or just lose altogether the things that don't paint the right portrait?" I nodded almost imperceptibly.

Harry sighed, then spoke gently. "If you want to be a spin doctor, go work for a politician. If you want to be a reporter, write the truth.

A writer's job is to look the world dead in the eye and write what she sees. Because, you know, if no one ever shows us the truth, we can never learn from it."

I didn't reply. Harry had done a pretty good job of verbalizing the struggle that had been going through my mind here in the dark of my office for the past hour. He got up and walked to the door, but stopped before he went out.

"And another thing, if it's any consolation," he added. "A real person is never the stereotype. There may be elements of the stereotype, but they will be diminished by the total perspective. The more real you make Ricky for the reader, the less stereotypical he will appear. And the more interesting."

He walked out, and I realized I had never had a decision to make after all. I just had a story to write.

Pulling up in front of the duplex where Ricky's grandmother lived, I fished around in my car for the photo she had lent me. I'd made a copy and hoped to use the opportunity of returning the original to talk a little more with her about Ricky. I rang the bell to her apartment, but there was no sound inside and no one came to the door. On impulse, I walked down to the first floor and knocked on the door of that apartment, but my knocks rang hollow inside.

Giving up, I went outside. On my way down the walk to my car, I waved at the next-door neighbor who was working in her yard—a tiny, white-haired woman with an apron over her thin housedress. She shouted over to me, "She went to the funeral."

I went over to talk. "Was that today?" I was disappointed. I would have liked to have been there to cover it.

She looked at her watch. "Yep. It's been over for an hour or so by now, I'm sure."

"How did you know that was the apartment I was visiting?" I asked, impressed.

"The first floor hasn't had a renter in two years. Plumbing problems, I think. Who are you?"

The question was blunt and I smiled. Someone was watching out for her neighbor. "I'm Lane Montgomery, reporter for the *Louisville Daily*. I'm writing an article about Ricky Simms."

She wiped the black skin of her forehead with the back of her gardening glove. "I'm Mattie Siskell. Nice to meet you. Mrs. Watterston said there was a reporter here asking questions about Ricky the other day, but I thought it was a man."

"That was probably me. I wrote a short article about Ricky and the editors liked it so much they wanted me to do something longer. So, I'm back."

"Well, he was a popular kid, no doubt."

The comment surprised me. "Was he really? I got the idea from his grandmother that he didn't have any friends at all."

"Yes, ma'am. Everyday after school kids coming in and out of that place. He had lots of friends, white and black. They were quiet, though. They never caused me any problems, and teenagers make me nervous, you know. 'Course, most of these kids were young. Not many big teenagers."

"Did Mrs. Watterston know about this?"

"I don't think so. We never talked much. She works all day and when she comes home she's tired from bein' on her feet all day. I mentioned about Ricky's friends to her just yesterday and she looked relieved, you know. She didn't know he had so many friends. I think it helped her to know he did. They was always gone by the time she got home. I think Ricky asked them to leave before his grandma got home so she could rest when she got in."

"So you knew Ricky?"

"A little bit."

"What was he like?" Maybe I was finally going to get some perspective on this kid.

"Spoiled rotten." She didn't smile.

"I take it you don't mean that in a good way."

She shook her head. "It started after his daddy left the family, and it got worse when Ricky's mama was killed in a car accident. His grandma felt so sorry for Ricky—that those awful things had happened to him—that she couldn't do nothin' to hurt his feelings. She couldn't bring herself to punish him for anything, to say no to him, nothin'. If he wanted it, he got it, what she could afford. If he didn't want to do it, he didn't have to. Anything so he wouldn't cry. 'Course, a kid raised like that grows up thinkin' the world should bow down to him. It's a big shock when he gets older and it don't. He gets angry, really angry at the world, because he thinks it's turned on him. In a way it has, I guess, and it's not his fault."

"His grandmother seems to think Ricky took good care of her."

"He took care of her, but he didn't respect her. I never heard such back talk from a child."

"Sounds like you've raised children yourself," I said.

"My husband and I raised six. And they all turned out pretty good, if I do say so myself." She grinned. "But Ricky, he was headed for trouble. The way he died, well, it makes me wonder if he'd already found it."

"Do you know any of his friends? I'd like to talk to some of them. Nobody else seems to know he had friends."

"Naw. I just saw them coming and going. Well, now, there was Trina. She's a white girl. She was close to Ricky as flies on flypaper." She fanned herself with a gardening glove.

"Trina. Do you know her last name?"

She thought a moment. "Garby. Garby's her last name."

"You said they were close. Boyfriend and girlfriend?"

She shrugged. "I never saw anything like that. Oh, then there was Lamont. Lamont Wallace. He's a black boy who was Trina's friend, too. But he ain't been around here since I don't know when. I don't think he liked Ricky. I don't blame him for that. Those are the only two I ever talked to." I wrote the names down. She watched me, then added, "I'll tell you who you should talk to. Go down to the Butchertown Youth Club. All the kids around here goes there. Ricky used to hang out there with the rest of the kids. Talk to them."

She gave me directions and I wrote them down in my notebook. I handed her my card. "Mrs. Siskell, if you see either one of Ricky's friends—Trina, or..." I glanced at my notes, "Lamont—please call me." She nodded. We shook hands goodbye.

I drove back to the paper by the interstate, with my windows down and my inefficient air-conditioner running full blast. The radio said that a hurricane was organizing over the Gulf of Mexico and could present itself as a threat to the Florida panhandle. I envied Florida, however inappropriately of me. The only moisture we had seen in Louisville in days was the heavy blanket of humidity that lay perpetually over the Ohio River valley.

Back in my office, I sat down and tried to clear a space on my desk big enough to work on. It seemed to me that if something as awesome as a hurricane could organize itself over the ocean, then just once my desk could organize itself. I had a message that Bev Holloway from Homicide had called, so I picked up the phone and dialed her. She picked up. "Bev. It's Lane."

"Hey, girl. I've been trying to reach you."

"What've you got for me?"

"A new development. We've got a suspect in custody for Ricky's murder."

"Wow, great!" I said admiringly. "Who?"

"We're not releasing the name. It's a juvenile."

I considered that a moment. "These stories about kid killers always give me the willies," I confessed.

"Yeah."

"Well, tell me what you can—or a little more than you should!" I grinned as I picked up a tablet and hunted around on my desk for a pen. "How did your crackerjack detectives cleverly solve the case?"

"Well, it wasn't too clever," she stated dryly. "More like dumb luck."

"Really?"

"Yeah. We had a guy doing an undercover buy down in that end of town from this fifteen-year-old kid who deals in small stuff—you know, a joint here or there, a little powder cocaine occasionally. We weren't interested in the kid, really, until all of a sudden he starts shooting off at the mouth about how he killed Ricky Simms."

"You're kidding! What a break for you."

"It blew our undercover guy away; he couldn't believe his luck. This kid's buddies were really impressed with his bragging until we sent the uniforms in to arrest him."

"I guess. Did he say why he killed Ricky?"

"He said Ricky had been a regular cocaine customer, but lately he'd gotten tired of looking at him."

"What? That doesn't make sense."

"This kid—the one who says he killed Ricky—identifies himself as a skinhead."

"Good grief. I guess he retracted all that pretty quick when the uniforms stepped in."

"Nope. They said he looked pretty stunned at first, but he hasn't backed down on his story one bit. He's proud of it, he says."

I ran my hand through my hair. "Kids can get their heads so messed up," I said into the phone. "But I bet you folks are pretty proud of yourselves, even if solving this did involve a little dumb luck."

"Yeah," she replied, her voice lacking enthusiasm.

I hesitated, but Bev didn't volunteer anything. Something wasn't quite right. "Bev? Are you there?" I asked.

"Uh-huh. That's all."

"Are you sure?"

"Yeah. Listen, Lane, I'm swamped right now. I'll let you know if something else comes up, okay?"

"Bev—?" She hung up before I could ask her anything else.

I pulled out the yearbook that Tinsley, the assistant principal, had given me and looked up the names of the students that Mattie Siskell had mentioned. Mattie had said that Trina Garby was as close to Ricky as flies on flypaper, so I was very interested in hearing her opinion about a teenage skinhead confessing to Ricky's murder.

I found her picture in the sixth grade section. She looked small for her age. I flipped to the back to check her name in the index. There was one other page number next to her name. I thumbed back to page thirty-six to find a photo someone had taken in the school hallway of Trina with her arm around a boy about her age.

She was so thin she looked delicate, but she dressed to communicate another message: She was tough. Don't mess with Trina. Her jeans sported the obligatory rips and tears, her T-shirt and oversized jacket were a foreboding black, and her necklace was a silver chain with a skull pendant. Nevertheless, her face was in a full-blown smile. She stood next to a kid who was dressed neatly, as if his parents actually had some say in what he wore when he left the house. He grinned as widely as Trina. He was black, but he was not Ricky. I scanned through the notes I had taken from Mattie and found the other name she had mentioned—Lamont Wallace, Trina's friend. Checking the index and then turning to the page, I confirmed it. This was Lamont.

I pulled the phone directory out of my desk drawer and looked up Trina's last name, Garby. There were three. I hit pay dirt with my very first call. Sort of.

"Hello?" A gruff male voice answered.

"Hello," I said cheerfully. "Is this the residence of Trina Garby?"

There was a long silence. "Who is this?" the voice demanded sharply.

"I'm a reporter for the *Louisville Daily* and I'd like to talk to her about an article I'm writing."

"What's your name?!" He demanded.

"Lane Montgomery," I complied. "Are you a friend or relative of Trina Garby?"

"That's none of your business!" He barked. "Why are you trying to find my daughter?"

He seemed unaware that he had answered my question. I smiled to myself. "I'm writing an article about a friend of hers and I understand she could answer some of my questions. Is she there? Would you mind if I talked to her?"

"Where did you say you worked? The newspaper?"

"The *Louisville Daily*." My head rang as the phone slammed into the cradle on the other end. Strange man. I pushed aside the phone and reached for a file folder. No sooner had I opened it than my phone rang. "Lane Montgomery," I answered.

"So, you do work for the paper." It was Garby.

"Yes, sir. Does this mean that I can talk to Trina?"

"She's not here."

"Oh." I was wondering why he had called me back, then. I took a different tack. "Would you happen to have the number of her friend, Lamont? I could talk to him instead."

"I don't know a Lamont."

I sighed. "Could I speak with Trina's mother, please?"

There was a pause on the other end of the line. "Trina's mother is dead," he finally said.

"Oh. I'm so sorry to hear that." I thought of the photo of the rebellious little girl. "Mr. Garby, if you wouldn't mind, would you please have Trina call me?"

"I'll do that if you do me a favor." This sounded more like a command than a request. "If you see her first, you call me."

"What?"

"Trina's run off."

"Sir, have you called the police?"

"I don't want the police in this. This is a family matter."

"Sir, you never know. I think you should—"

"Don't tell me how to run my life. If you see her, you call me. If I see her, I'll have her call you. Is it a deal?"

I agreed. I asked for his work number in case I couldn't reach him at home. He rattled it off, and I wrote it down on an index card, which I folded and stuck in my wallet.

"Now, if you see her," he said gruffly, "don't say anything to her. Just call me and tell me where she is. I'll let you talk to her after I go and get her."

"Yes, Mr. Garby."

"All right then. And don't call the police. This doesn't have anything to do with them. Understand?"

"I understand. No police."

With that, he hung up on me. I pressed my phone receiver into the cradle, let it back up, and dialed the police.

"Missing persons, please."

I got connected immediately. The conversation went quite well until I came to the part where I had to tell them who I was. After the officer determined that not only was I not related in any way to Trina,

I had never met her, the interrogation ended quickly with a curt comment that if the father wasn't concerned, I shouldn't be worrying the very busy police about it.

I decided to take a break. Sitting back in my chair, I unfolded a copy of the *Metropolitan Inquirer*—Ann's paper—and nearly fell on the floor. The headline for the day read, "Tenants Live In Slum Conditions While Management Agent Lives High On The Hog," byline, Ann Alexander. What grabbed my horrified attention, however, was not the headline, but the huge photo of Gerald Barnes that accompanied the story.

It wasn't a photo from the *Metropolitan*'s files. It was one of the photos I had taken the day before yesterday. Underneath the photo, in tiny print, it read, "Photo by Ann Alexander."

This meant, of course, that Ann had developed the roll. She had probably dropped it off at a drugstore, because Ann didn't know the first thing about photography. I had to wonder what she thought when she saw most of the photos I had taken on that roll—shot after sensual shot of herself in that black dress.

Maybe it was time for a vacation. Katmandu must be lovely this time of year.

Chapter Five

The next morning, I took Mattie Siskell's neighborly advice and visited the Butchertown Youth Club. I entered the old red brick building through a small glass foyer. The smell of car exhaust hung heavy and hot in this space from the noisy street just outside. Walking down the warm hall, I stuck my head in the first office I came to. A short round African-American woman with horn-rimmed glasses sat inside, pecking away intently at a desktop adding machine. I said "Excuse me," and she peered up over her glasses.

"Yes! How may I help you?" Her rich voice burst forth with sudden cheeriness.

"I'd like to talk to someone about one of the children who used to frequent the club."

"Sit down, sit down." She stood and motioned to a chair. Only shoulder height to me, she was about as wide as she was tall. I smoothed my skirt and barely managed to slide my body between her desk and a filing cabinet to reach the chair. The amount of furniture that had been squeezed into this office challenged the laws of physics.

She sat down and took off her glasses. I know you're never supposed to say this about overweight people because they say that it's all they hear, but she had a very pretty face. She put her glasses down on a stack of receipts and introduced herself.

"My name's Marjorie Riker; I'm the director of the Youth Club. How may I help you?" She continued. "I do hope you've come to volunteer."

"Well, no, not exactly. But I would like to ask you some questions about a child who used to frequent your club," I repeated myself.

"Certainly, certainly," she bubbled. "So, you're a photographer?"

She was referring to the camera bag I was now rifling through in order to find my notebook and pen. "Uh...yes." I answered absentmindedly.

"It would be wonderful if you could spare a few hours this summer

62

to teach some of our children photography!" She clasped her hands together with glee.

"I, uh, I..." I pulled the notebook and pen out of my camera bag and set it aside. "That would be very rewarding, I'm sure," I continued, "but I'm a reporter with the *Louisville Daily*, and I just don't think I could spare the time." I handed her my card.

"A newspaper reporter?" She said, taking the card. "Oh, the children will love that!"

Apparently she still hadn't registered what I was saying. "I'm researching an article about a young man who was killed in Butchertown a few days ago. Ricky Simms." She nodded in recognition at the name. "I heard he spent some time here."

"Please don't take this wrong, you have a very trustworthy face," Ms. Riker leaned across her desk. "But may I please see some sort of photo identification?"

"That's fine; I appreciate your asking." I went through my camera bag again.

"You look legit and all, but one must be careful when it comes to children, you understand." I pulled out my driver's license and my press pass. She looked carefully at both and handed them back to me. "So," she began, satisfied I was who I said I was. "Ricky Simms. That was a shame, a shame. What do you want to know?"

I set the camera case on the floor again and gave her a suggested list. "What activities did Ricky participate in here? Did he have any hobbies? Who were his friends? His grandmother worked and didn't know a lot about what Ricky did at home when she wasn't there."

Ms. Riker shook her head. "Until a couple of years ago, Ricky was very involved with us, especially in basketball. He believed it would be his ticket out of poverty. But when it became apparent that he wasn't going to have the height to play in high school, much less college, his heart was broken. Absolutely broken." She looked sincerely distraught. "We tried to interest him in other avenues of accomplishment, but he couldn't be persuaded. Of course, he was still young. We might have been able to reach him after he got over his disappointment. But for the time being, there seemed to be nothing that we could do. He'd lost his hope."

"His hope?"

"Yes, Ms. Montgomery, his hope. That was the key." She clasped her hands and leaned toward me as if sharing a confidence. "Think about it. What gets you out of bed every morning? You have a dream, that's what. A belief that today, for instance, you're going to get a front-page story—or even better, a photo that might win the Pulitzer Prize. Or maybe your hope is that some young man you've been eyeing is going to ask you out to lunch today. Or maybe you have higher goals—more altruistic, perhaps—that today you're going to be the reason one child's life finally makes sense, and in turn that is going to make the world a better place. But you do have a belief, as private and personal as it is, that life is going to be better tomorrow or next week or in some indeterminate future because of something you have the power to do today. That is hope, Ms. Montgomery. And that is what Ricky lost somewhere along the way. Hope can be very difficult to sustain among the poor, the underprivileged, and the oppressed. When one feels powerless to effect change in one's own life, when the prospects for a better life—whether better materially or spiritually—become dim, a person loses hope. And a person without hope and the self-esteem it brings can allow awful things to happen to him or her."

"Are you saying something happened to Ricky?"

"Ricky became involved in drugs."

"So you don't blame Ricky for the drug involvement—he was a victim?"

"Absolutely people are accountable for their actions. What Ricky was doing was wrong. But please understand that I knew and loved Ricky—I saw him as a person, not a drug statistic. I believe that drugs are evil. But I believe that our drug problem has its genesis on a systemic level as well. We must be realistic, Ms. Montgomery. The avenues of advancement are still limited for women and minorities." She shook her head, then looked up at me. "When is the majority culture going to learn that limiting the access of minorities and women to the power structure creates these horrible consequences?"

"The police informed me last night that a teenage skinhead admitted to killing Ricky after selling him cocaine out on the street."

Marjorie Riker looked at me strangely.

"What is it?" I asked.

"That seems very odd to me," she said. "Was this kid—the killer—a supplier?"

"A supplier?"

"Of drugs."

"According to the police, the boy who killed Ricky just dealt in small amounts of coke occasionally. Why?" I sat back in my chair.

"Because I can't see why Ricky was making a buy out on the street."

"But you just said that Ricky took drugs."

"Yes—but Ricky was a dealer."

I took a moment to comprehend what she had just said. "A dealer?"

"Yes. It doesn't make sense to me. I can't picture a skinhead choosing a black boy to deal for him. But I wonder why Ricky would be making a buy, if not from his supplier? And why would he be doing that out in the middle of the street? From everything I knew about Ricky, he was your typical scared kid dealer. He only dealt to people he knew, and he only did it in the safest place he knew to do it—at home. It doesn't add up."

I was taking notes as fast as she was talking. I didn't know why I hadn't put it together before—the crowds of kids at his home after school, but gone before his grandmother came home; the shoes his grandmother couldn't possibly have afforded—stolen, I suspected then, but now realized probably were bought with drug money.

"Are there any friends of Ricky's I could interview?"

"Well, there would be Lamont Wallace. Outstanding young man. He's going to make something wonderful of himself. Lately, though, he and Ricky hadn't been getting along. Trina Garby was still good friends with Ricky, though. Ah, yes, Trina. Good child."

I looked up at her. "Good child?"

"Yes," She nodded to herself as if anticipating a future victory.

"If she hung out with Ricky, are you sure she isn't also involved in drugs?"

"Oh, no," Ms. Riker stated flatly. "Trina would never take drugs. She completed our 'Kids Against Drugs' program."

She stated the fact as if it was beyond dispute. Deciding not to challenge it, I took a tangent. "Tell me about Trina. Is she here often?"

"Almost every day. She's involved in our basketball program, too, just as Ricky was. Basketball is our most popular program."

"I would like to talk to her if you see her. I had a very short and strange conversation with her father last night. All I really learned from him is that her mother is dead."

"I'm afraid I don't know a lot about Trina's home life. She's very closemouthed about her family. I suspect she doesn't talk about it because it's not a good situation."

Not a good situation seemed about right, recalling my phone call of the night before. "Please have her call me if you see her," I asked, indicating the card I had handed to her.

"Certainly," Ms. Riker agreed. "But come to think of it, I haven't seen Trina for a couple of days."

"Neither has her father, apparently."

"What?"

"Her father told me yesterday that she had, quote, 'run off.' He didn't seem concerned enough about it to call the police, however. I wondered if maybe this was a common occurrence with her."

"I don't know. But perhaps you should talk to our basketball coach. Perhaps he's seen her."

"Yes, I'd like to talk to him—about both Ricky and Trina." I closed my notebook and shook my head. "You know, kids getting involved in drugs isn't something you get used to. It's something you feel in the pit of your stomach."

"You see, that's why what we do here at the Youth Club is so important." She leaned toward me over her desk, picking up her glasses to wave in the air for emphasis. "We try to show these kids, first of all, that they have self-worth—that they are important simply because they are human beings. Secondly, we try to show them that there are career avenues that they can take that will someday allow them to move on to better lives. They could be doctors, teachers, musicians, ballet dancers—or newspaper reporters."

I looked up at that last word. "I understand what you're saying," I stated gently, suppressing a smile, "but as I said before, I don't have the time."

"Of course. But let's go find Coach Perret. I'll show you our building on the way." I slung my camera bag over my shoulder and followed her out of her office and down the hall. She pointed out a room on the right. "We have a pharmacist who comes in once a week and does kitchen chemistry experiments with the kids. They make volcanoes out of vinegar and baking soda, that sort of thing. Last year one of our boys started college at the University of Kentucky's pharmaceutical school because of that class."

She indicated the room across the hall. "Here we teach kids about business. A woman comes in who started her own dress shop. I now have three girls and one boy who want to start their own businesses when they graduate from high school. Follow me." She led me into a long, narrow room. As we stepped inside, she waved with a hand and said, "I thought this could be your classroom."

Windows ran all along one side, filling the room with sunlight. There was a chalkboard on my left, and corkboard on the wall behind me. The room was filled with tables and little chairs. I could almost see the children looking up at me eagerly.

"It broke my heart when I heard about Ricky," she said intently. "We try, but we can't save them all. In the end, it's their decision. But

66

there are others. You may be able to rescue one of them."

I hesitated, then said, "Maybe if I came in just one hour each day for a week—say, eleven to noon?"

"When would you like to start?" she asked.

"How about Monday?" I offered.

"Oh, I don't know," she backtracked. "You're awfully busy with this story. Are you sure?"

"Yes," I said. "Maybe I could interview some of the other children about Ricky."

"Of course," she exclaimed. "I hadn't thought about that! I guess you and the kids will be helping each other. Well, then!" she said gleefully, "Let's let you talk to Coach Perret!"

As she turned and headed out of the room, I suddenly realized how absorbed I had become with this woman. She had the charisma of someone who really knew what she believed. I smirked at myself. I was developing a little bit of a crush on her.

I followed Ms. Riker as she panted down a flight of steps to the basement, perspiration standing out on her chocolate brown arms. From the far end, I could see shirts and pants being tossed into the air from an invisible source. "Let me introduce you to Sherri," she said. "She helps out a few hours each month in our clothes closet." We walked back toward the textile tornado, and Ms. Riker pulled back the curtain of clothes hung on a wire to reveal a tall, athletic-looking African American woman.

"Oh, hi, Marge!" she said, before turning to look at me.

"Sherri!" I exclaimed.

"Lane!" she shouted, hugging me.

"Well, I see you two know each other," Ms. Riker smiled. "I'll let Sherri introduce you to Coach Perret. He's right outside on the basketball court. Ms. Montgomery, I'll see you Monday at eleven. Only the future will tell how important a sacrifice you have made."

"Thank you, Ms. Riker."

"Marge," she corrected, heading up the stairs.

"So you're volunteering for the Rev now, too?" Sherri asked.

"The Rev?"

Sherri grinned and nodded toward the stairs. "Marge. You didn't know she was a minister?" I shook my head. "So, she's looped you into volunteering, too!"

"I'm not quite sure how she did it," I smiled.

"Yeah. Funny how that happens," Sherri laughed. "I call this place 'The Black Hole.' You can enter, but you don't ever leave. I came in here two years ago with a friend who was volunteering, and Marge got ahold of me then. I work in the clothes closet and tutor chemistry. I'm not sure why I do it. Maybe it's the kids—I love them. Or, maybe it's because I have the tiniest little bit of a crush on Marge!" She smiled. "Let's go outside—I'm tired of being in a dark basement on such a beautiful day!"

We went back up the steps and outside onto a small paved playground. The light was blinding after being in the basement, so we moved into the shade of the building. At the opposite end of the playground, a barrel-chested black man in a T-shirt and shorts was blowing a whistle, overseeing a basketball game between six youths of about the age of twelve or thirteen. I wasn't surprised that the club's basketball program was its most popular. In fact, I was pretty certain that the average Kentuckian found the basketball coaches of the University of Kentucky and the University of Louisville more recognizable than the President of the United States.

"That's Richard Perret," Sherri told me. "He's a high school health teacher, but he gets bored out of his mind during the summers, so he spends most of his time here." She smiled at me. "Can you imagine? If I had my summers off, I'd spend the whole time at the beach!" She turned to me. "So, what brought you here?"

I gave her a quick review of the profile piece I was working on, then concluded. "What got under my skin, though, was all the attention that story three years ago got when a white kid was killed downtown. The media was all over that until it was solved. Now we've got the same sort of situation involving a black kid, and nobody notices. There's no public outrage." I looked at Sherri and shook my head. "Are we ever going to be able to end it, Sherri? The racism, I mean."

She gave me a look. "Please tell me you don't think I know the answer to that because I'm black."

I frowned at her. "I don't assume you know the answer because you're black. It's just a question that's been on my mind a lot the past couple of days."

"Girl, don't you think if I knew that I'd be head of the United Nations or something?" She swatted at me and I laughed. She continued. "I do know one thing, though. Do you like buffets?"

"What?"

"Do you like buffets? You know, like seafood buffets."

"Yeah. A lot."

"What's your favorite thing on the seafood buffet?"

"Lobster, I guess."

"Say you died."

"I died?"

"Yeah, you died, and you woke up, and all around you there was this harp music playing, and stretched out in front of you was a mile long buffet table of lobster. Lobster and more lobster as far as you could see. And there was this nice little table with a white tablecloth and candles on it, and you could eat all the lobster you wanted for free. What would you think?"

"Sounds like heaven all right!" I laughed.

"So say you ate all you wanted until finally you were so full you crawled into this warm little bed there beside your table and fell asleep. Then you woke up, and there was the lobster buffet again, full of fresh lobster as if you had never eaten there in the first place."

"I could handle that!"

"Sure you could! So you eat and eat, then go to sleep, and when you wake up, there it is again, full of lobster!"

"Lobster again?"

"Sure! You love lobster! So you eat and eat and eat until you fall asleep, and you wake up, and there's more lobster..."

"More lobster? Don't I ever get anything else?"

"No! Because, you see—you're not in heaven. You're in hell!"

I looked at her a moment. "So what's your point?"

"All I'm saying is that I don't think what everyone wants is a colorblind society, even if that's what they say they want. That's not how we should try to end racism. I think it's great that we come in all these different colors and cultures and ways of being. I mean, I like being black. I love it. I wouldn't want to be white, would you?"

"Very funny."

"And I think when God looks down on us He doesn't want to see one big lobster buffet."

I smiled at her. "Good point. Sherri, do me one favor. Call me if you see Trina Garby or Lamont Wallace. I want to talk to them."

"Anything for you, girl!" She stretched, then moved to a lighter topic. "So? What's been going on lately? I haven't seen you in months. Are you seeing anyone?"

I shook my head.

"Girl, you need to get out more." She winked, and we started catching up. We had been traveling in different circles, and both had information on people that the other hadn't seen in a while.

"What about Ann Alexander?" I asked too casually, but Sherri didn't seem to notice. "Is she seeing anyone?"

"I don't know for sure," Sherri answered. "Last I heard, she was dating a doctor—a gynecologist, I think. I've heard some people say it's serious for Ann, but I'm not sure. You know what an enigma Ann is." She shook her head. "I don't know why someone hasn't snatched up Ann forever and ever," she added, "because that is one beautiful woman. But who knows? Maybe the gynecologist is the one!"

Sherri's comment irritated me, so I changed the subject. "Hey, I haven't asked about Meredith! How is she?" Sherri and Meredith had been together twelve years now, ever since they met in college. Sherri discussed Meredith in glowing terms until something distracted her.

"What is it, Sherri? What's the matter?"

"Oh, nothing," she looked back to me, then gazed out past the playground again. "It's just...well, Richard—the basketball coach. Can you see him now?"

I squinted as I looked across the bright playground. The kids and Richard had finished their game and wandered off the court during my conversation with Sherri, and now four of the young people were getting into a car with Richard. I could barely make out their figures through the chain-link fence because Richard had parked nearly half a block away.

"Yeah. I see him. But you look worried."

She shrugged. "It's just that...well, it's against club rules to take the kids anywhere in your own vehicle." She smiled. "I don't know. I'm sure it's nothing."

"Maybe they've got some kind of field trip planned today."

"That may be it," she said. "Field trips are posted on the bulletin board in the front hall." She shrugged and began talking about Meredith again. I listened to her, but watched Richard Perret's little yellow car as it drove out of sight with all four boys aboard. After a bit, Sherri said she had to get back to work on the clothes. We hugged, and she went down to the basement, while I went back into the building at the first floor level and headed for my car. In the foyer, on impulse, I stopped and checked the bulletin board. No field trips were scheduled for today.

Back at the office, I called Detective Holloway. She picked up the phone right away. "Bev, either I have something new for you, or you're holding out on me."

"What do you mean?" Her voice was cautious.

"I learned today that Ricky wasn't just a user. He was a dealer."

She hesitated. "Yeah."

70

"So you knew that?"

"We knew."

"Then why was he buying coke from a skinhead, Bev? Does that make sense?"

"It's possible."

"But not likely, do you think? You don't think the skinhead's a supplier, either, do you?"

"No. We think he's a low-level dealer like Ricky."

"So your premise doesn't quite add up."

"That's up to the lawyers, Lane. We just get them off the streets."

"I think your job is to get the guilty ones off the streets."

"He is guilty," she snapped. "The skinhead deals to kids just like Ricky did."

"So he's guilty of dealing. But maybe not of murder."

Bev got very quiet on the other end.

"Bev, are you still there?" She murmured a yes. I spoke gently. "I want your professional perspective on this, Bev. So tell me. Do you believe this kid murdered Ricky?"

"I'm not sure, Lane. Everybody's acting like this is wrapped up, but I'm just not sure."

"Does anyone else feel that way?"

"Yeah. But we're in the minority."

"Well, did his description of what happened fit?"

"That's the thing, Lane..." She paused and I got the impression that she was looking around to see if anyone was listening. "He didn't really tell us anything more than what he could have learned from living in the area."

"Why would he confess to murder if he didn't do it?"

"Status. Status among his friends. Status in a gang."

"But surely once the police entered the picture he'd have admitted he lied."

"Nowadays, Lane, kids think you're hot stuff if you've been to jail. And he'll get out; he's a juvenile. This little murder will be attributed to hormones or something."

"I guess this means you haven't found the murder weapon."

"He said he threw it off the Second Street bridge. That's a bit of a walk, but not impossible."

"Why isn't anyone questioning this, Bev? Are they so eager to chalk up another win for the department that they're willing that a real killer might go free?"

"It's not so much that, Lane, as...well, we know Ricky was a

71

dealer. He wasn't an innocent little kid. And this other kid—the skin-head—he's been trouble in the neighborhood for years. He's the kind that scares old ladies. And you should hear him talk—it's nasty, especially where minorities are concerned. It makes your hair stand on end. I think that my brothers and sisters in blue are just finding it too tempting, you know? It's so easy to just relax and say, well, that's two troublemakers we won't have to worry about anymore."

"Bev—"

"I know, Lane. I'm not comfortable with it either. I'm just trying to explain the atmosphere at the moment. Things may change." She sounded tired.

"All right. Thanks for the info." I changed the subject. "Hey, is that boyfriend of yours still living with you? What was his name? Larry?" Before I hung up, I thought I'd better get the conversation on lighter ground. Bev was a good source, and a reporter is only as good as her sources.

"Yeah, Larry. Yeah, he's still living with me. But I don't know, I'm getting kind of tired of him. He's absent-minded, and it gets on my nerves."

"Really? Absent-minded?" Bev was smart about a lot of things, but not necessarily relationships. She tended to go through men like running shoes.

"Yeah. Like he's always leaving the cap off the toothpaste so that when I use it it's all dried up on the end. And he never can find his keys—but he expects me to know where they are. And he's always leaving the toilet seat up."

"I hear that one a lot from straight women."

"It makes me crazy."

"Well, maybe those things aren't big problems, Bev. Maybe you could work them out."

"Well, I haven't thrown him out yet. Mostly because I don't see much else out there. The man pool isn't looking too good right now. Are the girls looking any better?"

"No," I smiled. "I'm not seeing anyone right now."

"Aww," she sighed into the phone. "You deserve someone special, Lane, you know that? You hold out for her, 'cause you could make it work. Don't fall for the first skirt that gives you the eye. And when she moves in with you, and you get to that point in your relationship when you're not sure whether or not the two of you can make it work, you just console yourself with the fact that no matter how hard she is to live with, you're never going to fall into the toilet in the middle of the night."

At about seven-thirty I walked out into the parking lot, but my car wouldn't start. I went back into the building, found someone with jumper cables, and tried to jump-start the battery. When that didn't work, I called the auto club and waited around for a towtruck.

The driver told me I needed a new battery, but that the real problem was probably my alternator. I told him that that sounded about right since I had been buying new batteries at the rate of one every few months for about a year now. The trouble was I could always afford the new battery, but never the new alternator. He grinned at me and told me he'd tow my car to the shop a block from my house. I could pick it up tomorrow.

As it was getting dark, I went back into the building and wandered up to the newsroom to see if I could bum a ride from anyone to get home. A small crowd, including the news intern Tiffany and four others, were gathered in front of the TV watching the cable news. As I walked through the door, a commercial came on with a woman advertising plastic wrap. "Look at her hair!" Tiffany bubbled. "Don't you hate it?"

"Could someone give me a lift home, by chance?" I asked.

"I can!" Tiffany perked up.

Bad idea. I was about to ask if anyone else could give me a lift home when Tiffany ran up to me. "Get your stuff," she said. "I'm ready to go now!"

I went back into my office for my things, met her on the news floor, and we walked down to her car together. She rattled on about couldn't I just not stand Ronald, who worked in the mailroom, and wasn't he just a real nerd? I contemplated whether my best chance of survival would be to close my eyes and hum all the way home. But halfway there, I thought differently. Maybe this was my chance to open Tiffany's eyes a little and express my concerns about the article she had written about the gay rights parade.

"Tiffany," I interrupted her stream-of-consciousness monologue, "I want to talk to you about something."

"What?" she said perkily, flashing her brights at a car that was driving toward us with its brights on.

"Your article awhile back, about the gay rights parade—I didn't feel you accurately represented the people who participated in that parade."

"What do you mean?"

"Well, first of all, you dwelt on the drag queens, the topless women, the...more 'colorful' aspects of the parade."

73

"They were there."

"Yes, I know they were there. But you portrayed them as something to be ridiculed, not as people deserving of respect. And then you ignored all the others—the average, run-of-the-mill gay citizens. The majority of the marchers. The ones that don't frighten old people."

She laughed at my joke. "But I wanted to cover the really gay people."

I winced. "Average, ordinary gay people are just as gay as drag queens and topless lesbians."

"Well, then they aren't as interesting."

"I disagree. I know the drag queens and the topless lesbians and gay mothers on unicycles make good stories, but the ordinary gay people are people, too. They deserve attention."

"But who cares about reading about them?"

"I do."

"C'mon, Lane," she said. She stopped at a light. "Say a tornado hits the town of Brandenburg. You go in to cover it. What are you going to take pictures of?"

"What do you mean?"

"What are you going to take pictures of? You're going to take pictures of the damage, aren't you?"

"Yeah. What's your point?"

"Well, you aren't going to take a picture of a house that's still standing and write something under it like, 'The tornado didn't come anywhere near this subdivision.' You're going to cover what's interesting, aren't you?"

The question was rhetorical. "But Tiffany, don't we have a responsibility as reporters to try to give our readership an accurate portrayal? To get beyond the stereotypes of people, to look beyond the 'show' and report the real story?"

Tiffany exhaled, exasperated. "You learned it, Lane, your first day of journalism class. Everybody learned it. All news is censored—merely for the reason that no one can report everything. So journalists are going to report whatever is the most interesting, because that's what sells papers. You've got to admit it, Lane," she said in a sing song voice, "that's the nature of the media beast!"

"But Tiffany, if we only report the carnival aspects of stories, how are we going to break through peoples' stereotypes of minority groups? How is the average person supposed to get past his or her stereotypes of black people as criminals if every time they open the paper or turn on the TV news they only see African-Americans as criminals? Shouldn't we be showing Mr. John Q. White-Citizen the African-American citizen who's the cornerstone of his or her community?"

Tiffany smirked. "Bor-ing," she sang out.

"And how is Ms. Jane Q. Straight-Citizen supposed to get past her stereotypes of gays and lesbians when all she's sees in the media about us are stories about AIDS, promiscuous sex, and scenes of gay marches from San Francisco or Louisville that are portrayed like a Mardi Gras in June?!"

"What do you mean, 'about us'?"

Oops. I sighed. Well, maybe it was for the best. My respect for Tiffany grew a little bit in that moment, her catching my slip like that. Maybe she would turn out to be a reporter after all. "I didn't know if I should tell you or not, Tiffany. I'm a lesbian. I hope you're okay with that."

"You're a lesbian? I see. That's nice. Do I turn left here?"

"Yes. Go left."

"Yeah, don't worry; you're okay with me. Consider it a non-issue."

I looked at her. "Okay. It's a non-issue."

"Lane, what I'm saying is that you can't expect the paper to be the hero on issues of racism, sexism, and homophobia. That's just not its job."

"I disagree, Tiffany. I think if we chose to make it happen, our paper—and the media in general—could be a powerful influence to eradicate ignorance. The media has the power to show the public that people of all races and sexual orientations are diverse within their own groups, and that no matter how odd some of them may seem because of your own personal world view, they are still people deserving of respect. Harry would say, 'If you want to write entertainment, go write for Hollywood.' He says that if no one ever shows people the truth, they can never learn from it."

"Yeah," she looked at me brightly, "but would that sell papers?"

"Tiffany—"

"Lane, the only thing that's going to get rid of racism, sexism, and homophobia is for everyone to get outside their little social cliques and get to know people who aren't just like them. But people don't want to do that. They want to hang out with people who are like them. Straight people hang mostly with straights, gays with gays, whites with whites, blacks with blacks—because it's comfortable. But the only way we're going to end racism, sexism, and homophobia is by getting to know each other, one person at a time."

I had to admit that Tiffany made a certain amount of sense. I was reluctant to buy into her argument, however, because it seemed that if the end of isms depended on everyone getting to know each other, we'd be working on this problem until the end of the world. But the criticism had validity, even in my own life. I had African-American friends—some. I had straight friends, but I didn't call them to go see a movie. What about men? Did I understand them? I sort of understood Harry, so I thought. But other than that, my sexual orientation put men on the periphery of my social circles. I sighed. Good grief. It had been a long day if Tiffany was making me think.

We were approaching my apartment. "Here, Tiffany. Stop here. This is my apartment." I bent over and started fishing around the dark floorboard for my camera case and file folders.

Tiffany pulled to the curb. She put the car in park and turned to me. "Lane, I think you're a very attractive woman—"

"What?" I finally put my hand on my keys, which had slipped off my file folders.

"I mean, you're attractive; you know, any woman would think you were beautiful."

I froze, my head still under the dash. Was Tiffany telling me she was gay?

"I mean, you are beautiful. No doubt about it...breathtaking, even. All the men talk about you at the paper."

I sat up. "They do?"

"But..." Tiffany hesitated. "Oh, I hope I'm not breaking your heart or anything, but...you see, I'm not gay."

I looked at her. "So?" I was waiting for more information.

"So, I mean... I won't be going up to your apartment with you tonight."

I looked at her, stunned. "I don't remember inviting you, Tiffany."

"It's not because I don't find you attractive—"

"Tiffany, do you think just because I'm a lesbian I was planning to seduce you once we got to my apartment?"

"Now, you're taking this wrong."

"I'm not taking it wrong. Why do you think I wanted to sleep with you? I hardly know you!"

"You're a very nice person, Lane. I'm just not...like that."

"Tiffany, I know you're not 'like that,' and I don't want to go to bed with you—I assure you."

"Now, see, this is what I was afraid of. Now you're angry with me!"

"Tiffany, I promise I would have been angrier with you if you'd

76

tried to follow me upstairs!"

Tiffany's eyes flashed. "What's that supposed to mean?"

"Just what I said—I don't want to sleep with you! I've never wanted to sleep with you!"

"What? You're saying that I'm not attractive? Is that what you're saying?!"

"That's not what I said." This conversation was getting really weird.

"Get out of my car! Get out! I'm sorry I gave you a ride home. And to think that all this time I considered you a role model!"

I climbed out of the car gratefully. The moment I closed the passenger side door she screeched away from the curb and sped down the street. I sighed loudly. So much for that one-person-at-a-time, getting-to-know-you conversation.

Chapter Six

Sunday I walked to the shop to pick up my car. I wrote out a check that meant I'd be paying my water bill late, then used my cell phone to call the office and check messages. Janice answered the phone.

"Yeah, there's one for you, Lane..." I could hear her fishing around on her desk. "Here it is. Someone called to say that they know where you can find someone named Lamont. Go to the middle school basketball court at one. They'll meet you there."

"One?! It's twenty till already! Who left the message? Who am I supposed to meet?"

"I don't know, Lane. I didn't take it."

"Thanks, Jan. I'd better run."

Normally, for safety's sake, I wouldn't agree to this kind of meeting, but I didn't have time to change the circumstances. Although I was dressed in casual jeans and running shoes, I hung up from the call and jumped into my car. Catching nothing but green lights all the way, I was still ten minutes late.

When I walked onto the outdoor basketball court, it was empty. I scanned the space around the court. The school was about a hundred yards down a gradually sloping hill, but there was no one around the building and all the lights were out. On the other side of the court, fifty yards or so from the edge of the school property, was a large complex of run-down apartment buildings. No one was in that direction either, so I turned back to face the school, sat down, and leaned my back against the basketball goal. Maybe I had missed my appointment, or maybe the person I was supposed to meet was late, too. I would wait, just in case.

I had been sitting for about twenty minutes in the sun when a car pulled into the school parking lot down the slope from me. It was an old Chevy. It circled the lot, stopped for a moment, then pulled out again, disappearing down the road. Apparently not my appointment.

Silence again. My legs were going to sleep, so I stood and shook them out, then leaned against the post. The only sound was my own breathing.

All at once a cold chill ran down my spine. Something was wrong, but I couldn't place it. Had I heard something? I listened. There was nothing. Perfect stillness.

That's when it struck me. Everything had become weirdly still. There was no breeze on this hot day, but now even the birds had stopped singing.

How strange, I thought. How bizarre. What had happened to the birds? Then the sharp crack of a pistol shot sounded from behind me, and a bullet sizzled by about six inches from my left ear.

Now, everyone knows that the best reaction to being shot at is to either hit the dirt or run for cover. It's in all the TV shows. I, however, stood there as if nothing had happened. Why? Because strangely enough, there is a small minority of people in the world, to which I belong, who don't react in the most advantageous way in situations such as this. Let me explain.

Imagine an average person is on her way to the grocery store in her car, when suddenly someone rear-ends her at a stoplight. Her first response, after the expletives, is probably to think, Look what this guy did to me! Look at my car! What's going to happen to my insurance?!! as she jumps out of her car with her wallet and proof of insurance. That is the normal response.

However, when someone like me is rear-ended, his or her response is more along the lines of, I'm sitting at a stoplight. I haven't even moved. I couldn't have had an accident. I think I'll go on to the grocery. In fact, I have this theory that a good percentage of hit-and-runs are perpetrated by people who are in this sort of denial. They think, I'm on my way home to fix supper. I couldn't have run over that jogger. I don't do things like that, and off they go.

I don't know if this denial occurs because of a reluctance to deal with a sudden change in the parameters of reality, or because of a natural and innate slowness of the brain, I just know that I do it. And so, as that first bullet whizzed past me, I stood there thinking, It's a beautiful day. No one could be shooting at me. I'll just wait for my appointment. As the second bullet zinged off the goal post at my back, just above my head, it suddenly occurred to me, someone is shooting at me. That's when I peed in my pants.

I dove onto the ground in front of me, eating gravel. When the third bullet ricocheted off the goal post, inches above my right ankle, I decided to run for it. I jumped to my feet and took off at the speed of light.

Winston Churchill said that the most exhilarating thing that can happen to a person is to have someone shoot at you and miss. I beg to differ. To me, exhilaration is beating the deadline with thirty seconds to spare, or opening a Christmas present from my mother to discover it's not a book about the top ten things nice men look for in women. This, however, was not exhilaration. This was stress.

I had a downhill slope to the school, but not wanting to give who-ever-it-was who was shooting at me an easy shot, I ran a zigzag pat-tern like a duck in a shooting gallery. I don't know if that's really the best pattern to run, but I figured if they give prizes for hitting a duck that does that, it must be harder to hit one. I'm sure I looked excep-tionally stupid, but at the moment I wasn't thinking about my image.

As soon as the slope leveled out, I hightailed it to the school and rounded the corner of the building. At this point, I had to take a breather. Despite being in excellent shape, I was gasping for air. Even more to my surprise, I discovered that I was shaking almost convul-sively.

The shooting stopped. Still gasping, I quickly looked around the corner of the building. Not a soul in sight. I scanned the apartment complex at the top of the slope from where the shots had come, but it was as if those bullets had come out of thin air. I listened. There were no more shots, no more sounds, no more movement of any kind. After a minute, the birds began to sing again.

I took two deep breaths and let them out slowly. Control, I thought. Control. Get a grip. You lived. I made a one-hundred and eighty degree turn and stopped dead in my tracks. I was looking into the face of an apparition—a face that was unfamiliar and yet somehow familiar.

I blinked—afraid to budge—but the ghost didn't disappear and didn't move. He simply stood, motionless, about five yards from me, with ter-ror on his face. He was a small boy, and as I realized I was looking into the face of a real person, he let a tennis ball, which he had apparently been bouncing against the side of the building, fall from his hand onto the pavement. Otherwise, he remained spookily motionless.

I began to regain my orientation. This wasn't an apparition, but a face from the yearbook. This was Trina's friend, Lamont.

Suddenly we were running. I don't know who started it, but we were flying—I, in pursuit of him, and he, as if I had an axe in my hands. We were halfway across the schoolyard before I tackled him. He screamed bloody murder, and I had to put my whole weight on him to hold him down. He made this quite uncomfortable.

"Let me go! Let me go!" he was yelling over and over, while I kept screaming, "Be quiet! Be quiet!" right back at him. I finally clamped my hand over his mouth. "I want to ask you some questions!" I screamed at him, before I realized I didn't need to yell anymore.

He tried to yell something through my hand. Out of curiosity, I pulled my hand away. "I can't breathe," he said.

"Oh, sorry," I apologized, taking some of my weight off him. He scrambled up and started to run again. I was faster. Yanking him back down, this time I sat on him. "We're going to talk," I said.

He was face down this time. "Man, lady! Where'd you learn to run like that?!"

"Lots of practice," I replied.

"Let go of me!" he demanded again, kicking. "I ain't done nothing!"

"I know," I agreed.

"I can't breathe!" He whined.

"That only works once," I stated. "Answer my questions and I'll let you up. First of all, who was shooting at me?"

"Somebody who thinks you're ugly!"

"Very funny. Who was shooting at me?" I leaned into him a little harder.

"I don't know!"

"Do you know why someone would shoot at me?" I asked.

"They shoot guns over there all the time. They shoot the birds off the telephone wires and outa' the trees!"

"That's a pretty sick form of entertainment."

"They was probably shootin' at the birds, not you!"

"I was the target. Trust me," I countered. "Who was shooting at me? Did you see them?"

"Are you a narc?" He tried to twist around to get a better look at me.

"Did you see who was shooting at me? Was it a man or a woman?"

"I didn't see. I just heard it."

I grabbed him by the arms and lifted him roughly to his feet. He started to bolt again but I reached out faster and grabbed his collar, pulling him back to me. "Listen, Lamont," I yelled. "I don't have time for this. This is important. Who else have you seen here today?"

His eyes widened at my use of his name. "No one, ma'am. Just you."

"All right, then. I want to talk to you about Ricky Simms and Trina Garby."

Lamont began arguing immediately. "I don't have nothin' to do with that. I don't! I swear! I stay outa' drugs! That don't have nothin' to do with me!" Suddenly, he looked like the twelve-year-old that he was, but I didn't loosen my grip on his collar. Not yet.

"Why should I believe that?" I said firmly. Apparently he was under the illusion that I was a police officer, so he was talking fast in order to keep himself out of trouble.

"It was Trina hung out with Ricky. Not me. My daddy tells me to stay away from those people. But Trina did it to get back at her mom."

That comment stopped me. When Herbert Garby, Trina's dad, told me that Trina's mom was dead, he hadn't indicated that she had died recently. "Why did Trina want to get back at her mom?" I asked Lamont.

"You better ask her about that."

"Trina's run away from home," I countered. "I can't find her to ask her."

"I know. I don't mean Trina. I mean ask Trina's mom."

I faltered slightly. Struggling to make sense of how I was supposed to interrogate a dead woman, I asked, "You mean, Trina's stepmother?"

"No," Lamont's eyebrows lowered. "She doesn't have a stepmom. Ask her real mom."

At that, I let go of Lamont's collar. Somewhere I had made a wrong turn and I wasn't in Kansas anymore. I took a deep breath. "Lamont, I need your help." I reached for my press pass, which was in my back pocket, and handed it to him. "Do you know what this says?"

He glanced at it without trying to read it. "That you're a narc?" he asked.

"Not exactly," I answered, putting the pass back into my pocket. I scanned the schoolyard for any movement as I spoke. "Lamont, would you go on a ride with me so we can talk? I'm not sure either one of us is safe here."

Lamont agreed and got right in the car with me, apparently still believing I was an undercover police officer. I struggled with the impulse to lecture him then and there about ever getting in a car with a stranger, but that certainly wouldn't have advanced my purposes or afforded Lamont any protection from whoever had been shooting at me. He got in the car, and we headed to the nearest service station.

"You do know that Trina is missing?" I asked.

"Yeah. Trina's mom is real tore up about it."

"Lamont, does Trina live with her mom or her dad?"

"Her mom." Lamont was eyeing me suspiciously. He was beginning to figure out that I wasn't the omniscient being he had taken me to be at first.

"What's Trina's mom's name?"

"Mrs. Coleman—Teresa."

"Do you know where Trina is, Lamont?"

For a moment, I thought Lamont was going to cry on me. Then he became very stoic. "Mama said she's probably dead. I saw Ricky and Trina getting on a bus together the night Ricky got killed. They were goin' to Ricky's house. Mama said probably one of the men who works with the drug dealers killed Ricky and Trina, and they just haven't found Trina's body yet. She said that's what happens when kids gets involved with drugs."

"Did Trina take drugs?"

"No." Lamont was firm. "Trina said she'd never take drugs."

"Then why was she hanging out with Ricky Simms, Lamont?"

"Trina kept telling me it was to make her mom mad."

"Why would hanging out with Ricky make her mom mad?"

"Probably because her mom didn't want Trina bein' friends with any kid who was a dealer."

"Why did Trina want to make her mom mad?"

He shrugged. "I don't know. But Trina and Ricky hung out at Trina's place all the time."

"Do you know Trina's dad?"

Lamont shook his head. "Trina's talked about him."

"Well, Trina's dad is worried about her. He asked me to call him if I found her. If you see her, will you call me to let me know?" I handed him one of my cards and fifty cents, which I kept in the ashtray. "Do you know who Ricky got his drugs from, Lamont?"

Lamont started to say something, stopped himself, then decided to speak. "A old woman who lived in another building from mine talked to the police, and a dealer beat her up an' she's in the hospital. I heard my daddy talkin' about it to my mama."

I looked at Lamont, considering the import of what he had said. "Then never mind, Lamont. But keep that card and call me if you need me for anything, okay?"

Lamont hesitated, then said, "I think maybe I know."

"What?"

"Where Ricky got his drugs."

"Was it a teenage white boy?"

Lamont looked at me. "No."

"Who was Ricky's supplier, then? Who gave Ricky the drugs he sold?"

"I don't know for sure."

"Who do you think, then?"

"I think maybe he got the drugs from the man who fixes stuff in our apartment buildings. That's how Ricky met Trina. He rode over here with the handyman in the handyman's car."

"Do you know the handyman's name, Lamont?" Lamont shook his head. "Do you know anyone else that Ricky might have gotten his drugs from?" Lamont didn't answer, he just stared straight ahead.

Since he was clamming up on me, I changed the subject. "What do you want to be when you grow up, Lamont?"

"A lawyer. Rev. Marge told me I would make a good lawyer. But Mama says I have to work harder in school if I want to be a lawyer. My grades went up this year."

I pulled into the service station. "Lamont, it's probably better if you don't tell anyone that you talked to me."

Lamont nodded.

I parked and told Lamont to stay in the car, then rummaged around in my back seat until I found a pair of sweatpants. I'm one of those people who never cleans out her car, but now and then this comes in handy, like when you need a kitchen sink. I stepped into the restroom and changed into sweatpants, because when I said earlier that I peed in my pants, I meant that literally.

After my wardrobe change, I tossed my jeans into the trunk, pulled out my wallet with Trina's dad's daytime number in it, took out my cell phone, and dialed the number I had written next to the words "work phone." After three rings, someone picked up.

"O'Malley's Pub," an unfamiliar male voice answered.

"Is a Mr. Herbert Garby there?" I asked, trying to speak loudly enough that he could hear me over the television and clatter on his end of the line.

"Nope."

"Does he work there?"

"Nope."

"Will he be in later?"

"How should I know?" I could tell by his tone that this conversation was boring him.

"What's your address?" I asked. As he gave it to me, I wrote it on the back of the card. "Would you give Mr. Garby a message for me if he does come in?" I asked.

"Lady, what do I sound like? An answering machine?" he retorted, hanging up on me.

"O-kay," I said measuredly, hanging up my phone. I got back in my car.

"I'm hot," Lamont said irritably.

"Sorry," I said. "I'll get a breeze going here in a minute. Can you show me where Trina's mom lives? I want to talk to her."

"Sure," he answered. "Turn right from here."

I pulled out and drove about a half-mile before he told me to make a left and stop. We were now parked back in the school parking lot. Lamont pointed at the apartment buildings on the hill above us. "She lives up there," he informed me.

"Great. You mean Trina's mom lives in the same apartment complex where someone just tried to kill me?" He nodded. "Do you know another entrance? I'll make a nice big target if I march up that hill again."

He showed me the way to a parking space a couple of streets over, where we got out of the car and walked across a grass lot to the apartment buildings. Lamont then led the way through the complex while I followed several yards back in case someone should start shooting at me again. After awhile, Lamont indicated a building to me and held his fingers up in a peace sign. It took a moment for me to understand that he meant apartment number two. He walked on, and I went into the building.

Trina's mom's apartment was in a simple dilapidated quadplex. The door to the front hall dragged as I opened it, and as I stepped in, a roach ran for escape from under my feet. The tile floor in the foyer was filthy, and a single burnt-out bulb hung from a wire in the dark entranceway. There were four mailboxes on the wall to my left, but the locks had broken off two of them and their mouths hung uselessly agape. On the second mailbox was printed the name Coleman. I turned to the apartment door and knocked.

"Who's there?!" a woman's voice came from inside the apartment.

"I'm Lane Montgomery," I shouted through the closed door. "Is this Ms. Teresa Coleman?"

A deadbolt turned and the door opened a few inches and caught by the security chain. A red-headed white woman in her mid-thirties pushed her face partly through the opening. "What do you want?" She asked sharply.

"Just to ask you a few questions," I replied.

"You better be with the police," she said, "or you're going to have a very big hole in you." That's when I heard the click of a handgun being cocked behind the door.

My first impulse was to run, but a quick glance at her apartment door convinced me to stay. The doors in this building were of the cheap pasteboard variety, and ammunition fired from a squirt gun would have probably found its way through the door to me. I put my hands up and decided to talk fast, instead.

"All right, all right, all right, I've got ID," I blurted out as quickly and as reassuringly as I could, referring to my press pass. "I'm going to reach for it now. I don't have a gun."

I moved my right hand steadily and slowly to my back pocket, where I felt the soft material of my sweatpants. Bewildered for a moment, I came to the slow and painful realization that I didn't have a back pocket. I had changed into my sweatpants at the service station, and my press pass was still in my jeans in the trunk of my car. Teresa Coleman shifted a little and the slim barrel of the gun appeared in the opening below her face.

I learned in college that one of the symptoms of fear is thought racing. Now I got to experience it for myself. I tried to think how I could persuade this woman not to kill me, but trying to read the thoughts flying through my brain was like trying to read the lips of the actors on a fast-forwarded video. When I did manage to understand one, it was ridiculous. I actually considered pointing to the ceiling, shouting, "Look at that!" and running. Fortunately, however, I figured out in time that doing so would only get me shot in the back instead of in the front, so I started talking, hoping something intelligent would come out.

"It's in here somewhere, one of these pockets, where did I put that thing?" I felt in my shirt pockets, wishing that my press pass would somehow appear there against all the laws of nature. And then it occurred to me—that one little lifeline came floating down that just might save my neck.

I kept talking. "But, didn't you call for an exterminator?"

She paused for a few seconds. "Yeah. But that was weeks ago."

I tried not to sigh audibly or fall on the floor out of sheer relief. People who live in infested apartment buildings are constantly calling for exterminators to come chase the cockroaches from their end of the building to the end someone else lives in. I took a deep breath and determined to have a whole new opinion of that life form from here on out.

So far so good. "My office just got the message to me this afternoon." I stopped the frantic search for my pass, hoping she'd forget that part.

"That sounds just like him," she complained. "...my landlord. I'm surprised he called you at all. We've been on him about this for months." She was running with the bait. "He don't take care of nothin' around here."

"Other people have told me exactly the same thing," I said, shaking my head.

"Why aren't you wearin' a uniform?" she suddenly blurted out, suspicion in her voice.

I tried to prevent a stupid look from crossing my face. "I'm here to take a look at the situation," I said. "I don't do the spraying. Someone else does that. I'm allowed to wear whatever I want."

"Oh," she said. She closed the door and undid the chain. "Take a look around, then."

I stepped in as steadily as I could, my knees like water. As she shut the door behind me, she released the hammer on her revolver and tossed it on the couch. This was one nervous woman, although I figured that living in this particular apartment complex had something to do with it.

"Sorry if I scared you," she said, standing next to the door in a housecoat and slippers. "I'm a single mother, and a woman alone in a place like this's gotta take care of herself."

"I'm fine," I lied. "So, you're a mother. How many children do you have?"

Teresa Coleman's face grew strained. "One girl, Trina," she said, walking to the couch and sitting. "I don't know where she is. She ran away—just up and left. Didn't take nothin' with her." Her hands trembled as she sat down.

"I'm sorry to hear that. When did that happen?"

"Tuesday morning's the last I saw her. I waited here all night for her to come home. She didn't." Her voice caught as she spoke.

"Did she have someone to run to—an aunt or uncle, a friend, her dad?"

She shook her head at each of my suggestions, then laughed when I mentioned Trina's dad. "That man?" she said derisively. She stood again and began pacing the room. "He don't care 'bout his daughter. He makes twice as much money as me, but I don't see none of it. You'd shake your head if you know'd all I do to keep food on the table. You'd think he'd wanna help feed his own daughter, but he's out spendin' his money on beer. He hardly ever sees Trina. Still comes by to see me, though. It don't stop him from comin' by to see me, if you know what I mean." Her sneer softened somewhat. "He's a weak man," she said softly. "Just a good ol' boy who don't care about

87

nobody but himself." Her voice trailed off.

"Have you called the police?"

Teresa's eyes narrowed. "I don't need any help from the police," she said, taking a drag off a cigarette from the ashtray on the sofa table. "But if they touch Trina, I'll kill 'em myself. I'll kill 'em," she said firmly.

"They? They who?"

Turning to me sharply, she said, "You're supposed to be looking for somethin', ain'tcha?"

I took my cue. "Yes, ma'am. This won't take long." Teresa Coleman turned to a TV talk show and I went down the short hallway.

The rest of the Coleman apartment consisted of a small kitchen and two bedrooms, but the smaller of the two bedrooms looked like a converted walk-in closet. I flipped on the light and walked in. This had to be Trina's room. There was a small cot against the wall, a pile of clothes in the corner, and a basketball in the middle of the floor. I got down on my knees and went through the pockets of every item of clothing in the corner, went through the bedding and ran my hands underneath the mattress. All I came up with was lint.

Frustrated, I turned and sat on the floor, leaning against the cot. I picked up the basketball, twirling it in my hands. "Property of the Youth Club," it said. I looked around. Nothing on the walls except for a picture of a TV star and some clippings about college basketball. The only other personal possession was a doll. I set the ball back on the floor and continued my search.

I didn't find anything unusual in the bathroom, but on the table next to Teresa's bed was an ashtray that held a stack of burnt matches. On the floor beneath her bed I found a crack pipe. I shook my head. I wouldn't be surprised if Trina was considering dealing as a career option. Her mother was a user. I put the pipe back where I had found it, went to the kitchen and made some noise under the kitchen counters for good measure, then walked into the living room, where Teresa Coleman was still watching television. "You've definitely got roaches," I said. "Is there anything else I should know about?"

"Mice," she said.

"I'll put that on my report," I said. I waited for her to make a move to walk me to the door, or wrap up the conversation, or acknowledge me in any way, but it wasn't going to happen. She just continued to stare at her loud talk show, her pale blue eyes somehow sunken in a paler white face. I wondered if she ever left the apartment.

I let myself out the door. Outside I glanced around for Lamont, but he wasn't in sight, so I walked to my car and headed to Trina's father's house.

Garby's neighborhood was perhaps two miles from the apartment where Trina lived with her mother. His house was in the middle of a row of tiny shotgun houses built so close together that if a wind toppled the house on the end of the street, they would probably all fall in the same direction like a line of dominoes. I went through the front picket fence of Garby's little blue house and walked to the door. His place was neat and well-kept, but the trash cans from the house next door were full to overflowing. The weeds in that yard had not been pulled in so long they were peeking their bushy heads through Garby's side of the fence.

I rang the bell and took a closer look around. A confederate flag sticker was displayed in the window of the front door, along with a sticker warning that the premises were protected by an alarm system. I doubted that. I rang the bell again. Still no response. Thinking that perhaps the bell wasn't working, I knocked. When that got no response, I decided to check the back.

I walked down the narrow driveway. The backyard was as well kept as the front, except for a dilapidated wooden garage that was leaning precariously to the left. It looked out of place; if I had been Garby, I would have pulled it down and carted off the pieces. I mounted the steps to the back door and knocked again, not really expecting a response at this point. There was a potted plant to the side of the door—geraniums. I was impressed. Garby put a lot of effort into this property.

Walking back to the front, I was about to get in my car when I saw a heavyset man with a black frizzy mustache step out of a bus at the corner. The bus door closed with a hiss and pulled away, and the man trudged up the sidewalk toward me. The closer he got, the more he eyed me, so I figured this was probably Herbert Garby, wondering who was parked in front of his house.

"Mr. Garby?" I yelled while he was still a good distance off.

"Who are you?" he yelled back gruffly, not slowing his pace.

"I'm Lane Montgomery, the reporter from the *Louisville Daily*. We talked on the phone briefly."

"What do you want? I didn't invite you to my house."

I walked directly to him, purposefully standing between him and his house. "Mr. Garby, why did you lie to me?"

He stopped. "What are you talking about?" he barked.

"You lied to me, Mr. Garby. You told me that Trina's mom was dead."

"Did you see her?" he retorted.

"Yes."

"You call that alive?" He glared at me, then walked around me and toward his house.

"Are you referring to Teresa Coleman's drug problem, sir?" I started following him to his house.

"What do you think? Do you think a man can hang around and watch a woman do that to herself forever? I couldn't. It just got worse and worse. I wanted to take Trina with me, but that would've killed Teresa." He made the turn into the yard, talking with his back to me. I followed.

"Mr. Garby, why won't you call the police about Trina? Do you know that Trina was last seen with a teenage drug dealer who was murdered the same night Trina disappeared?"

Garby turned on me so sharply I thought he was going to swing at me, but he just looked at me—fear, if anything, on his face. About the time I caught my breath, he growled threateningly, "And did you know that you are trespassing on my property?"

"Yes, sir. I'm going," I stated dryly. I turned slowly and walked to my car.

"Don't forget our deal," he shouted to my back. "I see Trina, I call you. You see Trina, you call me. After I come get her, you'll get your interview. I swear."

I lifted my hand in acknowledgement, too angry to turn back to him, and got in my car.

Back at home, I decided I needed a distraction to unwind. A movie would be good. I reached for the paper, which was lying on my dresser, and in the process knocked one of my picture frames to the floor.

I picked it up. It was a photo of my parents. It was the same photo that they had included in their church directory. They attend a very large, prestigious church that I less than lovingly refer to as "First Fundamentalist." Within the walls of that sacred building they preach a gospel that bears some resemblance to Christianity, although not a strong one, as far as I'm concerned. My personal proof of that is that the fundamentalisms of any religion bear a lot closer resemblance to each other than to their respective faiths.

The photo and frame were fine after their tumble. I wiped a little bit of dust from the glass with the corner of my shirt before I set it back on the dresser. But before I could catch myself, I had glanced to see if the light on my answering machine was blinking.

Chapter Seven

I grabbed a hamburger and headed for the theater. I don't know where my mind was when I picked the movie, however, because the one I saw had a gunfight every five minutes like it was a commercial break. I felt like I was reliving my day all over again. I left the theater exhausted, figuring my last chance for sanity was to go to Hearts, the popular local lesbian dance club. When I arrived, they were playing taped music for the dance floor, which was filled with women. I took a seat and scanned the room, checking to see if I knew anyone in the crowd.

All at once, my breath was taken away by the turn of a head. I think I actually thought: what beautiful lips, what a perfect chin, what an aesthetic line to her neck. Then I realized—it was Ann. She was seated on the far side of the room. I started that way.

"Lane! Lane!" Someone was trying to get my attention. I turned to look. Mindy Pincher was waving at me. I waved back, but unfortunately that only encouraged her. She walked up and took my arm affectionately. "Well, well, well! Look who finally got her nose out of the newsprint!"

Mindy Pincher was... How do I put this? ...very attractive on first notice. Unfortunately, however, first notice with Mindy is all but forgotten after about two weeks. I should know, because I was enamored with her for about two weeks. Mindy turns heads; she's also very fashion conscious. The hair is always perfect; the clothes are always just right. She usually reminds one in some spooky way of whoever is the latest box-office draw. I met her during a Demi Moore phase; she's been in and out of those. Then I saw her a year later and she was Sandra Bullock. I was quicker to pick it up that time, but by then I had figured out what to look for.

Sometimes she goes retro. In fact, tonight I was detecting a very subtle Marilyn Monroe. It was nice to see she has an appreciation for the classics. Personally, I don't see why gay men should have all the fun doing female drag, anyway. Mindy ran her finger up my arm, á la

Marilyn Monroe. "Come sit with me, Lane," she cooed. "I'm here all alone. I'd love some company!"

She laughed a sensual laugh, albeit a contrived sensual laugh. I laughed too, but I was trying to see through the head of a woman seated three tables away in order to catch a look at the woman with whom Ann was having such an engrossing conversation. Was it the gynecologist Sherri had told me Ann was dating?

"I haven't seen you in ages," Mindy said, pulling me into the booth next to her. The tone of her voice suggested a breathy neediness, which only exaggerated the Marilyn effect.

"Well, you know how busy I can get." I looked back again to see who Ann was sitting with, but now I couldn't see her because Ann had turned in a way that was blocking the woman from my view.

"But Lane, you don't ever even call me."

"I know. I've been following this story. It's really kept me tied up."

All right. So that was a lie. I just didn't have any desire to call Mindy. And there was a reason for it.

Although Mindy came across with a great image—however peculiar, with the movie star look alike thing and all—that's all she had. Other women seemed to have figured out the same thing. It took me three dates to realize that Mindy was all image and no substance. I'm no psychologist, but I suspected the actress imitation thing sprung out of the fact that Mindy Pincher had no idea who Mindy Pincher was.

Nevertheless, every time we bump into each other and she wants my attention, I give her another chance to show some substance. Who knows? People change. "So," I ventured, "what have you been up to lately."

"Oh," she looked at me blankly. "You know. Work."

I nodded and looked across the room again for Ann, but she was gone. I could now see the woman who had been seated next to her, however. She was attractive, probably of foreign or maybe even Native American heritage. I felt a slight panic. Was this the one? I kept staring at her as if by doing so I could discern whether or not she was a gynecologist.

"How about you?" Mindy smiled.

Oh, no. I wasn't going to let her get by with that. I wasn't finished with the exam yet. Mindy was good at asking questions. In fact, it took me until the middle of our third date to realize that from the moment we had met I had done all the talking. The fact that it took me until the middle of the third date to figure that out enlightened me about myself, anyway. I learned that as soon as I insisted on asking the questions, the conversation collapsed. I realized at that moment, that, in effect, I had been on two and a half dates with myself. I have to admit that I was rather disturbed by the fact that I had had a really good time, too. "So, what do you think about the latest welfare bill they just passed in Congress?" I asked her.

She shook her head. "I didn't hear about it. What was it about?"

I'm sure she had heard about it. Everybody had heard about it. It just passed through her brain without stimulating a cell, so she couldn't remember it. "Never mind then. Seen any good movies lately?"

"Oh yeah. *Racer.*"

I was initially surprised she could give me an answer, until I remembered that *Racer* had been playing to rave reviews all over the country. She had given me a safe answer. I decided to throw her a curve. "Oh, really? I didn't like it."

"You didn't?"

"No. It just felt too manipulative. You know, they build up all this anger in the audience at the beginning so you find yourself approving of all the violence in the end."

"Yeah. I know. That's what I thought," she said, changing her answer. "I felt manipulated."

"But you liked it."

"Well, not really."

So far, same old Mindy. Nothing there. But she was looking at me hungrily, too hungry—approaching desperate—for female companionship. I could tell already I was going to have a difficult time getting away from her tonight. I sighed. One more try. "Have you tasted the 'Death by Chocolate' dessert over at Frankie's yet? I had it the other night for the first time. Everyone's talking about it."

"Yeah," she responded enthusiastically. "What did you think? Did you like it?"

I looked her in the eye. "You first."

She stared at me tensely, afraid to answer, panic all over her face.

Same Mindy. "I'll be right back," I excused myself. "Can I bring you something to drink?"

The pressure gone, she relaxed noticeably. "Whatever you're having."

"Sure." I scooted out of the booth. As I stood, I felt a hand on my shoulder. Ann spoke from behind me.

"Hello, Lane. Care for a dance?"

Folk wisdom holds that some people carry an electrical charge in their bodies so strong that other people can sense it. Considering how

I feel when Ann touches me, I could be convinced that she's one of those people. At that moment, if I'd had my hands on the battery, I could have jump-started a car.

I looked over to Mindy, who was staring wide-eyed at Ann. "Do you mind, Mindy?" I asked. "She's a friend of mine."

Mindy sat blank-faced, staring stupidly at Ann with her jaw hanging open. I wasn't too surprised. Looking at Ann in the state Mindy was in can cause overload.

"Well, if you don't mind," I said, "I'll be back in a little bit."

I took Ann's arm and began guiding her toward the dance floor, but Ann moved ahead of me, leading the way. Looking back toward me, she smiled. She was going to make me pursue her.

I excused my way through the crowded tables and down the steps to the dance floor, trying not to look as impatient as I felt. By then, Ann was already smoothly making her way through the bodies moving to the music. I pushed my way through a crowd that had seemed to part like the Red Sea for Ann, but which was now swallowing me. When I finally came within reaching distance of her, she sensed it. Turning to face me, she took my hand, pulling me to her. As if on cue, the music changed to a slow song.

Ann reached for my other hand and, swaying slowly to the beat of rhythm and blues, pulled me closer, placing my hands in the curve of her waist. She moved them down, slightly so that they rested just where her hips curved outward. Then she put her arms around my neck and pulled me closer. My mind blurred slightly at the scent of her perfume.

"Your friend is very attractive," Ann said. "It's funny, though. She reminds me of someone. I can't quite pin it. But she seems nice."

I smiled at Ann in reply, but other than that made no comment. The lights turned to blues as we moved on the dance floor. I couldn't help looking down at Ann's body—the perfect shape of her breasts, her narrow waist, the firm hips that moved beneath my hands. Ann pretended not to notice me observing her. I slowly looked back to her face in the low light.

"Is she your date tonight?" Ann asked.

Maybe it was the lights moving above us, but I felt dizzy. I wanted to say no, there could never be anyone but you, but thinking of the gynecologist, I said, "Yes."

"That's good, then," was all she said in response.

I wanted to say something more, but I was overwhelmed by the feel of Ann's body in my hands. Already, I wanted to own it, to possess her, to make her move and bring her to incredible pleasure according to my will. I was losing it fast, here.

Ann must have seen the tension of desire in my face, because she smiled reassuringly as she reached to take my hands off her waist and put them behind her. This brought me closer to her, but at least this way I couldn't keep obsessing over the rhythmic movement of her hips. Maybe I'd even be capable of conversation.

Ann leaned closer to me without touching my body. "Well, she's very attractive," she said. "Good for you." She smiled at me and tilted her head to the side, leaning back so that we turned together on the dance floor. She rose again in my arms and pulled so close that I could almost feel the warmth of her skin on my face. She spoke low to me. "Lane, back to the question I wanted to ask you..."

Question? What question? We hadn't said anything about a question. Then it hit me. She was referring to the question she had said she wanted to ask me that day in my office—how long ago had that been? Four days ago? Ann had this annoying habit of picking up on long-lost conversations and continuing them as if there had never been an interruption.

"You wanted my opinion about something."

"Um-hmm." She began playfully running her finger around the collar of my blouse. "What's the connection between horse racing and a lot of cash?"

"Uh—let me see, don't tax my brain here—it wouldn't be gambling, would it?"

She pretended to pound on my chest with her fist. "But that isn't it! He's not a bookie! There's all this laundered money and it's tied to the horses some way but I can't figure it out!"

"Ann, there are all kinds of scams you can run where horses are concerned."

"It's not that kind of thing! It's not that...complicated."

"Well, maybe if you could fill me in on the whole story."

She frowned and shook her head. "Never mind. I shouldn't have brought it up."

She gazed at me for a long time as if there was something important she needed to tell me, but instead of speaking she pulled herself back into my arms, bringing her face softly next to mine.

She was holding me as close to her as I could possibly be without anything but our arms touching. Her face was now so close to mine I could feel the heat of her soft skin. Her breath was warm on my neck, and she clasped me closer—yet still our bodies were not touching. I don't know how she continued to move with the music and not touch me. I looked down the line of her neck to her shoulder, partially

95

exposed by the V-neck of the top she had tucked into her tight jeans. Our bodies were close, so close, that the slightest forward movement on my part would bring the length of our bodies together. "Lane," she whispered softly to me. "Lane—"

She stepped back. "Lane, I think your girlfriend wants you."

It took me a moment to adjust. It seemed as if my eyes had gone out of focus. I looked up and over to the table where Mindy was now standing. I must have been on Mars not to have heard her.

"Lane! Lane!" Mindy was shouting over the music. "Don't forget that drink you were going to get for me!"

I turned back to Ann. She was looking at me strangely, with an emotion I couldn't quite decipher. What was that look? What was it?

The expression left her face, and she smiled warmly at me. "I guess you'd better get your date her drink, sweetie. Talk to you later." She backed away from me and then turned, disappearing quickly into the crowd.

I had a thousand things I wanted to say to Ann to stop her, but whenever you try to say a thousand things at once, they always bottle-neck somewhere below the larynx. Then it was too late; she was gone. I made my way to the bar, and brought Mindy her drink.

Because Mindy couldn't think of anything to talk about, she started asking me questions. I tried to answer, but got completely tongue-tied when I saw Ann leave with the gynecologist/not a gynecologist. Because Mindy didn't know what to do if she couldn't get me to talk, all she had to fall back on was drinking. She asked if I would get her another drink. Preferring to be alone for a while, I agreed.

As I waited in the crowd at the bar, my mind puzzled over Ann's expression when Mindy called to me on the dance floor. What had that look been? I couldn't decipher it. It had not been meant to communicate to me; it had slipped unintentionally over her face, exposing her in a moment of vulnerability. What had it meant? What had Ann been feeling?

I got the drinks and walked back to the table. Mindy thanked me, and as I handed her the drink, the answer came to me. I suddenly realized what I had seen on Ann's face, and it hit me like one too many Kentucky bourbons. The cup slipped from my hand and bounced onto the table, cascading its contents onto the floor and all over Mindy. Mindy jumped up and yelled, grabbing a napkin and wiping her dress. "Lane," she complained, "what was that?!"

Jealousy. That's what Ann had been feeling. Jealousy. Over me.

When I got back home, I had a message from Sherri on my

machine. I held my breath as I dialed. Maybe she had seen Trina at the Youth Club. Meredith answered. She asked me to hold while she got Sherri.

"Lane, I called Coach Perret." Sherri said when she got on the line.

"Great!" I responded. "Can I talk with him?"

"Yeah. He said how about Tuesday morning over breakfast? He's got this thing for this breakfast place on the corner down from the Youth Club. He eats there every week. Will that do?"

"Sure, Sherri. That'll be great. Thanks."

"I'll be there, too. I hope that's okay."

"Of course."

"And another thing…" Sherri hesitated. "…I didn't mention that you're a reporter or anything. I just told him you're a new volunteer at the Youth Club."

"Okay." I was a little confused. "But why? If I'm going to interview him, at some point I'm going to have to let him know I'm a reporter."

"I guess so. But you remember what happened on Friday when we were standing out next to the basketball court? How Coach Perret suddenly disappeared with all those kids in his car?"

"Yeah."

"Well, after I got home I started thinking. That's not the first time I've seen that. I was talking to Meredith about it. You know, sometimes you see stuff but the pieces don't click together for you. I think this happens a lot, whatever Perret's doing. Richard Perret will leave, and suddenly a bunch of the kids are gone, too. Don't you think that's mysterious, Lane?"

Sherri was obviously caught up in the drama of the whodunit about Ricky's murder and Trina's disappearance. "Well, Sherri, then Tuesday morning—" I began.

Sherri interrupted. "I know a couple of other times I've seen kids walking to Richard's car with him. Once as I was pulling out of my parking place, I saw him drive by with his car piled with kids. That's against Youth Club rules!" Sherri was breathless reporting this to me, almost like a teenager describing the latest episode of her favorite soap. "I don't know what he's doing, Lane. But that time I saw him with his car full of kids, Trina was in the car. Whatever Perret's doing, she's a part of it."

"All right, Sherri," I said, absorbing the new information. "Thanks for setting this up. I'll see you Tuesday." I hung up, thoughtful.

Chapter Eight

The next morning at the Youth Club—my first day teaching photography there—I talked about the use of light in composition, but on such a basic level that the kids understood and even seemed to enjoy it. After class, I struck up a conversation with several of my 'students.' It wasn't difficult. They seemed even more interested in learning about me than photography.

"Did you know you wanted to be a photographer when you was a kid?" asked Charlie, a chubby white boy with wavy blond hair and freckles.

"Well, in high school I figured out that I wanted to be a reporter. I didn't take photography until college, and I only did it then because it's kind of handy to be able to take your own photos if you're a reporter. But it was during those classes that I learned that I loved it. I guess it's because photography is so different from writing. I mean, writing is kind of a left-brain thing and photography is very right—"

"What?" asked Latasha, wrinkling her tiny face at me. "What's left-brain and right-brain?"

Charlie laughed. "Latasha's only asking 'cause she don't have one."

Latasha glared at Charlie in a way that said she'd get even with him later. I scolded Charlie gently, then rephrased myself. "What I meant was that I love reporting because I love chasing down facts and figuring things out. Reporting is about facts. Photography is more about...art."

The conversation gradually turned from me to them. Latasha was the one who brought up the subject of Ricky Simms. She described him as "her friend who got shot and died." She was just old enough to realize that maybe death really was final. "I liked Ricky," she said. "He was nice to me."

Thirteen-year-old Harvey looked at me and said, under his breath, "Ricky was a bad kid."

Latasha contradicted her brother loudly. "Rev. Marge says there's no such thing as a bad kid! She says kids can do bad things, but there's no such thing as a bad kid!"

Harvey settled his lanky frame into a chair next to Latasha. "Yeah, you're right, Latasha. I've got no business speaking bad about the dead."

Since Harvey was close to Ricky in age, I decided to ask him a few questions. "Harvey, did you know Ricky well?"

"We used to hang out. Before the drugs."

"What was he like?"

"Aw." He grinned suddenly. "Funny. He used to be so funny! He could make you laugh!" He drew out the word, as if he was remembering some particular joke. "And if you were his friend, well, that was it! He stood by you to the end. He was the type of guy, well, he'd go into a burning building after you if he had to... Know what I mean? ...because you were his friend."

"What happened? Why did he get into drugs?"

Harvey shuffled in his chair. "I think it was 'cause he didn't want to work at anything. When we were little he used to always talk about how he was going to do all this big stuff. He was going to be a movie star, or have a band, or be this big basketball star, but he never worked at it."

A girl named Paula, I had seen out on the basketball court with Perret, settled into the chair next to me. "Ricky was all talk," Paula complained. "But I know why Ricky got into drugs!" Paula looked around the room, as if she had information no one else had. "Because it's easy! A lot of money, not a lot of work!"

Harvey looked at her, then back at me. "I think Ricky was kind of spoiled," he concluded.

"I'd like to talk to his friend, Trina Darby. Do you know where I could find her?"

Charlie interrupted loudly. "I know Trina! Trina's cool!"

I turned to acknowledge Charlie, but a deep male voice sounded behind me. "You know what, kids? It's time for basketball!"

I turned around. Coach Perret was standing in the door. "How about it, Charlie?!" he bellowed cheerfully. "How about you, Latasha? Paula, c'mon downstairs!" The kids obediently scooted out of the room. Coach Perret looked at me, an odd look, as if he was analyzing me, then followed them down the stairs. I was left alone.

I wondered how long the coach had been standing there and how much he had heard. I also wondered about the look he had given me.

Shrugging it off, I collected my equipment from the classroom, then walked downstairs and locked it in my car. About half an hour had passed since the kids had left my classroom, and I could hear them on the basketball court. I walked to a bench that was outside the fenced basketball court, sat down, and watched. Coach Perret was following the kids up and down the court, panting alongside them with the whistle in his mouth.

The basketball game came to a close at about a quarter till noon and Perret and the kids straggled into the club building. Thinking I could get a few words with the coach, I went back in the building and walked down a couple of hallways toward the door to the basketball court, but the group was nowhere in sight. Confused, I went out onto the playground, but they weren't there, either. Soon, however, I spotted the group of them through the fence—boys and girls, some of whom had been in my class—wandering down the street to Perret's car. I hesitated a second, then turned and went through the club door, jogging to the front. On the bulletin board under "field trips," nothing was listed for today. I stuck my head in Marge's office. She stopped typing and looked up at me over her glasses.

"Marge..."

"Um-hmm?" she gave me a half grin.

"Any field trips planned for today?"

"Oh! I wanted to tell you something. Our janitor said there was a reporter in here a couple of days ago asking about Trina and Lamont."

"Really?"

"Yes. And you."

"Me? Listen, Marge, about the field trips—"

"Yes, you. The janitor said you may get a call."

"A call?"

"Yes, you know you gave me your card. I told the staff to call you if they saw Trina and I put your card on the bulletin board. The janitor pointed it out to the reporter."

"What kind of reporter? Newspaper? Radio? TV?" Apparently the news that the police weren't so sure they had the right guy had leaked out to someone else.

She shrugged. "I didn't ask. But he thought that maybe this new reporter might call you with some information you could use."

Fat chance of that. I was losing time. "Marge, about the field trips..."

She looked at me. "What about them?"

"Are there any scheduled today?"

"Nope, I don't think so. But check the bulletin board." She started typing again. "Why? Did you want to plan something?"

But I was already on my way out the door. I got in the Jag, and on the third try, started the car. I whipped it around the corner and punched the accelerator. Two blocks ahead of me I could see Perret's car, full of young basketball players, making a left. I briefly sped up, then slowed just enough so that my right wheels didn't leave the pavement when I made the turn. I had Perret's car in sight again, a block ahead of me now. I didn't want to get too close.

I followed him to a supermarket where Perret dropped the kids off at the door, then circled the parking lot until the children reappeared, their arms full of grocery bags. The kids and the grocery bags all got into the little car—I can't imagine how—and Perret pulled out again, heading for the expressway.

After a very few minutes we exited onto a street of moderately priced, neat houses with medium-size lawns. Perret pulled into a driveway and the kids tumbled out. I drove on past the house, circled the block, then parked about halfway down the street where I had a good view. Soon the kids rounded the side of the house carrying rakes, hedge trimmers, garden hose, weed trimmers, and a lawn mower. I leaned back in my seat and groaned. I doubted I was going to discover anything unusual here, but I would wait, just in case.

I rolled down my window to let in a breeze, and with half-interest watched as the young people mowed, raked, trimmed, watered, and worked up a sweat. An hour and a half later, the kids threw aside their lawn tools and got the grocery bags out of the car. One of the girls who had been in my class, Paula, pulled a bag of potato chips out of the top of one grocery bag and tossed it to one of the boys. Then, carrying their bags, they wandered around the house to the backyard. I'd never seen so much food for six kids' lunch in my life. Oh, well. Growing children.

I figured they were simply eating lunch, but out of curiosity, I decided to drive around and peek down the alleyway. Most of the kids had gone into a small shed that stood in Perret's backyard. Only ten-year-old Latasha sat outside the door on an overturned bucket, munching her sandwich. I could hear the sound of muffled laughter and of voices, but I couldn't distinguish words. This was about as exciting as watching the kids rake grass. Nothing was going on here except Perret letting some kids earn a little extra money doing yard work. Since it was already after four, I decided to take off a little early and go to the country.

"Grandmother, I'll be fine," I fussed. "I don't need to wear that." We were standing on the enclosed porch off the den.

"Yes, you do!"she argued. "We're going to be out in the sun!"

"It's late in the day!" I countered.

My grandmother smirked at me. "What nice young girl is going to want to go out with you if you get leathery skin like an old man?"

"I wear sunscreen," argued.

"Are you wearing sunscreen now?"she asked.

"N-no…" I stuttered.

"Then wear it,"she said firmly, pushing the sun bonnet into my hands.

I held the bonnet in front of me. My grandmother had made it herself. The material was a tiny flower print. The long ribbons were meant to be tied under the chin in a bow. And all around the hood, which acted as a sun visor, was a frilly fringe of lace. "But, it's so…nineteenth-century," I complained.

Grandmother finished tying the bow of her own bonnet under her chin. "Lane, you're not properly dressed for the garden without it."

I grimaced. That would have been true sixty years ago. My grandmother had grown up wearing bonnets in the garden and had never noticed the change in fashion. "But, what if someone sees me," I whined.

Grandmother frowned at me. "Lane," she fussed, "in my garden, the only things that've got eyes are the potatoes!" She hobbled past me and out the screen door.

Obediently, I tied on the bonnet and followed her. We walked down the path to the garden together. My grandmother looked like something out of a Norman Rockwell print. I looked like a baby doll on hormones.

We stopped by the shed for a couple of hoes. When we reached the garden, it was humid and the sun was intense. Grandmother moved to the green beans. With one hand she leaned on her cane. With her other hand, she chopped between the plants with the hoe. I moved to the row opposite her, got down on my knees, and started weeding.

"Well, what's the latest scoop?" my grandmother asked, eager for conversation while we worked. Grandmother had never been a person for gossip where her friends or family were concerned, but she considered politicians, entertainers, and anyone in the news fair game. In fact, it was understood between us that whenever I picked up her groceries, I was to pick up a tabloid or two with the milk and bread.

"I'm sure I should be asking you that." I looked up at her and grinned. "What do you want to talk about? Hollywood? D.C.? Or Louisville?"

"What happened with the boy you told me about? The one who was killed? I never saw any more about that in the paper."

I updated my grandmother on Ricky's story. I explained to her how I'd discovered he was a drug dealer. I told her about following the coach and the kids in the car. She laughed when I told her how much junk food they had bought at the grocery, and how I had discovered the big secret about the trips was that the kids were doing yard work. I didn't tell her about how someone had used me for target practice at the middle school, however. That would have just upset her.

Grandmother changed subjects. "Your mom and dad came by for supper yesterday. They weren't very hungry, though. They'd had lunch at your great aunt Gretchen's."

"If they ate at Gretchen's they won't be hungry for a week. I'll bet she'd even made her Dutch apple pie for dessert."

"And your mom told that story again about the family reunion, the one about you when you were a little girl and that old cloth doll aunt Gretchen gave you that you loved so much."

I sat back on my heels and looked up at my grandmother. "I remember that doll! Gretchen made it for me—it had a hand painted face, and it was dressed like a cowgirl. But I don't remember what story you're talking about."

Grandmother grinned. "Oh! You don't remember that one? Well, you had taken the doll with you to Gretchen's for the family reunion because you took it everywhere. You couldn't have been more than three years old. And you were kind of young to be traipsing around like that, but you were following your cousins all over the farm and dragging that doll with you, and when you got back to the house that little cloth doll was filthy.

"Of course, your aunt Gretchen had made that doll for you, and your mother was terrified that Gretchen would see the doll dirty!" Grandmother grinned. "You know how that would embarrass your mother! So, with all those people at the reunion, your mother sneaks off to Gretchen's basement and puts the doll in the wash. Well, when she goes back afterwards and pulls the doll out of the washer, the face has washed off!"

I laughed. "Oh my gosh! I bet Mom was horrified!"

Grandmother smiled. "Oh, it was worse than that. An hour later, your great aunt Gretchen comes down to the basement to get some ice out of the freezer and finds your mother sitting on the basement steps crying almost uncontrollably."

"Really?"

"Oh, yes." Grandmother shook her head. "Your mother isn't worried about what Gretchen thinks any more. Your mother just can't bear the fact that your little heart is going to be broken when you see what she's done to your favorite doll. So while Gretchen is comforting your mother and they're figuring out how to fix the situation, all of a sudden you show up on the basement stairs. Oblivious to the whole thing, you take the doll from your mother and drag it back up the steps. For the next two hours, you drag that doll with you wherever you go and never notice it's missing its face. Finally, your aunt Gretchen distracted you with a piece of her Dutch apple pie. She slipped the doll away from you and painted on another face for it while you ate. Your mother said you never knew the difference!"

I laughed and shook my head. "I never heard that before."

My grandmother smiled. "Probably because your mother still gets a little choked up when she tells it."

I looked at my grandmother. "She does?"

My grandmother nodded. "Well, sure, honey! You'll understand when you have children. It's hard to think you came close to breaking your three-year-old's heart—even twenty-five years later!" Grandmother grinned and pointed to the row behind me, made up of little mounds of plants. "Look! There's a couple of yellow squash! Why don't you pick them and I'll fix them for supper!"

After supper I drove home. I had slept fitfully the night before, having dreams filled with guns and chases and I needed rest. But it wasn't meant to be. A storm rumbled into the area about dusk.

People from places like California and Washington State think they've experienced thunderstorms until they come to Kentucky and have the bejeebers scared out of them. Kentucky is second only to Alaska in its number of streams and waterways. That means high humidity which, combined with our Southern heat, produces rain that rattles windows, lightning that puts your teeth on edge, and thunder that from a distance sounds like the footsteps of God coming. What people from other regions don't understand is that our thunderstorms are the reason the Bible Belt is located here and not in the northwest.

I pulled a pillow over my head and tried to sleep. Twenty minutes later, however, I heard my phone ringing through the feathers. Too groggy to answer it, I let the caller leave a message. I was surprised to hear a young voice whispering into the machine after the tone. I pulled the pillow off my head. It was Lamont.

He spoke timidly. There was traffic noise in the background, indicating he was calling from a street payphone. "Ms. Montgomery...the name of our handyman is David Case."

David Case. Lamont was giving me the name of the man he believed was Ricky's drug supplier. Lamont fumbled with the phone, then gave me Case's phone number. "I hope this helps you," he whispered before the dial tone clicked in.

I was stunned. This was a courageous act. Lamont had told me what happened to people in his neighborhood who ratted on the dealers, yet he had gotten the information and called me anyway. I sat up in my bed. There were still heroes.

Throwing off the covers, I grabbed my phone book and flipped through the c's until I found a "D. Case" that matched the number Lamont had given me, then wrote down the address. In a minute I was dressed—including a light jacket for the rain—and on my way. I'd figure out for what when I got there.

I pulled into the parking lot of one of the city's nicer apartment complexes and gave a low whistle. David Case made a good living as a handyman; I should switch professions. The storm had eased to a light rain. I parked and ran into the lobby, getting damp but not soaked. A quick glance at the mailboxes told me that Case's apartment was on the fourth floor.

I took the elevator, then read apartment numbers until I was facing his door. The hallway was empty; the only sound a television blaring from the apartment at the end of the hall. Case's apartment was silent.

I thought about knocking but, wondering if he was alone, decided to listen first for any sounds within the apartment. Gently, I pressed my ear against the door.

A squeak came from the hinges as the door swung open. Leaping back a good three feet, my mind raced with lies. But no one was there. The hallway that greeted me was empty. I eased forward. Apparently, the door had been open the entire time—closed only enough to give the impression of being latched. This was strange. Very strange.

"Hello?" I called out, a little too timidly. I tried again. "Hello—is anyone home?" That sounded better. I stepped into the foyer. "Excuse me, is anyone home? May I use your phone?" I could think up someone to call if it was offered. But there was no answer. I walked on into the hallway of the apartment. Maybe he was just in the bathroom. "Hello? Is anyone here? I'd like to use the phone, please." The bathroom was dark, but there was an occasional light on throughout the rest of the apartment. Why not? If he could afford an apartment like this, it didn't look like he needed to worry about electric bills.

I turned and went back down the hallway to the other end of the apartment. Nothing was unusual in the bedroom except that it was a mess, but I certainly wasn't going to be the one to pass judgement on that. From the bedroom I went toward the living room. As I rounded the corner, something moved.

Something had moved. I was sure of it. I had heard it—or had I glimpsed something? My eyes searched for the source. Then it registered.

On a table across the room a fax machine was spitting out a single sheet of paper. I walked over and looked at the sheet in the tray. It was a list of addresses without names, maybe eight on the page. But a list of what? Two addresses I immediately recognized—Trina's apartment number and address, and Ricky's. Ricky's had an ominous X drawn through it, as if it had been recently removed from the list but the sender hadn't bothered to retype it. There was no sender's address on the page, but the bottom right corner read, "Page 2 of 2."

Two of two? I was looking at page two. Page one had to have been sent seconds ago. So where was it?

I raised my eyes and looked slowly around the room, suddenly struck by the sensation that I wasn't alone. A chill began to crawl across my skin. I raised my hand and took the fax partly from its tray.

"Who's there?!!" A booming male voice demanded. I turned sharply, instinctively dropping the fax back into the tray.

"Who's there?!!"

The voice was coming from the foyer, my only route of escape. Apparently Mr. Case was now home, wondering why his front door was standing open. All at once I figured out the old telephone bluff wasn't going to work after all.

Footsteps moved cautiously down the hallway in my direction. A deep voice called out, "You're a dead man, mister. Count on it. You're a dead man."

I was the dead mister to whom he was referring, of course. Frantically I scanned the room, which was woefully lacking in hiding places. I dismissed offhand the single closet in the room; it would be the first place he looked. Along the wall next to me was a window with a floor-length curtain, but I figured my white running shoes would be just a little too obvious peeking out from underneath.

Case's furniture leaned toward minimalist contemporary, which meant he hardly had any furniture, and what furniture he had was made out of ugly sticks. The only table in the room had a glass top. I panicked. It's not the recommended thing to do at a time like this, but I did. Only by sheer willpower did I manage to quit critiquing the decor so I could figure out a place to hide.

On the far side of the room next to the closet was an overstuffed sofa. It was pulled out from the wall just enough that most men wouldn't be able to hide there, but I just might be able to slip my body between it and the wall. I only wished to high heaven, though, that I had been a medallist in the fifty-yard dash because I was out of time. I ran silently across the room, then went up and over the back of the sofa, slipping quietly down between it and the wall. As I settled in the dark space behind it, I would have screamed if Ann hadn't clamped her hand over my mouth.

"What are you doing here?!" I whispered sharply, pulling her hand away from my mouth.

"Just shut up and pray nobody walks in on this guy!" she whispered back, turning away from me.

There was a moment of breathless silence, then I heard Case step suddenly and swiftly into the room. He hesitated, listening. My heart was pounding so hard I was sure he could hear it. Ann was in front of me, and I could see her struggling to breathe evenly. "I heard you. I know you're there," he shouted. "Put your hands in the air and step out slowly."

We froze. Neither Ann nor I were so much as taking a breath. I've never needed oxygen so much in my life, but I know when to drop a bad habit.

"I said step out!!" Case bellowed.

Ann trembled involuntarily and began to lift her hands. Silently I reached forward and took hold of her wrists, holding them to her sides.

"Good enough," Case said. "You're dead."

Case's heavy footsteps approached, then he stopped, hovering next to the sofa. My mind emptied in the endless pause of waiting for him to act. Then in one frightening, sudden move, he threw open the closet door.

Case sighed dramatically at the empty closet. We'd given him quite a scare. He sniffed, then wandered into the next room. "Come on out," he called from time to time, but without much conviction.

Ann was trembling. Without a sound I put my arms around her. Her breathing was quick and shallow. I lowered my head slightly, feeling her soft hair against my face. She breathed the slightest sigh of release, so I tightened my embrace.

Minutes later, Case shut the front door, then came back into the room. He turned on the television, then collapsed, hard, onto the sofa. His mother had probably told him his whole life not to throw himself around on the furniture like that, I thought. Obviously, we were going to be stuck in this spot for a while.

I was all right with it for all of ten minutes. After all, he probably couldn't hear us over the noise of the television. Then desperation set in. I've never been claustrophobic, but it's amazing how a phobia can develop simply by thinking you're glad you don't have that particular one. Why is it a law of nature that as soon as you realize you can't allow yourself to move under any circumstances, the only thing in life you can think about is how badly you want to move? It's like someone telling you not to think of an elephant. Sure enough, next thing that pops into your head—

I closed my eyes and tried to imagine myself in wide open spaces, but got distracted when my left leg went numb. Next I tried remembering the Gettysburg Address, but that failed miserably after I couldn't get beyond the first sentence. As a last resort, I decided to concentrate on my breathing—if it worked for a woman during childbirth, surely it would work for me. I concentrated—breathe in, breathe out, breathe in, breathe out, breathe in, breathe out. I gave it up after thirty seconds. It just didn't seem to work when you were hyperventilating.

After what seemed like hours later, the only logical course of action seemed to be for me to jump up and scream for Case to just shoot me. I shut my eyes tightly and held my breath, then slowly, slowly, opened my eyes and exhaled.

Ann rested lightly in my arms. She leaned against her left knee with her right leg tucked under her, her body holding all the tension mine did. I wondered how she was coping. My face was close to hers but not touching, and I could feel the heat of her skin against my cheek. The usual fragrance of her perfume was missing, and in its place the warm clean scent of her skin. My eyes traced the line of her shirt tucked into tight black jeans, then over and down her long legs, then back to the soft profile of her face. Gratefully distracted, I allowed my gaze to travel down her neck to where her collar hung open underneath her black leather jacket. Selfishly I let my eyes follow the line of her shirt to where it buttoned modestly at the spot her breast began its curve. She inhaled, and I watched as her breasts lifted gently, the collar tilting. The next time Ann inhaled, I watched again, as if at any moment the collar would lift and reveal more of its soft secret.

It was a sophomoric pastime, but it worked. Five minutes later, I still had my sanity. I'd figured it out. The trick was to concentrate on Ann's breathing.

Something in my brain unknotted at last. I gazed back to her face, where I could see the occasional flutter of her eyelashes, the profile of her full lips. She inhaled slowly, as if any movement too sudden might attract attention. With every breath she took, her body exerted a gentle, seductive pressure in my arms. Only our arms touched, but the space between us was starting to burn me.

I closed my eyes and breathed in and out slowly, taking in the scent of her. My heart began a strong, purposeful pounding; my arms heated where they enclosed her, touching her ever so lightly. A sense of urgency came over me. I wanted to turn her in my arms, press my lips against hers, draw her body to mine and—

"Lane..."

I opened my eyes.

"Lane—he's asleep," Ann mouthed to me.

"How can you be sure?" I asked silently.

"I can hear him snoring," she whispered, so close her lips brushed against my ear.

I looked at my watch. "Are you willing to bet your life on that?" I asked.

She read my lips, then nodded. Silently we crawled out and stood up, our legs numb. I hardly glanced at the man sleeping on the sofa out of the simple fear he would feel my glance and wake up. But as soon as we reached the hallway outside the apartment, Ann stopped and turned to me.

"What?" I whispered.

"I need to see what kind of gun he has!" She turned back to the open door of Case's apartment.

I gripped her arm. "Are you crazy?"

"I have to know!"

"You have to know?!"

Before I could argue further, she disappeared back into Case's apartment. Holding my breath, I waited. If I heard anything, or if Ann didn't return within a couple of minutes, I would run to my car and call 911.

I waited and listened. Nothing. After awhile, the elevator door opened, but no one was there. It closed again.

I crossed my arms and quietly took a deep breath. How long had she been gone? I looked at my watch. That did no good. I hadn't checked to see what time she had gone back in. I had no way of knowing how much time had passed.

I waited another sixty seconds. Okay, so maybe I wouldn't leave to call 911. Maybe I'd just go check on her myself. I slipped through the door and back into Case's apartment.

In the hallway, I neither saw nor heard any sign of Ann; the only sound was the television coming from the living room. Stopping first at the bedroom door, I leaned around the doorframe to look. On the table next to Case's bed was an automatic pistol, 9 mm perhaps. But there was no sign of Ann.

My heart beat faster. Where was she? I went back down the hall to the living room, moving silently. As I peered cautiously around the corner, I could see that Case was still sound asleep, sprawled on the sofa in nothing but his jeans, his head hanging over the arm awkwardly, one foot propped up on the glass-topped table. He was a tall, lanky white man with unnaturally bright blond hair. He snored quietly. And not three feet from him, Ann was pulling the page from the fax machine— Page 2 of 2.

Of course, I thought. Ann was the one who had page one of the fax when I discovered it missing. She must have pulled it from the machine just before I walked in on her. Ann glanced at page two, then put it in the right pocket of her jacket. Sudden irritation flared up inside me. How could I have been so stupid? I had had that page in my hands before Case had walked in on me. Now Ann had it! Fuming silently to myself, I returned to the outside hallway.

"Did you see the gun?" I asked when she returned.

"Yes. It's an automatic, 9 mm." she whispered.

I didn't respond. We rode the elevator down in silence, but when we stepped into the lobby she turned to me, quietly serious. "What are you doing on my story?!" she demanded.

"Your story?" I retorted, surprised by the sudden change in mood. "Your story? What are you doing on my story?!"

"I got there first."

"You mean you were trespassing first!"

"I was not trespassing!"

The elevator doors opened behind us. Both of us reacted, startled. I exhaled. "Could we continue this conversation elsewhere?" I whispered. "I'll meet you at The Pier."

Frowning, she nodded. I held the door for her as we stepped out of the building.

We parked our cars behind the restaurant and walked the narrow

110

dim alley to the door without speaking. The hostess led us through the restaurant and out the back, seating us on a covered deck overlooking the river. We were the only people in the restaurant tonight, the rain having discouraged the usual crowd. We pulled off our jackets as the waiter walked up, barely taking his eyes off Ann long enough to get my order.

After he left, Ann picked up her spoon and began playing with it in silence, alternately pressing designs into the white tablecloth and looking up to consider me. Her eyes were as green as I'd ever seen them. Behind her the moon shone through rushing translucent clouds, an Arab dancer drawing silk scarves across her face. I watched the heavy mist rising from the river and waited for Ann to speak first. The only sounds were the river lapping against the bank, the light rain on the grass, and the soft clatter of dishes from the restaurant kitchen. Finally she spoke. "Why did you decide to investigate it? Both our papers buried the story."

I leaned toward Ann. "You remember that white kid who was killed downtown three years ago? Do you remember the coverage that got?" Ann nodded. "Well, it's just so typical," I continued, feeling a little of the old anger rising up in me again. "A Caucasian kid gets murdered and it's front page news for a year, but when an African-American is the victim, it disappears into the depths of the newsprint swamp."

She shook her head slowly; her eyes lit with admiration. "Good angle, good angle. I hadn't thought of that."

"I think it bothers me more because I don't think of this city as particularly racist," I said. "We're not the Deep South here. Believe me, I've seen more racism up north than I've seen in Louisville."

"You're fooling yourself if you think racism doesn't exist here."

"Don't exaggerate what I'm saying."

"Remember, you move in the more enlightened circles." She raised her eyes to meet mine, and in that moment my mind went blank. I sat there, unable to think of anything other than how terribly beautiful she was. Her skin was flawless, her eyes thickly lashed, her lips full, sensuous, soft, meant to be kissed. When I didn't respond, she repeated herself as if I hadn't heard her.

I considered her words. "That's fair," I replied. The waiter brought our coffee, and I took a sip. The storm may have raised the humidity, but it managed to bring the temperature down to coffee-drinking bearable. It tasted good even in the warm night.

"So what about you?" I asked. "What brought you to trespass in the apartment of one Mr. David Case?"

She looked me in the eye. "I wasn't trespassing."

"Right."

"I wasn't!"

"I see. He just invited you over to spend the night behind his sofa."

"The door was already open, like it was when you got there."

"I know why the door was open when I got there."

"He must have left it open accidentally."

I nodded. "And you just accidentally dressed head to toe in black, too."

She hesitated—a slip I rarely see from her. "Black is in right now. This is the monochromatic look."

"And you accidentally forgot to wear any perfume?"

She shrugged. "I don't always wear perfume."

"That's convenient, because it's notorious for giving away a good hiding place."

Ann frowned at me, ever so subtly. "I said, I don't always wear perfume."

I smiled at her. "You stick to that story and bat your eyes a little more and the jury is bound to find reasonable doubt."

A smile fluttered across her lips involuntarily, then disappeared. She looked down at her coffee cup. "My reasons are personal. I actually met the victim. Just once."

"You met him?"

"Yes. He worked for Barnes. You remember Barnes? I think you took his photo once."

The flush started at my temples. This was a quick return parry to me for cornering her about breaking into Case's apartment. I had forgotten about the pictures. I had forgotten that she had developed them. I had forgotten that I planned to move out of town because of them. Call it selective amnesia, but I had forgotten. Now all I cared about was controlling the color that was spreading across my face.

She grinned that ironic grin at me, the one where I'm never sure whether she's laughing with me or at me. "They were very good, you know—the photos. I showed some of them to one of the staff photographers and told him a friend had taken them. He said you should consider exhibiting. Although, for some reason, he seemed to think you were a man."

That did it. I knew my face was burning a bright red. Ann pretended not to notice and turned the subject back to the murder.

"I wanted to do something—I don't know—just because I'd liked him. At first I collected the usual—the 'good citizen' stuff, his church work, etc."

I leaned forward in my seat. "You got those kinds of quotes? That's what I was looking for, but I didn't find it." Of course, I hadn't visited Ricky's church, either.

"Did you hear about his paper route?"

"No." She was irritating me. How had I missed this stuff?

"He didn't use a penny he earned from that paper route for himself, you know. He created his own sort of citizenship award, giving that money to someone he'd heard about who had done something exceptionally kind or good during the past year. He named the award after his mother. Quite a self-starter for his age, don't you think?"

I nodded, but my mood was declining fast. Where had she come up with this information? "One of the TV news shows did a piece on it a few years ago, but I thought it deserved mentioning again. And have you met his wife?"

My jaw dropped open. "His wife?" This had moved from strange to bizarre. "And how old is she?"

"Twenty-seven."

"Twenty-seven? Twenty-seven?" I was gaping at Ann, completely confused.

"I know, I know,"Ann nodded. "The age difference is kind of shocking."

"Shocking?" I was raising my voice. "I'd call that what it is! Statutory rape!"

"Lane,"Ann frowned. "I didn't know you were such a prude."

"Prude! Good grief, Ann! Would you marry a fifteen-year-old?"

"I don't think that's a reasonable comparison, Lane." She stared at me. "Anyway, she's beautiful, has an MBA, started her own company, and makes lots of money. You wonder what she saw in someone with an eighth-grade education."

I shook my head. "That's sick, Ann."

Ann looked at me, dumbfounded. "You've surprised me, Lane. I thought you were more open-minded than that."

"I am open-minded,"I shot back. "I'm very open-minded. But the wind isn't whistling through my head!"

"Good grief." Ann ran her fingers through her hair and took a sip of her coffee.

"Why did she marry him, Ann? Did that question ever occur to you?"

Ann looked at me, confused by my reaction. "She said it was because he was a good person. She said nothing was more sexy to her than a man who was really, truly good."

"And that didn't ring a little false to you, considering the age difference?"

Ann looked right at me. "Lane, we're both investigative reporters. Every day we go into work we get lied to. Do you want to sit there and tell me that after years of this I haven't developed some pretty good hunches?"

"You don't think the attraction had anything to do with the drugs?"

Okay, so that was a little stupid. But only in hindsight. However, Ann had shown me up far too much for one evening's conversation.

"I don't believe either one of them was involved in drugs," Ann replied sternly.

"Why?"

"They didn't strike me as the type."

"Oh, I see. That's convincing."

Ann glared at me. "The autopsy didn't show any evidence of drugs. Just because somebody gets shot in the head doesn't mean it was over drug money."

Shot in the head? I looked up at Ann slowly. We weren't following the same murder.

"Get real, Lane. Who would hire a sixty-eight year old man as a drug runner?"

I clenched my jaw so as not to change my expression. So that's why I had been so lost in this conversation. Ann had been talking about someone else. Ann hadn't figured it out yet. She kept talking.

"He was a good man, Lane. There is such a thing. You've been working for the paper too long—you've become jaded. He was a good man and his wife knew it. She loved him for it. When they pulled his body out of the river in Louisville, I knew Barnes was involved in some way. I don't know what Barnes has gotten into—fixing horse races or some other kind of scam…"

Horse racing. The murder Ann was following was related to horse racing. The murder I was following was related to cocaine. What was the connection?

"…but if you look close enough, Barnes has money coming in that can't be explained by that poorly run property management company of his. I think Franklin found out something he wasn't supposed to know, and Barnes made him pay for it. But you tell me," she continued with sarcasm, "what evidence do you have to support that they were on drugs? Or did I misunderstand—is this about the prescription kind?"

My face was devoid of all expression. To prevent myself from reacting to this latest information, I had forced every muscle in my face to relax. Now I wasn't sure I could make my face move on such short notice. I was right. I couldn't. Ann's eyes had already begun to narrow. She was catching on.

"All right,"she said slowly. "What is it? What do you know?"

"Nothing." My pulse had quickened.

"Don't hold out on me," she threatened gently. "We share on the street."

"Not in investigations."

Ann's eyebrows lifted. "You're following a different murder, aren't you? You're following a different murder and it led you to the same apartment."

I threw money onto the table and reached for my jacket. My heart was pounding; I could feel the familiar adrenaline rush that comes with finding a new piece to a puzzle. I had to get out of here and figure out how this all fit.

"Lane..." She put her hand on my arm. I stood up. "...what murder are you following?"

I pulled my jacket on and headed for the door. Inside, I waved at the waiter and stepped into the alley that led back to my car. Halfway down the alley, in the rain, Ann caught up with me.

"Lane..." Her voice was gentle. I turned to look into crystal green.

Ann looked down as she fingered the sleeve of my jacket. Lightly she ran her fingers up my arm. "Lane," she said again, and then pressed her hand against my shoulder, pushing me under the eaves of the building, out of the rain and against the brick.

She drew close, but instead of speaking she looked at me hard, objectively, her eyes studying my face as if pinning me against the building gave her the right. She tossed her head slightly to move her hair out of her eyes, then stepped back to look at my body, not taking her hand off my shoulder.

"Ann..." I began.

She responded with "shhh,"not taking her eyes off my body. She stepped in again, so close I inhaled the faint scent of her. Being close to Ann is always difficult for me, but this close, I was beginning to lose my mind. Her eyes came up to meet mine just as a breeze from the river caught her hair, tossing it around her face, catching wisps of it in her lips. With her free hand she brushed back her hair, then reached for my jacket zipper. As she eased it down she watched my eyes for any sign of protest. I couldn't have mustered a complaint if I'd tried. As the jacket fell loose, Ann turned back the collar and pulled it aside. Her eyes darkened as they lowered to my body. I closed my eyes to the sensation created by that look. "You are so beautiful, Lane,"she whispered. "So beautiful." Then low, as if to herself, she added, "So why do you have to be so intractable?" She let go of my shoulder suddenly, stepping back.

I opened my eyes. Her jaw tightened as she looked at me, betraying the desire she felt. "Not everything has to be a competition, you know," she whispered. She took another step back, making a striking silhouette in the moonlight. Then, running her fingers through her hair, she turned and walked away. I stood against the wall until I heard her car start, then drive off.

All right, maybe I'd been wrong not to give a little information after what Ann had told me; I had to admit that. A reporter who doesn't share on occasion soon finds herself in an information vacuum. I sighed, then reached into my jacket and pulled out the piece of paper I had lifted from Ann's pocket. The bottom corner read "Page 2 of 2." I read the list of nameless addresses as I walked to my car.

Back at home, I got on the website for Ann's paper, the *Metropolitan Inquirer*, and going into their archives, looked up the article Ann had mentioned writing. Ann said she had met the victim, and the article reflected the warmth Ann had felt for him. But the basic facts of the article were that the body of Noah Franklin, a resident of Versailles, Kentucky and a retired truck driver, had been found in the Ohio River in west Louisville. He had died from a gunshot wound to the head—on the same night Ricky had been murdered.

Chapter Nine

As I stepped through the door of the restaurant on Tuesday morning, Sherri waved at me from a table. I went to the chair she indicated and scooted in next to her.

"Get the 'Country Kitchen Plate'," she recommended. "It really is good." She glanced around. "You know, this is so exciting. I'm usually stuck in a lab all day—I don't get to help track down a murderer very often!"

I laughed. "Well, this is just an interview, Sherri. I don't think Coach Perret killed anyone."

Sherri frowned at me, as if I was ruining her game. "Lane! I watch the mystery shows. You know that everyone is a suspect!"

I smiled and shook my head. "It's just that I know a little more about the coach since the last time we talked. I really don't think he's doing anything—well—mysterious."

Sherri put her hand on my arm. "Lane, you have to keep an open mind. If you don't, you might miss a clue." She emphasized the word.

I nodded. "That's true, Sherri. It's just that yesterday I followed Coach Perret after he left the club and—"

Sherri shushed me and squeezed my arm. "Quiet, girl! There he is!" She leaned over and whispered to me. "You know, I took half a vacation day for this! This is so exciting!"

She waved at Perret just as she had waved at me. Perret made his way over and took a seat across from us. He was dressed in shorts and a T-shirt, ready to head for the Youth Club when he was done.

"Eaten here before?" he asked. I shook my head. "Oh, you're in for a treat!" He signaled the waitress. "So, the Rev's roped in another volunteer, has she? What are you teaching?"

We ordered coffee and juice, enjoyed breakfast, and talked. Coach Perret entertained us with his basketball stories. This was his tenth summer volunteering at the Youth Club. One boy, whose talents he had discovered at the Youth Club, was now playing professionally in Miami. Most of his stories, however, were not about children's lives changed through basketball, but about children's lives changed through contact with a caring adult. He spoke openly and happily, like a man with nothing on his conscience. That is, until I changed the subject.

"Coach Perret," I shifted the conversation, "I really appreciate your meeting with me. I would like to talk to you about Ricky Simms."

"Ricky Simms? Why?" Subtly, Perret's demeanor changed.

"I'm a reporter with the *Louisville Daily*. The paper assigned me to do a biographical piece because he was murdered. I know you coached him in basketball for a while."

"A reporter?" Perret looked accusingly at Sherri. Sherri shrugged, so Perret turned his glare back to me. "No one told me this was going to be an interview."

"Oh—I'm sorry, I said." The turn in Perret's mood surprised me. "I've enjoyed our conversation at breakfast very much, but I did want to interview you for the paper. If you're not open to that, then that's fine."

He looked me straight in the eye. "I'm not open to that. I don't want my name appearing in any article alongside Ricky Simms'."

"Is that because of his involvement in drugs?"

"That's none of your business."

"That's fine, then. If you prefer, we could just talk about Ricky and I won't quote you—"

He interrupted. "I have nothing to say about Ricky Simms."

"All right." I switched focus. "I'm also trying to locate Trina Garby. Her parents haven't seen her since Tuesday morning. She seems to have disappeared. Would you know anything about that?"

"No." He sat back in his seat. "Why are you asking me about that?"

Sherri looked at me as if she was processing something, then turned to Perret. "You haven't seen Trina at the Youth Club since Tuesday?"

Perret shifted in his seat. "No." Tiny beads of sweat broke out along his hairline.

She continued. "You know, Lane here isn't just any kind of reporter, Richard. She's an investigative reporter. We know about your unauthorized trips with the kids in your car. I think you'd better explain that."

I turned to Sherri and spoke kindly, but firmly. "Sherri, I really think you need to let me handle this—"

"Was that some kind of a threat, Sherri? What are you implying?!" Perret's face broke into a full sweat. "I don't know anything about Ricky and I don't know anything about Trina disappearing! I coach basketball. Sometimes I buy those kids lunch, take them to my house, and pay them to do odd jobs two or three times a week. I know that's against club rules, but frankly, I think the rules are wrong! I'm trying to give those kids a few opportunities, and I'm not going to let stupid rules stand in my way!" Perret wiped his mouth. "Well, ladies, I wish I could say it has been a pleasant time. At least it started out that way." He picked up his bill, then left to pay the cashier.

I rubbed my hand over my face and spoke calmly. "Sherri, I really wish you had let me handle that by myself. He left mad, and I hadn't even begun to ask him what I wanted to talk to him about."

Sherri ignored me. She watched Perret exit the restaurant, then laughed. "Just trying to give those kids some opportunities, huh? Opportunities in the drug trade, no doubt!"

I shook my head. "No, Sherri. I really doubt that."

Sherri turned to me, not even hearing me. "You see, all we had to do was apply a little pressure on him, and he started lying like a big dog!"

I sighed. "What do you mean, lying? When did he lie?"

"Acting so innocent and talking the way he did, about not knowing anything about Trina disappearing!"

"What are you talking about?!"

She turned to me excitedly and took my hands. "What night did you say it was that Ricky Simms was murdered?"

"Tuesday night."

"And Trina's been missing since then?"

"According to her parents, yes."

"Well, you know that story I told you about seeing Trina in Richard Perret's car, with some other kids?"

"Yes, of course."

She looked at me with import. "That happened Wednesday—the next day. At noon."

I looked steadily at Sherri. "So you're the last person to see Trina since she disappeared?"

Sherri shook her head slowly, with suppressed excitement. "Apparently not. But it sure looks like Richard Perret is."

This was significant, I had to agree. But Richard Perret wouldn't be talking to me again. I had lost my opportunity to get his side of the story.

"Where have you been?!"

Rosemary rounded the corner to my office as I was hanging up from a phone call with Ricky Simms' grandmother. I hadn't been in the office more than ten minutes and I could tell I was in trouble. "I had an interview this morning," I replied. I skipped the part about being at the Youth Club to teach my class. "Why?"

"I've been looking everywhere for you. I just sent Patrice to the Movieplex 10 to drive around the parking lot and look for your car."

"Well, lucky me, I caught the early show." I leaned back in my chair. "What do you want, Rosemary?"

"I want that profile on Ricky Simms. I've seen nothing on it. Nothing. This is a story you can do in your sleep!"

I took a deep breath and filled Rosemary in on all the details. She soon interrupted me with little tsking noises.

"Lane, I know that look in your eye. You're sounding too enthusiastic whenever you get to the parts about the murder, or the drug dealing, or—"

"Well?"

"You're supposed to be writing a profile—a biographical piece!"

"I know," I sat forward. "But have you been listening, Rosemary? There's a real story here! The police are allowing themselves to believe they've solved Ricky's murder in order to get a troublemaker off the street; they haven't got a lead for the second murder—"

"What have you found out about the second murder?" She stood back, tapping one little sandaled foot, skeptical.

I opened my file and threw the clippings on the desk. "Noah Franklin. Upstanding citizen. Single shot to the head, found downriver by some fishermen two days after Ricky was killed. Autopsy showed he was killed the same night Ricky was."

"Same caliber weapon, too, I guess?"

I hesitated, thinking of the nine millimeter handgun in Case's apartment. "No. Ricky was shot with a .32. Franklin was killed with a 9 millimeter."

She quipped. "Oh, that's certainly indicative the murders were related."

"Rosemary…"

"Not to mention the fact that Franklin was killed with a single shot to the head, assassination style, while Ricky had a .32 unloaded into his chest like it was amateur hour. Oh, and don't forget the bodies were found miles apart. What else do you have to relate these two murders, Lane?"

"These murders are related," I argued. "But I think there are two killers. Ricky Simms and Noah Franklin both had connections to the same businessman. Franklin worked for him. I just got off the phone with Ricky's grandmother. Ricky lived in an apartment he managed."

"What businessman?"

"Gerald Barnes."

"Gerald Barnes? Of Barnes Property Management?"

"Yes."

"Oh, good grief, Lane. Barnes is a well-respected businessman in this community, despite that nasty little article in the *Metropolitan Inquirer* about him last week. The man knows how to make money hand over fist. He started that property management company of his and built it into a multi-million dollar corporation within ten years. And he's a rather good-looking man for his size, too, I think," Rosemary threw in. "So why would a successful man like that be running around the city killing people? Besides, Barnes manages properties all over the city. I'm sure it's purely coincidence that Ricky lived in one of the apartments Barnes manages."

"Maybe, Rosemary. But I've been following Ricky's murder, and a reporter from the *Metropolitan* has been following Franklin's, and we found ourselves at the same man's apartment last night."

"And what did the man at the apartment have to say about all this?"

I hesitated just long enough.

"Never mind," Rosemary held up her hand, "I don't think I want to know." She turned to leave. "I'll give you four days. Four days! That's my final word on this, do you hear?" She turned and marched away from my office with her hands in the air, mumbling "Good grief!" and something about investigative reporters to no one in particular.

I spent the next couple of hours researching the rest of the addresses on the fax page I had lifted from Ann's pocket the night before, the page that included Ricky and Trina's addresses. I cross-referenced the addresses with their current residents, then looked up those names to discover any previous drug-related arrests. Four names turned up with records in drug trafficking. Since I knew Ricky had been a dealer, I was beginning to suspect that I held a list of dealers' addresses in my hand. Trina's address on the page didn't bode well for her. It looked like maybe Trina had flunked out of the Rev's "Kids Against Drugs" program after all.

A phone call to the office of Trina's apartment complex revealed Barnes was managing that property as well. A follow-up on the rest of the addresses on my page of the fax revealed the same thing. Barnes didn't own any of the properties, but his company managed them all.

Barnes would not have wanted to put his own property at risk. Property could be seized if it had been used in the drug trade. But managing the properties would work fine for Barnes' purposes. David Case was the link between these properties because he was the maintenance man for them, but there the hard evidence ended. No, your honor, Barnes would say. I had no idea my maintenance man was dealing drugs at these properties. I should have checked his references.

I stared at the phone. I had an appointment, but one other thing needed to be done. I took a breath and dialed. Marge picked up after six rings.

"Marge, this is Lane Montgomery."

"Oh, hi Lane! How are you?"

"Marge, I wanted to ask you a question. The other day at the Youth Club, when I stopped by your office, you said another reporter had been by to ask you questions about Ricky? And you gave her my card?"

"Who?"

"The reporter. You said a reporter was asking questions about Trina?"

"Oh—not me. Our janitor, Robert. He talked to the reporter."

I had passed Robert in the hall a few times and exchanged hellos. "Is he there? Could I ask him something?"

"Yes, he is. Have you got a few minutes to hold?"

I said yes. Eventually Robert came on the line. "Miss Montgomery? This is Robert. You wanted to ask me somethin'?"

"Yes. Hello, Robert. I understand that you showed my phone number to a reporter. Was this reporter an attractive white woman from the *Metropolitan* newspaper?"

"What? No, ma'am, he wasn't a woman. He was a man. No. This reporter—I think he was a reporter, maybe he was with the police. I don't know. But he came in that evenin' after you was first here. He was askin' questions about had I seen Ricky's friend, Trina. So I showed him your card that Marge stuck up on the board; I told him you was tryin' to find out about Ricky, too."

My chest was beginning to feel tight. "The reporter was a man?"

"Yes. Or he was a police officer. I didn't like him, though, like I like you. He wasn't as good-natured as you."

I spoke slowly. "Robert, what did this man look like?"

"He was a tall white man. Skinny, but strong. With yellow hair."

"Thanks, Robert," I managed to say. "You've been a big help."

Robert said a cheerful goodbye. As I placed the receiver back on the hook, I could feel the pulse beating in my throat. David Case had my name and number. David Case had known I was looking for Trina since Saturday. Nine out of ten, it was David Case who had shot at me at Ricky's school to try to scare me off the story.

A humid mist rose from the pavement as I sped through another curve outside the Kentucky town of Versailles. Rolling hills rose on both sides of the road, allowing me the occasional glimpse of horses—the racing kind, thoroughbreds. Always smaller than I remember, they looked fragile, gently raising their hooves like ballet dancers stretching out en pointe. When they raced my little car, they were so beautiful I had to remind myself to keep my eyes on the road.

Pre-Civil War slave-built fences lined many pastures, still serving the purpose for which they were built a century and a half or more ago. Above me a canopy of trees stretched out their arms, creating a verdant tunnel between the hills. I never understood why Daniel Boone had pronounced our grass blue. That was a lie; Kentucky invaded the senses with green. A Californian woman I interviewed years ago, visiting Louisville for the Kentucky Derby, had remarked that she had never seen such a beautiful state. "It's so green," she kept repeating.

I was on my way to pay a visit to Noah Franklin's widow—the beautiful twenty-seven year old with the MBA and her own company. Ann had been impressed. Now I would see for myself.

About three miles out of town I spotted the drive. I turned in and pulled up to an elegant, small, two-story colonial with a barn in back. A baby-blue BMW was already parked in the drive. Beside it was a black BMW sports car.

Racinda Franklin wasn't rich yet, but she was certainly doing better than average for a twenty-seven-year-old. During her last year as an undergraduate student, she had started an advertising company that specialized in the African-American market. By the time she graduated with her MBA, she had most of the African-American businesses in Lexington as clients, as well as a few very large, mostly white corporations who wanted to appeal to the local African-American market. As I rang the doorbell, I decided, if anything, Racinda Franklin was living beneath her means.

The door opened and a tall woman dressed in an ivory suit and heels greeted me, inviting me in. "Lane Montgomery?" she asked, shaking my hand. "I'm Racinda Franklin."

When Ann told me Racinda Franklin was beautiful, I had expected she meant the typical Americanized version of African-American beauty—light skin, small features, straightened hair perfectly styled. I find that look very attractive, and it's usually the look white Americans are referring to when they say a black woman is beautiful, but I learned long ago it's not the only look an African-American woman can pull off with impact. Racinda Franklin was the most stunning example I had seen of the other look.

Racinda's suit was conservative yet elegant; her hair was unstraightened and cut close to her head. Her skin was deeply black, which she accented with the ivory suit. Her lips were full and her nose and face broad, and she wore a minimum of makeup. The pattern in her large earrings hinted at Africa, and their shape had the effect of drawing one's attention again and again to the sculpted bone structure of her face. Her presence was commanding, and her beauty very African. I didn't wonder for a moment why every person in Lexington was throwing their money at her advertising company. Racinda Franklin had exactly the look for what she wanted to accomplish.

"Thank you for making the time to talk with me."

"My pleasure," she said. "Come in."

I entered a spacious foyer with ivory white walls and shining wood flooring. As I was about to remark to Racinda how beautiful her home was, a dark figure stepped into the foyer. I turned to see a large white man dressed in black business attire. It was Gerald Barnes.

I found myself holding my breath. As he walked to Racinda, he glanced at me and smiled. He had no idea who I was. Racinda Franklin offered her hand and he took it. Trying to be inconspicuous, I moved further into the foyer.

"Since you have company, Racinda, I'll be going," Barnes said.

"Oh, I was hoping you could stay," Racinda protested.

"I need to be getting back to work anyway." He squeezed her hand.

"If you insist. But we'll do lunch next week."

He grinned at her. "And I'm going to teach you to play golf. If you want to get the really big accounts, you're going to have to learn to play golf."

She laughed. "If you say so."

He moved around her toward the door.

"Oh, Gerald!" she stopped him. "Wait a minute. I want you to meet someone." I tensed as Racinda nodded toward me. "Lane, this is Gerald Barnes; he was a friend of Noah's. Gerald, this is Lane Montgomery."

Barnes' eyes darted sharply from Racinda to me. I felt my skin prickle. He knew my name.

"Ms. Montgomery works for the *Louisville Daily*. She's here to write an article about Noah. It might generate some new leads. Isn't that great?"

"That's great," he replied steadily. He was smiling, but his eyes were analyzing me. I smiled back politely, and he turned to Racinda. "Let me know if she comes up with anything," he said. "I'd like to know. I'll be in touch."

"Of course," Racinda replied. "Have a good day."

Barnes allowed himself another glance at me, then let himself out. Racinda Franklin closed the front door and began talking, but I found myself straining to hear the car pull away.

"He has been so wonderful," Racinda said. "And before my husband died, I hardly knew him. I think he's concerned about my living here alone after what happened to Noah."

"I see," was all I could answer.

"Thanks again for doing this," Racinda said, motioning me through the foyer. "The police seem to be at a loss. Every time it's mentioned in the news it just increases the chances that we'll discover some answers."

As we passed a room with a window, I looked out to the drive, but couldn't see the cars. I took a deep breath and tried to relax. I needed to get this interview on track. "Where did you get your name, Racinda?"

"It's a combination of my parent's names—Cynthia, or Cindy, and Raymond."

"You have a beautiful home."

"Thanks. I'm fortunate, business is good."

"So the papers say."

"You've researched me!" She grinned.

"It saves me from wasting time during interviews."

"The only way to go is to start your own business—that's what I believe. So what if I'm young? I didn't want to waste all that time working my way up, playing games, pleasing the right people, then hitting the inevitable glass ceiling and wondering if I didn't get that promotion because I was black, or wondering if the only reason I'd been given that promotion was because I was black..." She hesitated, as if she was suddenly concerned that what she was saying might offend me. "Anyway, all that energy spent in figuring out someone else's invisible rules seemed to me like energy better spent in other ways."

She led me into a sunlit room with polished wood floors and throw rugs, decorated mostly in an ivory color. She motioned for me to sit on the couch next to the fireplace as she sat across from me in a chair. I could see past her through the French windows to the barn just beyond the backyard. The green of the lawn showed brightly through the windows.

"Now, what would you like to know?"

"Why don't you tell me about your husband?"

She was thoughtful for a moment. "Most people didn't understand our relationship," she began. "He was quite a bit older than I; he didn't have my education. But I'm sure you read the *Metropolitan Inquirer* article that Ann Alexander did on him. You don't have to be young or educated to be an extraordinary person. He was a good man, Ms. Montgomery. That's what attracted me to him."

She hesitated a moment. When she looked back up at me her eyes shone with tears. "They found Noah's body in the Ohio River, in west Louisville. I'm sure you read that. The autopsy showed that they killed him first, then threw his body in the river afterward in an attempt to hide it."

I shook my head. "I hadn't heard that he'd been killed somewhere else."

"I have no idea why Noah would have gone to Louisville. The police officers..." She looked away from me, then back again. "...The police kept asking me questions that...well, I knew what they were implying. That he had gotten into trouble; that he had been drinking, or had gotten into a fight, or was somehow responsible for getting himself killed. I got so angry I could hardly answer their questions. Noah never touched alcohol, and he was a peaceful man, a good man."

"Had anything unusual happened to your husband before he was killed? Can you think of anything he mentioned that was out of the ordinary?"

"No, nothing! The police went through all this."

"Had there been any changes in his behavior in the last month, or longer?"

"No." She paused, looking at her hands.

"Ann Alexander said your husband had impressed her, that's why she wrote the article," I said gently.

"It was a touching tribute to him."

"I understand that you know Mr. Barnes because your husband was working for him when he died."

"Well, not exactly. Noah quit a couple of weeks before he died."

"Oh. What happened?"

"About three weeks ago he came in from a road trip..."

"A road trip?"

"My husband used to be a truck driver. Since he retired he pulls a horse trailer for racehorse owners."

"Racehorses? Gerald Barnes races horses?"

"Yes. He owns a farm outside Lexington. He races them here in Kentucky and in Florida."

"Oh," I shook my head. "This is new to me. I just knew about his property management company."

"Noah told me he was quitting after a race in Florida. He walked in and said he wouldn't be working for Barnes anymore."

"Did he say why?"

"No, not really. I was surprised, but, to tell you the truth, I was relieved. I didn't like Noah driving long hours, so the fewer the jobs, the better. We didn't need the money, after all. I didn't press him about it. I do know that Noah quit; Gerald didn't fire him. Noah seemed very angry, but he never said what about. When Noah had an uncomplimentary opinion about someone, he kept it to himself. But I don't think it had anything to do with Gerald Barnes."

"Did you know Barnes has a company in Louisville?" I asked. "He manages investment properties—like apartment complexes—for the owners."

Racinda Franklin looked up. "No, Gerald and I haven't ever really discussed his work. But I can't imagine Gerald Barnes would have anything to do with this. I just can't. Why would you kill the driver of your horse trailer? Noah was nothing to him. And do you see those roses?" She indicated a dozen roses blooming in a vase on a table next to the French doors. "Gerald sent me those when he heard the news about Noah. And he calls me every few days, just to see if there's anything he can do for me."

I bet he does, I thought to myself, looking at her. But she had made a good point. Why kill the driver of your horse trailer? Horse racing and cocaine had something more in common than Gerald Barnes. But what? What was the connection I was missing? "Do you know a David Case?" I asked.

She raised an eyebrow. "That man gives me the creeps. Yes, I know him. He's one of Gerald Barnes' employees. Gerald always insisted that David clean out the horse trailer for Noah after the Florida race trips, but all Case did was move the straw around. Noah always had to give it a real cleaning afterward. Noah didn't like David Case, didn't trust him. If Noah quit because of a person, it would have been because of Case."

I nodded, but didn't say anything. I suspected that David Case might have been the person who murdered Noah Franklin. Noah Franklin had been killed by a nine millimeter pistol, and David Case owned one. But there was more to this. There had been two murders that night, with different guns. Case probably hadn't committed them both.

"Ms. Franklin, do you know a Ricky Simms?"

She thought for a moment, then shook her head. "No. Should I?"

"How about Trina Darby? Have you ever heard of her?"

"No. Who are they? Do they have something to do with my husband's murder?"

I sighed audibly. "I don't know, I don't know. I wish I knew. I'm just looking for some connections. Maybe it's nothing."

I spent the rest of the interview collecting information for a biographical sketch, then brought the interview to a close. I took a few photos, and Racinda walked me to the door.

"Do you mind if I get a few outside shots before I go?" I asked, indicating my camera.

"Of course not," she answered. "And if I can be of any more help…"

"I'll call," I said. "And Ms. Franklin…"

"Yes?"

"I'd rather you didn't discuss the details of our interview with Mr. Barnes."

"Oh, of course," she said. "I wouldn't want him to know how Noah felt about David Case anyway. He might feel bad about that."

"Thanks." We shook hands. As the screen door shut behind me, I glanced toward the driveway, but the black sports car was gone now. I walked down the porch to the yard and got a couple of shots of the house. As I turned to my car, I caught sight of the barn. A thought occurred to me and I glanced back at the house, but Racinda Franklin was nowhere in sight. After a moment's hesitation, I walked to the barn. Peeking between the wood slats, I could see the shapes of the horse trailer and truck inside. Lifting the heavy wooden latch, I swung open the doors, then walked into the barn with its dirt floor and filtered sunlight.

The truck was blue and one of those oversized models capable of pulling a large trailer. The trailer was white, large, and capable of carrying four horses at one time. I walked around the trailer once, then started fiddling with the doors. There was a loud bang as the barn door slammed shut. I jumped and turned around.

"I'm sorry. I really didn't mean to scare you." Racinda Franklin was holding her car keys in her hand.

"Oh—I'm the one who needs to apologize," I began. "It's just that something occurred to me, but you had already gone back into the house…"

"About the trailer?"

"Yes." I took a step back. "Do you have the keys?"

"Sure, right here on my key ring," she said, stepping forward to unlock the trailer doors.

"You said Barnes always insisted that David Case clean the trailer for your husband after Barnes rented it for a trip to the track?"

"Right—the long trips, the Florida trips."

I nodded. "Has Gerald Barnes shown an interest in knowing who buys the trailer when you sell it?"

Racinda Franklin's eyebrows lifted. "Why, yes—how did you know? He said he was hoping I would sell it to a driver, like Noah. He said it was a nice trailer and he would like to be able to continue renting it."

I threw open the doors. The trailer had a strong odor of straw and manure. "Whew! Is this how David Case cleaned the trailer?"

Racinda nodded with disgust. "Yes. This is his job."

"I thought your husband always gave it a good cleaning after Case was done?"

She shook her head. "Yes—until this last time. It was strange. After Noah's last Florida trip—the one he quit after—he didn't want to have anything to do with this trailer. He didn't even come out to the barn anymore. Noah was very moody after that trip, right up until he was killed."

"I'll tell you what—have you got some old clothes I could borrow? I think I need to give this trailer a good cleaning myself."

She stared at me. "You're kidding, right?"

"Nope."

She continued to stare at me, but when I didn't laugh, she shook her head. "All right. Come inside. Everything you need will be in the barn. I have to get back to work."

Three hours later the trailer was spotless, even if I couldn't say the same for myself. Not only was it clean, but I had taken apart everything in the trailer that would come apart with the help of the small toolbox in my trunk. The cleaning had been necessary in order to look for any unusual seams in the metal. None had turned up, but that would have been too easy. I had crawled slowly on my back underneath the trailer feeling with my hands and looking with my flashlight for seams on the belly of the trailer, but that had turned up nothing. I had examined the windows and inspected the roof. What almost threw me was that I had taken apart the two spare tire storage areas separately, and found nothing. When I took them apart the second time, I pulled the spares out together and compared the compartments. That was when I discovered it.

I grabbed my screwdriver and, tapping around the left compartment, distinguished between hollow and flat thuds until I found the spot where I could just wedge the slot end of the screwdriver. Using the screwdriver as a miniature lever, I popped open the bottom of the tire compartment pretty as you please and shone my flashlight into the small space. I was a genius. What do horse racing and drugs have in common? Florida.

Gerald Barnes might have loved his horses, but they certainly gave him a legitimate and regular reason to make trips between Florida and Kentucky. If the area I had found was being used as I was imagining it, then someone was supplying Barnes with drugs—from Miami, perhaps—and getting them onto the trailer in Florida. From there, Noah Franklin had been unwittingly transporting them into Kentucky. David Case would show up under the premise of cleaning the horse trailer in order to remove the drugs.

The crude, handmade compartment I had discovered had probably been inserted by David Case on one of the Florida trips, when he had easy access to the trailer and Noah Franklin hadn't been around. The compartment could hold perhaps a kilo of pure cocaine. Cut and recut, that kilo would have kept Barnes in business at least until the next trip to Florida—making him a rich man in the process. From this barn, I imagined Case took the drugs to Barnes' dealers for cutting and redistributing by dealers—such as Ricky Simms.

Even if most of this scenario was true, I realized I could be jumping to conclusions about Barnes. Racinda Franklin seemed to like him; Case was who she didn't trust. Maybe it really only went as high up as Case.

But I doubted that. Every time I considered that David Case might be the man at the top, I remembered the fax I saw at his apartment—the fax with Ricky Simms' address crossed out. Case seemed to be taking instructions from someone else.

I went to my car and got my camera. I didn't have enough information to go to print with this yet, but I took some photos just in case my hunches turned out to be right later. Then I'd give my friend Bev Holloway at the Louisville Police Department a call. I couldn't be sure that what I'd found was significant. All I had found was a small empty compartment that might have been used to transport cocaine. I didn't know how Noah Franklin had figured it out, but my gut said that Franklin had discovered that this was exactly what his trailer was being used for, and that discovery had gotten him killed.

Chapter Ten

The cool water felt good running over my body. I closed my eyes and lifted my head to the showerhead, letting the water splash over my face. With my eyes closed, I pictured Ann as she had looked last night at the restaurant—the light of her green eyes, her soft black hair—then the slow movement of her hand as she opened my jacket, the mind-blurring nearness of her as she looked at me—

I yanked the bath towel off the rod, dried myself, then pulled on my jeans and a tank top and tucked it into my jeans. I was home and I was going to be comfortable. I went to the kitchen, unwrapped the deli sandwich I had picked up on my way home, and ate it in front of the local television news.

My cell phone conversation with Bev Holloway had gone well. She had been very interested in the compartment I had found in the trailer, and said they would be sending someone out to check it for traces of drug residue. I could tell from her tone of voice, however, that it wouldn't be on the top of their to-do list, which meant I would have to wait a couple of days or so for confirmation of my theory.

I finished my sandwich just as the national network news was ending. I carried my plate and glass to the kitchen sink and headed back to the TV. I had an exciting evening of reruns planned.

Halfway to the couch, my doorbell rang. I wasn't expecting anyone. Cautiously, I leaned into my door to look through the peephole. Thinking I had lost my mind, I opened the door.

Ann was standing in the hallway dressed to the nines in a blue-sequined evening dress. The collar encircled her long neck, leaving exposed her shoulders and slender arms. The dress fit snugly to her body, the hemline stopping at midway down her thigh. In her arms she carried a bouquet of long-stemmed red roses. She stood with her face turned toward the soft petals, inhaling with one long slow breath.

Out of this whole vision, my eyes came to rest on her neck. I wondered at the perfection of this one small part of her, just below her earring, and the delicate line of her jaw. She turned her head slowly and my eyes met with green light.

"Hello, Lane," she said, smiling demurely.

I didn't respond. I had forgotten my name.

She stepped toward me, placing the bouquet in my arms. "These are for you." She smiled again, waiting for a response. "May I come in?"

"Sure," I managed to say, stepping back and holding the door open for her. "And—thanks," I added, indicating the roses in my arms.

She wandered casually into my apartment and made herself comfortable on my sofa, crossing her long legs. A game show was now blaring away on the TV. I quickly walked over and shut it off, still holding the bouquet in my arms. "I hope I didn't interrupt anything," she said.

"Uh...no," I managed.

"Well, then," She smiled up at me, "better hurry or we'll be late." She held up two Arts Center tickets.

What?" I asked. "What are those?"

"Tickets for the ballet," she responded, as if I should have known.

"The ballet?"

"The ballet. You've heard about it—the Latin-American Company? One night only!" She leaned back and put her arm along the couch.

I was suspicious. "If you've come for the second page of the fax, it's not here."

Relief crossed her face. "You've got it? Thank goodness! I thought I'd dropped it."

"I've got it. But I'll make you a deal..."

She looked at me, frowning. "Please, Lane. I really don't want to think about work tonight. This is your personal life. You've got exactly half an hour to get dressed. And make it count—I expect to have the most beautiful date in the city tonight." She smiled at me warmly.

My mind was flying with deals I could strike with Ann for the information she had on the first page of that fax. But she was beautiful. Stunning. My resistance was fading fast. The ballet—spending the evening with Ann—or staying home and working in front of the TV. Let's see, was I an idiot?

"All right. Half an hour. I can do that," I mumbled. I started for my bedroom, had the sensation that I had forgotten something, headed for the kitchen, couldn't think what it was, headed back to my bedroom, realized that I was still holding the bouquet, turned to go back into the kitchen, and nearly ran over Ann.

"I'll take these and put them in a vase," she said, gathering the roses out of my arms. "You need to be getting dressed."

As I walked into my room, I could hear Ann laugh to herself in the kitchen. She was very pleased with herself. I was thrilled about the ballet tickets and she knew it. I shook my head. "Most beautiful date in the city," I whispered aloud, smiling. I knew who would have the most beautiful date in the city tonight. I would.

I went to my closet and started going through clothes. I didn't exactly have a huge selection to choose from for an event like this. I started to pull out my basic black, but decided it was too dark for a summer evening. Instead, I pulled the one other real option I had—my cream colored silk pants, jacket, and shell. I pulled it on quickly, put on my makeup and ran a brush through my hair.

Thinking of Ann seated in my living room in blue sequins, I went to my jewelry box and pulled out a sequined brooch the color of Ann's dress. I placed it carefully on the lapel of my jacket and stepped back to the mirror, analyzing myself. Perfect. Or, as perfect as I could hope for.

I opened my bedroom door and stepped into the living room. Ann was seated comfortably on my couch, absorbed in the game show that she had turned back on, which was playing low on the TV. She looked up as she heard me step into the room. She paused, then set down the drink she had fixed herself, never taking her eyes off of me. At last, all at once and almost as a whisper, she said, "My God, you're beautiful."

Her eyes met mine, and all I could think was how beautiful she was. "I'm ready," I said.

"I'll drive," she replied, standing and picking up her clutch.

"Great." I let her out, locking the door, and we took the stairs to the street.

Ann had the roof off the white T-top. We hardly said a word as she drove to the Arts Center. I lay back in the plush seat, closed my eyes, and let the warm wind caress my face. At one point I opened my eyes and looked over at Ann. She was looking at me. She smiled, put in a CD, and we were surrounded by music.

The Arts Center was crowded. The Latin-American Ballet Company had been promoted in a big way, and tickets had been hard to come by. Everyone was spit and polish and shimmer, but there wasn't a woman in the Center as beautiful as the one accompanying me. Ann walked next to me, occasionally reaching out to take my arm, telling me stories about her work and laughing at her own jokes. It isn't often that I feel my sexual orientation is anyone else's business, but Ann was such a vision that I found myself hoping that the people who passed us, whose gaze lingered just a little long, were thinking, Could they be together?

Our seats were on the main balcony, and as we walked down the aisle I noticed with amusement that nearly every man turned to watch as Ann descended the steps to our seats. As we sat down, Ann leaned toward me and laughed, "I think every man in the theater is watching you, Lane. Did you see that?"

I whispered back to her, "You forgot to mention the four women seated together in the lower left balcony. And thank you, but they had their eyes on you, Ann, not me."

I could tell from the look in Ann's eyes that she really believed they had been looking at me. As I struggled for something to say, the lights dimmed and Ann's attention turned to the stage. With reluctance, I turned my eyes away from her. The conversation was forgotten in a swell of music from the orchestra.

The company performed a variety of pieces, both classical and Latin. The Latin music was romantic, the grace and athleticism of the dancers breathtaking. One pas de deux was especially sensual. Ann, moved by what she saw, reached out and touched my hand. Not until that moment did I realize I had been holding my breath.

Afterward, we drove home in the hot night, and Ann walked me up to my apartment. She waited until I had unlocked the door, and then stepped inside while I turned on some lights. I thanked her one last time for the evening. She put her hand on my arm. "No, thank you, Lane," she said warmly. "And, by the way, I did have the most beautiful date in the city tonight."

She stepped toward me and I thought she was going to kiss me, but instead, she merely touched her cool cheek to mine and held it there for a moment before moving back. The sudden unexpected closeness of her took my breath away. She paused as if she wanted to say something more, but only said, "Good night," low, and turned to the door.

"Ann," I said, stopping her. She turned back to me, looking somehow childlike.

I stepped toward her. She was so beautiful standing there I could think of no other words but, "Ann, please stay with me tonight."

There was the slightest tremor in her voice when she answered. "I was afraid you weren't going to ask me."

I walked around Ann to shut the door, turning to her. She was within arm's reach of me now, so I took her hand in mine, drawing her to me, but she turned in my arms so that when my arms enclosed her, she had her back to me. I could feel the curve of her hips and her upper back lightly against the length of my body. She turned her head to look up at me, her face not childlike anymore, but like a woman. Her eyes searched my face for a moment, then she reached up and I felt her fingers first running through and then gently grasping my hair. Slowly, but with purpose, she drew my lips to hers. Her eyes were heavy-lidded pools that I thought I would fall into until my lips touched the warm soft velvet of hers.

She held me there, extending the kiss, her tongue caressing my lips one moment, her lips enveloping mine the next. With one arm I held her gently to me, while my other hand traced the length of her arm, down her side, over the cool curve of her shoulder, over the swell of her breast, until I caressed the concave curve of her small waist and out over her hips again...incredible, sequined softness.

No longer patient, my lips left hers and traced the line of her jaw back to her neck, searching beneath her earring for the spot I had found so captivating earlier in the evening. As my lips touched her neck, my hands moved from her hips to her flat stomach and up, until I touched and took her breasts in my hands. As I grasped her breasts firmly, Ann's head dropped back and she groaned softly. My desire rose so sharply at her response that my longing escalated from desire to pain. My hands dropped from her breasts to her hips; forcefully I pulled her hips to me, thrusting my body into her, her body draped over mine, her head lying back over my shoulder. She laughed at my loss of control, first reaching up behind her to grasp handfuls of my hair, then turning in my arms and pulling away from me. "Patience, darling," she said, taking my hand and leading me to the bedroom.

The bedroom was warm on this summer night. Ann pulled me toward her gently, smiling as if at some private, shared old joke between us. She placed her hands against my upper chest, leaving them there until the heat of her palms penetrated the silk. Then Ann's eyes met mine and she leaned toward me, her eyelids lowering just as our lips met with shocking warmth. Unrushed, her lips held my mouth while she began to explore my body through the silk.

The warmth of her hands was sensuous torture. Her lips left my mouth as she gave me tiny, teasing kisses up my left cheek. Her hands began tracing soft circles through my silk blouse as they moved slowly to my breasts. My breathing became quick and shallow. "So soft, sweetheart," Ann whispered in my ear. "You are so soft."

I reached to the zipper of her dress and began drawing it down care-

135

fully, slipping my other hand under the sequins as the two sides parted. Her skin was smooth, warm milk. I slipped both my hands inside the dress to her hips, pulling her close until the length of our bodies met. Her hands ran up my neck and she entwined her fingers in my hair.

My hands moved up her back to her shoulders. I slipped off the straps of the dress, enjoying the image as it slid lazily over her body and onto the floor. Touching her breasts, I traced soft circles over the silk that covered them. Ann kissed me, and as her lips played on my mouth, I encircled her breasts in my hands, lifting them gently. She moaned softly. I increased the gentle pressure of my fingers, continuing the slow circles of silk against her nipples, feeling them become erect beneath my touch.

"Ann…" I whispered. "Ann… I need you."

Drawing myself away, I grasped her arm and pulled her toward the bed. Aching for her, I stopped, only for a moment, just to look at her. Then, leaning forward to kiss the soft flesh above the satin cloth, I took off her bra, putting it aside. An involuntary sound escaped my throat as I looked down on her firm, curved body.

I reached for my collar, but Ann's hands were on me as she eagerly and playfully separated me from my clothes. I then lay Ann on the bed and eased myself onto her, every nerve firing as I fit the curves of my body into the warm curves of hers. She moaned softly as I pressed my mouth onto her waiting lips, separating them tenderly. Kissing her deeply, I let her feel my longing for her. She answered me by embracing me and pulling me tightly into her arms, holding me captive in the kiss.

I turned, pulling her on top of me. She continued the kiss, first stroking my throat, then my shoulders, then lightly running her fingers down my sides. Her hands returned to my face, then she buried her long fingers in my hair, touching and stroking me. My body was on fire for her. I turned her onto her back and began devouring her with my lips—first her face, then her neck, then tracing the curves of her body with my lips until I found the warm center of her. Ann gasped with an incoherent exclamation as I took her into my mouth, thrusting her hands into my hair, pulling me harder against her.

I held her to me as she moved, desperately wanting to meet the need of her body, but she was helpless against the commands I gave her with my mouth. I brought her close, then left her to kiss her stomach. I brought her close again, then left her to kiss her thighs. I brought her close again, but this time she struggled against me, calling out my name in a whisper, pleading. My name had never sounded as sweet as from her lips. I took her in my mouth, and with a warm touch from my tongue she cried out, shuddering, her hands grasping my hair, pulling me to her, until at last she was still and breathless.

I was crazy for her. I pulled her down to lie along my body beneath me, then raised her hips, enclosing her around me. I fitted her to me, then pressed into her, burying myself in the warm, hot center of her. The pleasure was piercing. I moved slowly at first, but the urgency rose sharply as our bodies moved together in a rhythm driven by my desire for her. I was surprised to begin hearing again her low, throaty moans. Everything became a blur of rhythm, the force of my movement increasing with her obvious pleasure.

"I want you all night, all night," I breathed. Ann was on the edge again. I clenched my jaw as I moved into her, waiting for her. All at once she arched into me, gasping, pulling at my back. The sound of her coming electrified me; I was transfixed, Ann's body an explosion of sensation beneath me.

At last, Ann released me, falling back into her pillow, reaching up to me with her arms. Liquid, I melted into her, running my fingers up and through her hair and pulling her face to mine gently.

I rested in her arms, then moved aside, needing separation. Moments later, Ann ran her finger over my lips and whispered, "That was wonderful. I just love foreplay, don't you?"

Forcefully, she turned me onto my back and then her mouth was on me, everywhere. Her lips were like burning brands on my skin, claiming ownership as they moved down my body. "Oh, God," was all I could say. "Oh, God, oh, God..."

At some point, in the wee hours of the morning, I awoke to Ann caressing me. She was whispering softly. "I know about Trina, Sweetheart. So please understand I have to do what I'm about to do."

She smoothed my hair, tenderly kissed my forehead, then turned on her side. Within moments, I could hear her breathing in sleep. I, however, suddenly found myself wide awake.

I awoke the next morning having no memory of falling asleep. It took time for me to orient myself because I had slept so deeply, but suddenly it all came back to me—Ann, the ballet, the lovemaking. I reached back for her, but something pricked my palm. I jerked my hand away and rolled over to look, but Ann was gone. On her pillow, however, was one of the long-stemmed red roses from last night's bouquet.

Chapter Eleven

Later that morning I was standing with Marge on the stairs of the Youth Club. "Who was here asking about Trina?" I said sharply.

Marge's eyes widened. "Some woman from the newspaper. I ID.'d her, of course. I even called the newspaper to confirm it."

Marge looked frightened. I couldn't imagine why my hysterical reaction to her innocent statement could possibly have done that to her. I made a conscious effort to relax and smile.

She watched my face for clues as she continued. "Her name was Ann Alexander. She's a reporter—" She interrupted herself. "Lane, I know you said we have to be careful where Trina is concerned, but this woman was legit. I certainly hope that you aren't going to tell me that the newspaper is part of a conspiracy to kill Trina?"

I shook my head stiffly.

"I was very impressed with Ms. Alexander, actually. Extremely intelligent—that's what I noticed about her at first—and poised and warm and very kind. And did I mention how beautiful she was? Her eyes could knock you over. And she was wearing this olive colored business suit with a skirt that came up to here," Marge indicated on her thigh. "Not too high to be inappropriate, you know, but just high enough to give her a very glamorous look. I honestly can't remember when I've seen such a sexy pair of legs..."

Marge was off and running with a glowing description of Ann. I am endlessly amazed by the way heterosexual women describe a beautiful woman. They use such sexual terms that you would think they were in love, until the glowing résumé ends at last with the typical "I just hate her, don't you?" Marge, of course, although straight as an arrow, didn't have that little mean streak in her, so I just waited until the long, rapturous description ran out of steam.

"When was she here, Marge?"

"Oh, early this morning, a little before seven o'clock. I was unlocking the building when she walked up to me."

So, Ann had left my bed around five-thirty in the morning, driven home, changed clothes, put on some make-up, maybe had a little breakfast, then had driven straight over here to start making my life miserable. I felt my expression hardening again. Marge seemed aware of this and spoke up.

"While we were talking, she mentioned she knew you. She was very complimentary—she has great respect for you." That didn't soften me, so Marge started talking faster. "I wasn't surprised that you two were friends, actually. You remind me of each other, somehow." I was now glaring at Marge, but I couldn't help myself. Her expression became helpless. "I'm so sorry, Lane. I can see I've done something terribly wrong. Have I put Trina in any danger?"

I shook my head, trying to relax for Marge's sake. "No Marge, no. It's nothing like that. This is…personal."

Marge sighed, heavily. "I'm so glad I haven't done anything to hurt Trina," she said, actually smiling. "But, this Ann Alexander, who is she?"

I thought of Ann moving beneath me last night, her silky skin, the low tones of her voice as she cried out my name. "An old adversary," I replied.

Marge patted my arm. "Well, as long as it's nothing I need to worry about as far as the children are concerned."

"No. No, not at all," I answered.

"Good," Marge said. "Because she's going to be teaching a class in journalism here next month." She turned and started easing her weight down the stairs to the basement. I shook my head and followed. Marge had even worked her magic on Ann.

I had agreed to help serve lunch to the kids today. Marge and I and two other volunteers made bologna sandwiches factory style. My entire photography class was there, as well as the boys and girls from the basketball court who had helped Perret in his yard yesterday, and a watercolor class that had been taught by the man to my left who was now spreading mayonnaise on bread.

I carried a plateful of sandwiches to a table and sat down next to the kids. Latasha, from my class, spent her meal squirting lemonade through her teeth at Charlie, who sat across the table from her. Eventually I got up and moved her and her sandwich to the other end of the table so Charlie could eat in peace. When I came back in, the basketball court gang nearly ran over me on their way out the door.

"You kids didn't eat much," I remarked.

"We're going to play!" one of the guys informed me.

"Stop bouncing that basketball in here!" Marge scolded. The guilty party caught the ball up in his hands.

Marge started cleaning up. Everyone else had left, and I knew she was swamped with work. "Marge, leave that—I'll put everything away and straighten up."

"You need to get back to work," she argued.

"I'll get it. You go on upstairs."

She smiled sweetly at me and made her way up the stairs. I put away the sandwich supplies, wiped down the tables and straightened the chairs. When I finished, I walked to the top of the basement stairs to leave, but there was no light switch at the top of the steps. I walked back down the stairs, only to discover the switch all the way across the room from the exit. Not very smart, I thought to myself. I looked around. There was one window. I shut off the lights.

Seconds passed while my eyes adjusted to the dimness. A strange little memory was nagging at me. What was it? I groped for the stairs. Reaching out for the handrail but finding only air, I stepped up onto the first step. My eyes were beginning to make out features. As I spotted the handrail and grasped it, my mind suddenly grasped the thought it had been groping for—Ricky's cellar.

Ricky had stairs leading to a dark cellar in his building. I had discovered it with sleuth-like sophistication by falling down them—except that no one ever went down to Ricky's cellar, other than perhaps the maintenance man.

That thought stopped me. David Case was the maintenance man for that property. It occurred to me that Ricky's building was just blocks from Gerald Barnes' Louisville office. And Lamont had told me that the last time he saw Trina—or Ricky alive—they had been boarding a bus for Ricky's house.

I had another stop to make. I ran upstairs, called out a goodbye to Marge, and headed outside. My car started on the second try and I pulled out slowly. I hit my turn signal and made a right. That's when I saw the flash of white in my rear view mirror.

My heart pounding, I signaled and crossed three lanes of traffic to make a left opposite the direction I really wanted to go. Maneuvering on this congested street was difficult with one eye on my rear view mirror, but I glimpsed the car again, nearly a block behind me. I drove half a mile and pulled into a convenience store.

Casually, I got out of my car and walked in to buy some gum. I took my time. Did I want fruit flavor, cinnamon, or spearmint? Hmm. Spearmint looked good. I placed it on the counter, fiddling around in my pockets until I came up with the correct change. I walked back outside, unwrapped a piece of gum, stuck the wrapper in my pocket, and chewed awhile, enjoying the day. Ten minutes later I got back into my car and pulled out again.

I drove several blocks, keeping one eye on the traffic behind me, but it looked clear. I signaled and made a right to head back to my original destination. Half a block later, at a different intersection, a little white T-top made a left and fell in line several cars behind me. I swallowed my gum. Ann was following me.

"No, no, no!" I yelled out loud, slapping my steering wheel. Of course, it only made sense. Ann needed Trina to complete her story as much as I did. But, investigatively speaking, I was a week ahead of her. She would be wasting her time to go back and retrace all my footwork. If she stayed close to me, eventually, she hoped, I would lead her right to Trina.

I punched the gas, circled the block, and headed into the city. I was going to have to lose her, somehow, but without indicating that I knew she was following me. If she figured me out, her guard would go up and I might never outsmart her.

The easiest way to lose her would be at a light. I paced myself as best I could in the traffic so that soon I was running yellow caution lights. At last, when I thought I had her, a chorus of car horns blared out behind me as Ann ran the light. That should humble her a little, I thought, because she knew she had attracted attention. Sure enough, she dropped a little further back, and the next light caught her.

As soon as she came to a stop, I made a right, then a left, and drove into the city. Seconds later, she reappeared again. I kicked myself. I should have made a left when she got caught by the light. She'd made a right on red and had caught up to me from there. The traffic in the city was creeping. I'd have a hard time losing her here.

I spotted a parking garage and pulled in. Racing around to find another exit, I was dismayed to discover there was only one. This was going to make it almost impossible to leave the garage now without Ann following me. I circled around and drove to the top of the garage, put my car in park and walked to the edge of the building.

I could see Ann from here. She had the roof off the car and was listening to music, looking very unperturbed by this little cat-and-mouse game we were playing. All she had to do was watch the exit for me to emerge.

I deliberated a few seconds, then began timing Ann as she circled the block. With the traffic and the stoplights, it took her about two minutes and ten seconds to leave the garage exit and return to the exit again. I would have to time myself so that I left the garage while she was at the opposite end of the block. I would have to push to make it to the exit in two minutes, but that was my best bet. If I gave myself more time than that, fluctuations in traffic might put her right in my path again, or a parking place might open up for her near the exit. I waited for her to circle to the point opposite the exit, glanced at my watch, and ran for my car.

I hit the down ramp as fast as I dared and began circling the labyrinth of the garage. My squealing tires echoed in the cavernous building as I prayed that all good little pedestrians were safe in their office buildings. I rounded the last curve of the level and hit the next down ramp flying. Second floor. One more down ramp to go and I was out of there.

I rounded the next curb and came up suddenly on bright red tail-lights. Screeching to a halt, I barely missed the back bumper of a car backing out of its space. The driver glanced over his shoulder and waved at me politely, as if he'd done something wrong. I backed up, and he continued out of his parking place. His trunk hood was bouncing lightly up and down where it hadn't shut because of some packages. I was hoping he wouldn't notice, but he did. He got out of his car, came around and slammed the hood down until it latched, then smiled at me in a Southern-gentlemanly way before getting back in his car. I wanted to nudge his rear bumper a little, but I controlled myself, creeping along behind him until he paid the woman in the booth and exited the garage. The woman then took my ticket. I glanced at my watch. The way I had it figured, I had ten seconds before Ann rounded the corner.

"Well," the woman began, looking at my ticket, "you didn't stay long!"

I shoved money into her hand. The gate began rising in front of my car.

"Wait a minute…you get change!" I heard her say in the distance as I tore out of the garage. The road was clear. I gunned it to the end of the block and whipped it around the corner, just as the first cars appeared at the far end of the block. I'd made it! I'd lost Ann.

I headed toward Butchertown. Pulling up in front of Ricky's grandmother's duplex, I threw the strap to my camera bag over my shoulder, then walked around to my trunk and pulled out a flashlight. I entered the duplex foyer, stopped a moment to take a breath, then opened the door to the cellar. Flicking on the flashlight, I descended the steps I had nearly broken my neck on a few days earlier.

Although it was bright daylight outside, it was dim and damp down here. I couldn't see all of the cellar at once because of structural walls and the narrow beam of my flashlight, and it put my nerves on edge. I kept repeating a sort of mantra to myself that I was alone here, I was alone. Alone wasn't great, but it was better than who I might run into. Case had to have been the one who had called the paper under the pretense of having information about Ricky. He had arranged to "meet" me at the school and fire a few shots at me to try to scare me off the story. This meant that he knew what I looked like. If I ran into him I wouldn't have the luxury of lying my way out of it, and he wouldn't have the luxury of letting me.

My flashlight teased apart heavy curtains of darkness as I walked forward. I made my way toward the old furnace, which flailed outward at me with its swollen tentacles. As I rounded the furnace, my heart stopped as something fluttered across my light beam. I froze, searching back over the area with my flashlight. I caught movement again, and shone my light on a spider the size of the palm of my hand. I backed away, and turning, walked slowly to the other side of the cellar.

One dingy window let in gray light despite the brightness of the day. There were more spiders, but none the size of the one I had encountered behind the furnace. Spiders were not what I had come looking for. Confused, I headed back to the stairs. If what I was looking for was not here, then perhaps my whole scenario of the crime was wrong.

Halfway up the stairs, I stopped. The stairs were slats of wood, unenclosed. I backed down to the cellar floor, and leaning into the stairs, shone my flashlight between the steps.

There was something I couldn't make out, so I walked around to the side, and shone my light in the area underneath the stairs.

Someone had attempted to dig a hole in the hard dirt floor of the cellar under the steps; then, probably hastily, filled it back in. Digging it wouldn't have been an easy job. It would have taken a pick as well as a shovel, and a lot of time and effort. The hole was several feet long, and about shoulder-width wide.

A shallow grave?

I wouldn't have jumped to such conclusions except for the large pool of what appeared to be blackened dried blood at the head of the grave, congealed on the hard surface of the dirt floor.

My stomach jumped. Fumbling for my camera, I raised it and took a few shots, then backed up and took a few less graphic shots of the stairs. Then, quickly, I headed to the steps. Reaching for the handrail, I pulled myself up and out of the cellar. Running out of the building and toward my car, I took long, deep breaths of the air that was shuddering through the trees on this bright, intensely beautiful summer's day. I opened my car door and got inside quickly, pulling the door shut next to me and locking it, as if that would provide some kind of protection against what I had just seen.

What a terrible place to die. What awful circumstances for a good man to find himself in. Noah Franklin had discovered he'd been used to transport drugs. Believing it was all Case's doing, Franklin must have debated for weeks whether or not to report it. Finally, he had decided to go to Gerald Barnes' office in Louisville to inform him what his maintenance man was doing.

But Barnes knew. It was his operation. He also knew that Franklin was a man of integrity, a man who couldn't be paid off or trusted to keep quiet—so Barnes quickly arranged for Franklin to disappear. The duplex where Ricky lived was a perfect place to kill Franklin—it was close, the first floor was uninhabited, and it had perfect cover in which to kill a man and dig a grave.

But then Ricky must have shown up with Trina, interrupting the murder or the burial, and things got messy. The kids got scared; they ran. Case was forced to dispose of Franklin's body in a different way—unplanned—hence moving the body from the place of the murder, and the sloppy job of tossing it in the river.

Steadier now, I pulled out my cell phone and called Bev at the LPD to describe what I had found. Within the hour, she pulled to the curb in front of me. A wiry woman in her early forties, she walked over to my car and asked me a few questions about what I had seen and if I had disturbed anything. Satisfied, she told me to stay in my car while she checked out the cellar herself.

Ten minutes later she returned, lit a cigarette, and asked me to join her in her car. When she had gotten off the radio with her department, I looked over at her. "What do you think?" I asked.

"I think your scenario of the crime is plausible," she said. "But now we're bringing in the folks who can tell us what's really down there." She flicked ashes out the window and tried to push her brushy blond hair out of her face.

"What do you mean?" I asked.

"I mean we're going to see if you have a story, or if some kid was down there last week burying his pet ferret."

"That would have been an awfully big ferret," I remarked.

She grinned at me. "Yeah, but we'll let science determine that."

"The grave will be empty," I said. "And the blood will be a match for Noah Franklin."

"I know that's your scenario," she said. "But we won't know for a day or two about the details. First of all we have to determine that it's human blood, that it's Noah Franklin's, that—"

"Yeah, yeah, I know," I said. "I want the story to myself."

"Of course," she nodded. "I'll let you know when and what you can go with."

We sat in her hot car in silence for a while. I took a deep breath, released it, and leaned back in the seat. "I know our killer was pushed for time," I said, "but burying the body in the cellar? It seems to show a certain lack of imagination."

"Yeah." Bev grinned. My heterosexual friend finished her cigarette and threw the butt out the window. "I bet he's a rotten lover, too."

I waited until the crime scene investigation unit arrived, asked them a few questions, then headed back to the office. On the way, I considered what I still needed answered. If the blood in that cellar proved to be Noah Franklin's, I had finally found solid evidence to tie the two crimes together.

But who had killed Ricky? Case would have been occupied with getting rid of Franklin's body, and Barnes certainly wouldn't have done it himself. Barnes would have had to call on someone else to get rid of Ricky and Trina—someone Ricky would have trusted enough to let get close to him.

So, who was the second killer? One little girl might have the answer, but I couldn't find her. And somewhere, she was either hiding or running for her life.

Back at the office, I started the article about Franklin, but my thoughts kept getting interrupted by a congealed black pool on a hard dirt floor. I couldn't shake it. Afterward, thinking it would help to talk to someone, I got up and went to Harry's office. He wasn't there. I asked around and found out he'd taken an early supper. At five-thirty I left a message with Terry that I was leaving for the day, then got back in my car and drove around to a couple of Harry's favorite spots. He wasn't there. He had probably gone home to eat with his wife.

I didn't want to bother him with this at home. I looked at my watch. It was six-thirty. I decided it was time to call it a day.

I took I-64 to go home, but found myself taking a left instead of a right on Grinstead Drive, heading toward Crescent Hill instead of home to the Highlands. I passed the old Crescent Hill Water Reservoir—a turn-of-the-century image that looks like something from an Impressionist's watercolor—and made a left down an oak-lined street. Parallel-parking in front of a handsomely renovated two-story, I went up the walk and onto the porch, which was dotted with potted trees and plants. Stepping to the door, I rang the bell.

Although I couldn't make out the figure through the cut glass windows of the front door, the footsteps were gratefully familiar. The door opened and Ann looked at me, perplexed. I suppose I shouldn't have been surprised at her reaction. After all, she had been following me all day. Now, not long after she gives up, I land on her front porch.

She frowned as she analyzed my face. Then she spoke softly. "Are you okay, sweetie?"

"Bad day," I whispered, low.

Ann was dressed in slim-fitting capris and a button-down blouse with the sleeves rolled up. She looked comfortable and comforting. "Is this something you want to talk about, or something I'm going to have to wait and read about in the papers?" she asked.

"The papers," I said.

"All right." She smiled soothingly and took my hand in her warm hands. "But come in. It looks like I have to put on a few more vegetables."

She pulled gently on my hand until I stepped into the cool, light front room. Closing the door behind me she said, "Make yourself comfortable."

Music was playing low on the sound system. The windows were open, and a soft breeze was brushing at the sheer curtains. From the kitchen, I could smell the mouth-watering scent of lemon-garlic.

"You know," I said, "right at this moment, in my apartment, I have two stale cookies."

Ann laughed. "And I'm sure if I had dropped by you would have shared."

I turned quickly. "I'm sorry. You're expecting someone…"

Ann shook her head and put a hand on my arm. "No," she said firmly, "I'm not. I've had a roast in the Crock-Pot all day; I was just fixing some vegetables to go with it. In fact, why don't you come back to the kitchen with me? I know you can't tell me much, but maybe we can just talk."

I nodded and followed her back to the kitchen. She set a stool for me at the kitchen island, poured a cold glass of wine out of the fridge for me, then left me to go into her backyard. In minutes she returned carrying two tomatoes, warm from the garden. I laughed. "You did it! You finally planted your own garden! Congratulations!"

"Oh, not really," she smiled. "It's very small. Just a few plants. But it's a start." She unwrapped some bread and put it in the oven, stirred the lima beans on the stove, then moved to the sink and rinsed the tomatoes. "What would it help you to talk about?" she asked.

I watched her as she got the cutting board and brought the tomatoes to the counter in front of me. "I'm not sure," I said. I watched her silently as she sliced the tomatoes. Eventually a question came to me. "When does it get to you?"

"What part?" she asked.

"The violence we cover."

She paused with the slicing and looked up at me, thinking. "When I'm not expecting it, I guess," she said after a moment. "When I haven't had a few minutes on the drive to the scene to prepare myself." She took a breath. "I was called in once to cover the story of a baby who'd been abandoned. But when I got there, I discovered that the baby had been left all day in a car in a parking lot. It was the middle of August." She hesitated a moment, looking at a point across the room, then went back to her slicing. "You get those stories at least once every summer, but this time I wasn't expecting it. I wasn't prepared. It completely threw me. I couldn't finish a thought for a week."

"Well, that's pretty much it. I think that's pretty much what happened to me today. I drove to a scene expecting to find some kind of evidence but..." I hesitated. "...What I found was a little more graphic than what I had bargained for."

Ann looked at me thoughtfully. Then she pulled a plate over to the cutting board and began arranging the tomatoes on it. "Sorry about my story, then. I'm sure that didn't help."

I reached out and put my hand on hers. "No—that's exactly why I came here, Ann. I needed to be with someone who's...been there. Someone who can understand. Even if I can't talk about it."

Ann picked up the plate and walked around the kitchen island. She gave me a quick squeeze around the shoulders, then put the tomatoes on the kitchen table. The window next to the table was lined with potted plants. "Fresh basil!" she announced proudly, then began picking some of the herb. "Do you like basil on your tomatoes?"

I smiled. "Sure."

She arranged the basil on the plate, then came around to the fridge to get the wine bottle. "I think you need another glass of wine," she said, refilling my wine glass. "In fact, I think you may need two or three more glasses of wine."

"No, no." I laughed. "I don't want to have to call a cab to get me home."

Ann handed me the glass. "I'll take you home," she countered. "Or." She hesitated, looking at me. "I won't."

Ann's eyes met my gaze. With one hand I took the wine glass, with the other I reached out and took her hand, softly brushing her fingers with my lips. For a moment, Ann looked flustered. She pulled her hand away and smiled. "I hope you have a little bit of an appetite, despite your day," she said.

The room was heady with the aroma of roast and garlic and baking bread. I laughed. "I wouldn't have a chance in this kitchen, no matter what kind of day I'd been through," I answered. "Here—let me set the table."

We ate in the kitchen, then chatted as we filled the dishwasher. At dusk, Ann led me to her living room. She opened the fireplace screen, struck a long match, and lit the candles that filled the grate. She blew out the match, rose, and walked to the CD player where she changed the CD to an old Sarah Vaughan album. She sat next to me on the couch. "Is this okay?" she asked. "Or would you rather go see a movie or something to distract you?"

The room was filled with the soft light of the candles from the fireplace and the glow of a streetlight through the window. I took several deep breaths. "This is fine," I began. "This is good. It's—"

Unexpectedly, something inside me let down. It was the alcohol, or maybe the music or the food, but some protective barrier in me broke. I could feel my shoulders tremble as I spoke. Ann drew closer to me, filling my arms with her body.

"I'm sorry." I whispered. "I didn't mean to...do this..." I tried to breathe. "I wasn't going to come here. I was going to go talk to Harry—"

Ann caressed my hair, shushing me. "I don't think Harry is what you need, Sweetheart," she whispered.

"Lane... Lane..."

I could hear Ann's soft voice in my ear. Groggily, I sat up. "I need to go home—" I began.

"No,"Ann said. "Upstairs. It's three in the morning."

I was too disoriented to argue. I followed Ann up the stairs and into her bedroom, where she sat me on her queen-sized four poster bed.

"Do you want to sleep in all this?" she said to me softly, indicating my clothes.

I shook my head and reached for my collar, but Ann's fingers were already there, loosening the buttons. Gently, she lifted the shirt over my head. I stood and kicked off my shoes, and as I looked back up, Ann was watching me, a soft expression on her face. She handed me a shirt to sleep in.

I pulled it on, then stepped toward Ann, reaching for her collar. "Here," I said. She looked down at my hands as I undid the buttons, then back up to me. I opened her shirt slowly, easing it over her smooth shoulders. I lay it neatly over the back of a chair, then helped her into a silk nightgown.

Ann turned and drew down the corner of the quilt and bed sheet. "Go ahead, get in," she ordered gently. I got into the bed and Ann followed. The bed felt marvelous, and I was deliciously sleepy. Ann reached up and turned off the lamp. She settled into the sheets next to me, the length of her body just touching mine.

I looked at the silhouette of Ann in the darkness of the room. She looked like life next to me—the very antithesis of that dark, cold entity which had gripped my chest next to the shallow grave. And she felt very much like love, the opposite of whatever it was that could bring one person to indifferently rip the life out of another.

Ann turned to curl up next to me and put her head on my shoulder. My eyes were adjusting to the darkness, and the sight of her body rising and falling with each breath gave me a sense of steadiness I hadn't felt since the afternoon. Gently, I reached up and brushed the hair from her face. She responded by placing her hand on my chest.

Her hand was warm, and layer by layer I felt the sleepiness fall away from me. I nuzzled her hair and kissed the top of her head. She leaned back on the pillow and looked up at me. I could tell she wanted to ask me something.

"Lane..." she hesitated as if she didn't quite know how to put it. "I'd like to ask just one thing about whatever it was that you saw today."

"All right."

"It wasn't Trina, was it?"

Even in the dark, I could tell from Ann's face that she had been afraid to ask the question. "No, Ann. It wasn't Trina."

She sighed. "You know, what happened to Ricky..." she trailed off, then started again. "We haven't talked about this with each other, but it's possible that when we find Trina, she may not—"

"Trina's alive," I said, answering the real question Ann was asking.

"You've found her?"

I smiled. "That question is cheating. But I'm going to answer it. No. I haven't found her. But I know she's alive."

"How do you know? Can you tell me?"

I knew for a fact that Trina was still alive because David Case had been at the Youth Club looking for her, but I couldn't provide Ann with details. I took a breath. "Ann," I started, "the people who killed Ricky and Noah. Well, think about it. Ricky was hardly more than a child. Noah was retired. Even many criminals would avoid killing the young or the elderly. The people who did this are cold. Dispassionate. They won't blink at killing a little girl. If I can't find Trina..." I looked at Ann, "...then you've got to. If one of us isn't the first to locate her, I don't think she has a chance."

Ann reached out and touched my face. "All right, all right," she said with conviction.

I took Ann's hand in mine, kissed it, then pulled her into my arms, wanting to feel the strong beat of my own heart, wanting to feel the surge of blood through my body, wanting to feel alive. I held her tight. Too tight. Ann pulled away, then kissed me hard.

"It's okay, Lane," she breathed. "It's okay. It's just you and me. You're okay."

She touched my hair, then kissed me again. Her lips were full and warm. Heat filled the pit of my stomach. Ann ran her fingers up my back and entwined them in my hair. She lifted her knee over my thigh, then drew me toward her so that I was cradling her in my arms underneath me. "You're not alone, sweetheart," she murmured. "I'm right here..."

Ann moved under me, slipping her thigh between my legs. "Come to me," she whispered. "Please." Her face was so close I could feel her breath on my skin.

Ann's slender body felt fragile in my arms. The heat of her body beneath me sent fire through my veins—a longing so strong that it screamed to my body I was alive. Tenderly, Ann caressed my face and neck. She ran her fingernails over my shoulders and back until I shuddered with pleasure. Taking locks of my hair in her hands, she wrapped them around her fingers and pulled on them teasingly, grinning at me.

I smoothed her hair, then traced a line over the soft rise and valley of her throat. Moving my hand under her nightgown, I followed the curves of her body, brushing lightly over her breasts and her waist. Her skin was warm against my palm.

I slipped my hand over her flat stomach, exploring downward over the length of her body. When my fingers finally touched the warm place between her thighs, I could feel she was already wet with desire for me. She lifted her hips to me, and gently moving my whole body into her, I entered her.

Ann gasped, almost a laugh of relief. "I've been wanting you," she said, her eyes searching my face, "since the moment you walked in the door tonight." She pulled me closer.

I moved into her again and she strained upward toward me, wanting me harder. I obliged, beginning an unhurried yet strong rhythm into her. Ann closed her eyes, letting her head drop back to her pillow, lost in feeling. I kissed her forehead, nuzzled her shoulders, then softly bit her neck. Opening her eyes, she laughed, then pulled tight at my back, arching into me. I moved over her and kissed her deeply on the mouth.

Her lips were warm, soft, and eager for mine. I held the kiss, exploring her mouth until she pulled away to gasp with pleasure at the increased force of my rhythm into her. Careful to maintain my intimate connection with her, I opened her gown with my free hand. Her nipples were taut, erect. Ann groaned as I drew the nipple of one perfect breast into my mouth.

Her breast was like silk, and I could smell the slightest scent of powder on her skin. A hot heaviness began to swell between my legs. My mouth consumed her breasts, first one, then the other, then moving to the soft place underneath her arm, then to her smooth shoulders and back to her throat. Ann murmured a soft, low sound.

I raised up on one elbow and shifted my body closer, never breaking my rhythm. Ann's arms tightened around the small of my back, pulling me even closer, wanting me stronger, faster. A brand was burning inside me, centering itself and demanding to be satisfied. Its flame grew with every brush of Ann's thigh. But it would have to wait.

Ann clasped me around my shoulders, pulling at them as she lifted her upper body off the bed, trying to meld her body with mine. "I want you…" she pleaded, her lips brushing my cheek. I leaned my body into her full force, rattling the bed, meeting her urgency. She gripped me tight, and then even tighter. Suddenly the sound of my name was replaced by a gasp, and she shuddered, long and close, in my arms.

Slowly, the warmth of her body fell away from mine as she eased herself back onto the bed, sated. My thighs and abdomen were tight with desire. I could smell the faint scent of her perfume and perspiration. It was intoxicating. I leaned over her and kissed her. Her forehead was slightly damp.

Lazily, Ann turned her head on the pillow to look up at me. She smiled. With her right hand she touched my face, then ran her fingers down my neck, over my breast, across my stomach, then softly gripped me between my legs.

I clenched my jaws against the surge that jolted through my body. Ann lifted the shirt I was wearing over my breasts. I moved over her as she ran her fingernails over and down my back and buttocks. Softly, she moved down my body, kissing and caressing my breasts, then my stomach. My body felt like a hot pistol ready to go off.

With a tease and then a soft touch of her tongue, Ann took me into her mouth. I couldn't breathe. With another move, she enveloped me completely, drawing me in. My body tensed, its heat hardening and centering itself explosively in the warm wetness of Ann's mouth.

Ann had complete control of me now. With every stroke of Ann's tongue my urgency grew, swelling into the warm, moist softness of her mouth. My legs trembled with tension. Her mouth owned me, stroking me over and over into an unbearable tautness.

Ann ran her fingernails up my stomach. She gently took my breasts in her hands, grasping them. I gasped, but Ann wasn't ready to let me go. The moist movement of her mouth was gathering every nerve ending of my body into one point, piercing me. Then, just as pleasure was about to turn to pain, her tongue touched the center of me. I grasped at the bed sheet as the warm colors of the room went dark and I became lost in an intense, powerful release.

Mid-morning the next day, Harry walked into my office. "You want me for something?" he asked.

I looked up from my computer, startled. "What?"

"Sorry," Harry teased. "Didn't mean to wake you."

"Oh—I was just doing some research on the internet."

"I don't think so—you were a million miles away," Harry laughed. "What were you thinking about?"

I felt my face flush. I hoped Harry didn't notice. "Nothing. I guess I just drifted there a second."

"Anyway, Terry said you were looking for me yesterday—that you needed me for something?"

I looked up at Harry, but couldn't help grinning to myself. "No, never mind. I found what I needed."

Harry ambled over to my desk. "Whatcha workin' on?"

"Trying to figure out who the second shooter was. Trying to figure out who killed Ricky Simms."

"Who's your suspect?"

I rocked back in my chair. "Richard Perret. The coach at the Youth

Club. A friend of mine spotted Trina in his car with some other kids the day after Trina's parents said she disappeared. Then, when I interviewed him, he went ballistic. Didn't want to have anything to do with the interview, and especially didn't want to have his name associated with Ricky's in any way."

Harry crossed his arms and glanced at my computer. "So, does he mention the murder on his homepage?"

I grinned. "I'll have to check on that. Right now I'm just searching our newspaper archives, where we publish arrests."

"What have you found?" Harry leaned in and squinted at the computer.

"Look for yourself." I hit some keys on the keypad. "He's got a record."

"For what?" Harry asked.

"Drugs."

Harry read the screen and whistled. "What do you think? Have you got your man?"

I sighed. "It's not that clear, unfortunately. These charges are almost twenty years old and are only for possession. He was arrested a couple of times in college. I can see two scenarios." I turned in my chair to face Harry. "One—the drug charges were a mistake of youth. Perret turned his life around, got his teaching certificate, managed to get a job, but the drug record has haunted him all his life so the last thing he wants is to be associated in any way with the drug trade. Or—"

"Or," Harry continued for me, "he never gave up drugs, now he's up to his nostrils in cocaine and it's about to catch up with him."

I nodded at Harry. "So to speak."

Grandmother and I sat in her kitchen breaking beans. It was after supper. Outside, night was falling. Through the screen window, the nocturnal insects were humming and I was beginning to hear the frogs call from the pond. On the stove, green beans were boiling on one burner and jars were heating for canning on the other. "When does basketball season start?" Grandmother suddenly piped up.

"Not until November, Grandmom. We still have football season to get through first."

"Well—I'm all ready for basketball season," she fussed. "I miss my Wildcats."

"Why don't you start watching football? The University of Kentucky sometimes has pretty good football teams, too, you know."

"Oh, I know." She reached for another handful of green beans,

153

which she plopped down in her lap on her apron. "It's just not the same."

"You sound like Mom and Dad."

"Have you talked to them yet?" she asked.

I looked up from my green beans, ready to take a little bit of a break. "Grandmom, I've really tried. Now and then, usually while I'm at work, I'll look at the phone and think, just call. But I don't. I don't pick it up. I don't know why." I broke a few more beans, then stopped again. "They don't call me. I feel like if I called it would just be so…fake. I don't know what to talk to them about anymore."

Grandmother sighed. "It's funny, I guess, to feel like you don't know what to say to the people you spent eighteen years of your life living with."

I nodded. "Yeah. I wish it were as easy with them as it is with you."

Grandmother looked up at me and met my eyes meaningfully. Then she smiled. "Well, all I can say is I talk to all of you and they're confused, too. They seem to think that ever since they've found out you're gay, you must be a completely different person from the daughter they knew. They seem to think that 'Poof!' You've become a stranger!"

I grinned half-heartedly. "Yeah. That's kind of how they treat me."

"Well," Grandmother continued to break beans, "keep trying. Because if you don't make the effort, they may not be able to, and you're going to lose each other forever. All I know for certain is that you'll keep drifting further apart if you don't talk." Grandmother picked up the corners of her apron, brushed off the strings and tips into the trash can next to her, and grabbed another handful of the green beans. "So—tell me about your newspaper story."

I filled Grandmother in on what I'd discovered since we'd last talked. I told her about my morning at the Youth Club, about serving the kids lunch and being reminded of the cellar at Ricky's apartment. I told her about discovering the apparent grave under the steps. I left out the part about the blood.

"Anyway," I continued, "a friend of Ricky and Trina's—Lamont— had told me that the night Ricky was killed and Trina disappeared, he had seen the two of them getting on a bus to go to Ricky's house. I knew Noah Franklin had been killed in one place but his body had been moved, so, when I remembered that cellar, I decided to check it out. When I found the partially dug grave, I knew that was where it had all happened."

Grandmother didn't seem to hear the last part. She giggled.

"Kids," she mumbled.

"What?" I looked up at her, surprised. "What are you laughing about?"

"Oh, I'm sorry," she said. "I was back to thinking about the kids at the club—about how you fixed lunch for them before you went to Ricky's duplex. You said that you and the other teachers made all those sandwiches for them and then the kids hardly ate anything."

"Yeah..." I was confused, but I grinned. "So?"

"Well, last time you were here you were telling me about following those kids in a car, and how they stopped at a grocery and bought bags and bags of food for lunch! Weren't those the same kids?"

I didn't answer. Grandmother looked at me. "Well? You never can figure about kids, can you?" She waited, then she laughed. "Lane, your mind is going a million miles an hour! Did you even hear me? Weren't those the same kids?"

I looked up. "Yes, for the most part, those were the same kids." I stood up and emptied my lap of beans. "Hey, I've got to go check something out, Grandmother." I grabbed my keys and walked around the table, kissing her on the top of her head. "You going to be okay here tonight?"

"Why, sure, honey. But why are you running off?" She squeezed my hand.

"Because you're a genius," I said on my way out the door.

I checked my trunk for my toolbox and lock pick set, then headed for the city and Perret's house. It was about ten o'clock now and dark, but I had a flashlight in the car. My mind was racing.

When I arrived in Perret's neighborhood, I pulled into the alley behind his house and drove to his backyard. I stopped the car and listened for any sounds of people outside who might become suspicious. All was quiet, so I grabbed my lock pick set and my flashlight and jumped the fence into Perret's backyard.

I walked to the shed and discovered there was no lock on it, so I opened the door cautiously. A strange smell of something decaying greeted me. I couldn't quite identify it. I turned on the flashlight and looked into the shed.

The shed looked as if no one had cleaned it out in years. I wondered where all the kids sat in order to have lunch, until I remembered that the lawn mower, the rakes, and assorted other tools had been out on the lawn while they were in here.

I flashed the light around the cramped space. The light caught and reflected off the plastic of a potato chip bag. I looked closer. Toward the middle of the shed were a couple of cereal boxes, pretzel bags, and assorted other junk food items. I stumbled over a broom and made my way further back.

My nose still hadn't adjusted to the smell of something rank in the shed. I flashed my light to the back of the shed. There were at least three more boxes of groceries in the back. Three large jars of juice sat on a shelf next to an assortment of garden tools. One was only half full. I smiled.

I started climbing around tools and old furniture. My foot hit something that ricocheted off a watering can. I stood still and listened for sounds of anyone from the house. I didn't hear anything, so I searched for the object. It was an open can of beans, some of its contents now oozing onto the shed floor. It occurred to me that was what the shed smelled like—a kitchen garbage can that should have been emptied a couple of weeks ago.

Something rustled in the back of the shed, and I raised my flashlight in time to see a can of soup hurtling through space toward me. Tiny lights swam before my eyes as it struck me full force in the head, knocking me sideways. I fell into some stacked kitchen chairs, dropping the flashlight, as a dark figure ran past me. Shaking my head, I stumbled to follow, still unsteady from the blow I had just taken. I limped between the junk piles and out into the yard. Not sure I was completely conscious, I managed to catch up to the figure at the fence and pull at her white T-shirt until she fell backwards onto me. She was fighting like she thought I was going to kill her. I rolled her over.

"Don't kill me!" Trina shouted. "Please don't kill me! Don't kill me!" All at once she gave up fighting and began crying, almost hysterically.

"Trina! Trina! Shhh!" I tried to quiet her. "I'm not going to hurt you! I'm here to help you!"

Her hysterical crying didn't subside. "Don't kill me, don't kill me, please—"

"If I was going to kill you, I would have done it already, wouldn't I? I'd have shot you as you went over the fence, or I would have had a knife. Or, I'd be trying to strangle you because you can't get away. Right?" It was the best I could do, considering the circumstances.

Her breathing slowed. "I...g-guess," she conceded.

"My name's Lane Montgomery. I'm a reporter. I know you're afraid. I'm afraid too, believe me."

I pulled her up into a sitting position. Right now, Trina didn't look a thing like her tough-girl photo in the school yearbook. Right now she looked like a scared twelve-year-old.

"Are you okay?"

She nodded. She didn't smell okay. She smelled like a kid who'd worn the same clothes and lived in the kitchen trash for a week.

"I'm going to take you someplace where you'll be safe. I know your mom will want to know you're all right. And your dad asked me to take you to him if I found you."

Trina sniffed. "My dad? My dad wants to see me?" I nodded. The ghost of a smile played at the corners of her mouth. "My dad. My dad wants to see me! I didn't think he cared what happened to me. I hardly ever see him."

I pulled her to her feet. "Do you have anything in there you need to get?" I nodded toward the shed.

She shook her head. We walked back to the shed. I retrieved my flashlight, then we got into the car quietly and I pulled out of the alley.

"Sorry about your head," Trina remarked.

My head was splitting. "I'm all right. It was a good defense. But you could have killed me."

"I don't like killing," Trina stated simply.

"Trina, I'm going to take you to the police. I've got a friend there who works in homicide—"

"The police? No! I want to see my dad!"

"What? Now?"

"Yeah."

"I thought we'd call both your parents from the police station."

"I want to see my dad!"

"Your mom would like to see you—"

"I want to see my dad, okay? I see my mom all the time. And you said he said he wanted to see me!"

I frowned. "Okay, okay." I turned the car and headed to her dad's house.

Trina gazed out her window. "The kids from the Youth Club told me what happened to Ricky."

"I'm sorry," I said.

"Yeah," she responded. Her voice wasn't much louder than a whisper. "When I thought they were going to kill me, I ran home, but Mom wasn't there. I didn't have my key to get in, but then I thought it was stupid to go home, they'd know where to find me."

"They who, Trina?"

"The men who killed that man—"

"What men?"

"Ricky and I got off the bus and went up the street to his house. When we got close to his house, we heard a loud sound. Ricky thought it was his friend working in the cellar—"

"His friend?"

"Yeah. The same guy who fixes things at our building works at his apartment building, too. That's who he thought it was."

"What's that man's name?"

"David. Ricky made friends with him because...well, David was around and Ricky was lonely, you know, with his grandma gone most of the time..."

"So what happened after you heard the noise?"

"Ricky said, 'Let's go see David,' so we ran down the cellar steps, and there was David with a shovel in his hand coming around the stairs and someone lying on the ground behind him. Then I saw blood on the floor next to the man. I think the loud noise we heard was a gun going off. Ricky stopped—I think he figured it out before I did. All of a sudden, the light went out in the cellar."

"What light?"

"Somewhere there was a light on in the cellar and it went out."

"Did David turn it off?"

"No. There was someone else down there."

"Did you see him?"

"Kind of, but not really. He was all the way across the cellar and it was dark. He was big. Fat. But I heard him. He turned out the light and said, 'That's a shame. So young.'"

No wonder Case was still looking for Trina. The second man was Gerald Barnes. Not only had Ricky and Trina witnessed David Case with Franklin's body, they had seen Gerald Barnes. Barnes was too careful to disassociate himself from his crimes to let them escape. "Then what happened?" I asked.

"Both of us started running up the stairs as fast as we could in the dark. When we got out into the yard, Ricky yelled, 'Run home! I'll meet you there!' Then we split up—he ran one way, I ran the other. I don't know how long I ran, but when I finally got home, it was dark. Mom was out, and I didn't have a key. Then I thought, it's stupid to be here. David knows where I live, and he might even have heard Ricky yell at me to run home. So I ran to the Youth Club."

"Why the Youth Club?"

"I don't know. I guess I always felt like the people there liked me. I hid out close to the building until it opened the next day, then I went in. Coach Perret was taking kids to his house to do yard work, so I went along, but then I stayed in his shed. He didn't notice I didn't leave with the others. My friends brought me groceries twice a week, told me what was going on, what happened to Ricky. They said they'd let me know when it was safe."

"Trina, why didn't you go to the police?"

She shrugged.

"Was it because of the drugs?"

She looked at me, frightened. "I don't deal. Ricky was a dealer, but I ain't. I don't take drugs."

"Why did you hang out with Ricky then?"

Trina looked away from me. The streetlights were alternately lighting her face, then plunging it back into the dark. "To make my mom mad. She hated Ricky."

"Why did she hate Ricky?"

"Because he was a dealer. She knew what drugs did to her and she didn't want me to end up like her. But I thought if she believed I was getting into drugs, she'd stop using them."

A logical approach for a twelve-year-old's understanding of addiction, I supposed. Just stop doing it. "Trina, I could be wrong, but I don't think David killed Ricky. Do you know who might have?"

"The other man?"

A possibility, but I doubted it. Barnes had already come too close to getting dirty for one night. I turned onto Trina's father's street. "Maybe. Do you know anyone else who might have been involved in drugs like Ricky, who would have known what Ricky looked like, and who Ricky might have trusted even when he was running for his life?"

She shook her head.

A thought occurred to me. "Do you know anyone who owns a red truck?"

She looked at me as if I'd changed the subject. "Yeah. My dad. Why? Do you need to borrow one?"

My blood turned ice cold. Of course, Trina wouldn't know anything about the eyewitness report of the red truck with the shattered headlight. That item hadn't even made the newspapers. I discovered I couldn't think of anything to say but, "Yeah, I need to borrow a truck."

Thankfully, my silence didn't clue her in to the connection I was making. She just kept talking about the truck. "Yeah, Dad lets us use it now and then to go to the store. Mom lets me drive it in the parking lot. I could drive your car. Want me to show you?" Trina's glance out the window was distracted. "Hey, you passed my dad's house!"

"I know." I was having to think too fast. I made a right to circle to the back of the house. "I just realized how awfully late it was. I wouldn't want to wake your dad." I made another right down the alley. "We'll call him in the morning. But I think I'll take a look at his truck tonight and see if it's big enough to load my sofa. Do you mind?"

Trina looked at me oddly, but just shrugged.

I pulled on past Garby's garage a little further than necessary so Trina would be facing away from me while I was at the garage. I was grateful for the darkness when I opened the door to my back seat and grabbed my flashlight and toolbox. "Be right back!" I assured Trina brightly.

I walked back to Garby's garage. A bush was growing at the corner of the garage blocking Trina's view of me. I pulled at a bicycle lock which was looped through the door handles of the shed. I could pull the doors apart a bit, but only enough to see that there was a truck inside, not enough for me to wedge my body through. I opened my toolbox and pulled out a slot screwdriver. Down on my knees, I worked at the rusty screws of the door handle until I had them all or most of the way out. When at last they wouldn't give way, I picked up my hammer and, using the screwdriver like a chisel, I managed to chip away at the door until the right handle broke loose and swung down to hang from the left door handle by the bicycle lock. I also broke a chunk off the handle of my screwdriver.

I turned on my flashlight and walked in. There was a truck, but it was green. I looked at it more closely. Yeah, it was green, but the paint job was amateurish. A paint gun lay to one side of the garage. I walked around to the front of the truck.

Sure enough, a large portion of the front and right side hadn't been painted, probably because of the body work that needed to be done. The grill was dented and the right headlight was smashed. The original paint color, which remained here, was red.

Trina's mother had said that her father didn't care about the children. She had called him "a good ol' boy who only cared about himself." I remembered his curt command to me to bring Trina directly to him without calling the police. Had Barnes expected Garby to kill his estranged daughter also? I had a lot more questions for Trina.

I swung the doors of the garage back into place. As I reached over to pick up my toolbox, I heard an engine rev from the direction of my car. Instinctively, I felt for my keys, but they were in my pocket. So, despite Trina bragging about how she could drive my car, she wasn't trying to do it.

The engine revved loudly again and then I heard the squeal of tires peeling out. Toolbox in hand, I ran into the alley just in time to see the taillights of a white T-top make a right at the corner. It was Ann, and she had Trina.

I ran for my car and jumped in, throwing the toolbox into the passenger side of the floorboard with such a thud that I thought it was going to fall through. Stupid! I was so stupid! How could I forget to watch for Ann after she had followed me all day yesterday?

I shoved my key into the ignition and turned. One...two...on the third turn my car started. I punched my accelerator with such force that the tires spit gravel. I shot down the alley and made a right. Ann was two blocks ahead of me, coasting through a stop sign to make a left. I followed. She was doing at least twice the speed limit. Ann made a right on the main roadway and floored it. She knew I was trying to catch her. I made a right and drove as fast as my car would go. Ann was hitting the lights on green, but after about three of them, the caution lights started to catch me. I was doing sixty-five in a thirty-five-mile-an-hour zone, and I was losing her. I speeded up. Ahead, I saw Ann take the east ramp to the expressway. I know I would have caught her on the expressway if a cop hadn't caught me at the ramp.

Thank heavens I had slowed down for the ramp or it probably would have been my license. The officer clocked me at just twelve miles over the limit. I spoke carefully, so that she wouldn't misconstrue the anger I felt toward Ann as being directed toward her. She gave me a pretty good lecture, but I think it came more from her frustration at missing ticketing Ann than it did from the fact that I had been speeding. Twenty minutes later the officer drove off, leaving me holding a ticket with a fine for sixty dollars that I didn't have. Ann was long gone.

I called Bev at the department, but she had left for the day and her partner, Mort, answered. No sooner had I begun to tell him what I had learned than he interrupted me. "Lane, there's a woman here, a colleague of yours, and she has the girl with her. We'll take it from here. Thanks."

I drove to the police station, but they wouldn't let me beyond the front desk. When I asked, the officer manning the front responded curtly. He told me that I could get whatever I needed from the police sheets, like everyone else.

As valuable as the information had been to me, I wasn't about to quote a twelve-year-old without input from the police and permission from her mother. There wouldn't be an article tonight. There was nothing left for me to do but go home.

Chapter Twelve

I awoke at five a.m., having blissfully forgotten the events of the preceding day for all of ten seconds. Then it hit me like a sledgehammer. Ann had beaten me to the Trina interview.

I knew I wouldn't get back to sleep so I didn't even try. Deciding that if I couldn't sleep, no one else should be allowed to either. I took a quick look in the book and dialed Garby.

"Whaaa...um...uh...hullo?" He choked out hoarsely.

"Mr. Garby, this is Lane Montgomery."

"Uh...who?...what?... Who is this?" He coughed.

"Lane Montgomery. I need to see you."

"What time is it?"

I glanced at my digital alarm clock. "Five fifteen."

"Five in the morning?! Who is this?!"

Apparently Garby was not a morning person. I answered his question for the third time. "Lane Montgomery. Reporter for the *Louisville Daily*."

"Oh...yeah. What do you mean, calling me at this hour?!" he bellowed.

Ah, there was the Garby I knew and loved. "I need to see you."

"Now?!" He roared.

Seemed like a good suggestion to me. "Yeah, that would be great!"

"NO!" he yelled into the phone.

"All right, then. When and where?"

"What's this about?" he growled.

"It's about your daughter."

"One o'clock then, O'Malley's." He slammed down the phone, missing the cradle the first time before he readjusted the receiver and I heard a dial tone.

I put on dress jeans, a jacket, and running shoes; made myself coffee and drank it. Sitting down to my computer at home, I started to work on my stories with the information I had gathered so far. By nine thirty, I had composed profiles of Ricky, Trina, and Lamont, along with a

162

companion piece about the drug ring. Now only the final details were missing. I stuck the disk and my keys in my camera bag and decided to go out for a quick bite to eat. Half an hour later I was walking out of a bakery on Bardstown Road with a doughnut in my hands, and I had an idea.

Camera bag at my side, I drove downtown to the office building that housed Barnes Property Management Company. As I walked into the carpeted lobby, a security officer nodded hello to me. "May I help you?" he asked.

I scanned the lobby. "Yes, you may," I answered. "But first, does Barnes Property Management pay for security in this building, or do the building's owners do that?"

"Oh, Barnes Property Management doesn't pay me. They just rent office space here."

"Ah, very good." I turned to him and smiled. "My name's Lane Montgomery. I'm a reporter for the *Louisville Daily*, and I was wondering if I could get your help on a story?"

Three hours later, I was finally leaving Barnes' building for my appointment with Garby. I spent the whole drive wondering how I was going to bring up this little issue of murder. At one-thirty, I pulled into O'Malley's without the vaguest idea in my head of what I was going to say.

As I stepped inside the dark little pub I looked across the room and—to my utter amazement—Herbert Garby sat ga-ga-eyed across the table from Ann. She and Garby were involved in an apparently delightful conversation. I walked straight through the crowded little pub to their table.

Garby looked up at me. "Look at you. You wanted to talk at five this morning, now you're late."

I looked at Ann. "What are you doing here?"

Garby looked back and forth between us. "You two know each other?!" He obviously couldn't understand why Ann would hang around someone of my caliber. The look didn't last long, however, as his attention turned back to Ann. "Can I buy you a beer?" he asked.

"No, thank you," she replied, actually batting her eyes at him.

I repeated my question to Ann. "What are you doing here?"

Garby glared at me. "This lovely young lady here found my daughter," he said.

"She what?!" I started. "She didn't find your... I...I was the one who found..." I realized it didn't matter. I turned back to Ann. "How did you know I was meeting Garby here?"

"Well, I was taking Trina and her mother to brunch this morning," she said. "We'd had a long night at the police station, as you might imagine, and Trina hadn't had a decent meal in a week..."

"And?"

"So while we were at the restaurant, Trina started saying how she hadn't talked to her father yet, so I got Mr. Garby here on my cell phone to talk to Trina—"

Garby interrupted. "And I told Miss Alexander that I was on my way here to talk to you."

Ann smiled. "So I rushed right over, naturally. I didn't want to miss anything!"

"But you already got your interview," I said.

"Not exactly," she argued. "The police are making me hold the article until they arrest the shooter." She meant David Case. "But they can't find him."

"They can't find him?"

"No," she shook her head. "He's not at home; he's not at work. They don't know where he is."

Something felt sinister about this. Ann shrugged, but she seemed to feel the uneasiness, too. "So I missed the deadline. I can print the article as soon as they make the arrest, along with whatever information I can add."

"So where are Trina and her mother?" I asked. "Did you just leave them stranded at the restaurant?"

"Of course not, silly," Ann said. "But since you asked, there is a little thing —"

"What 'thing'?" I asked.

"Well, I didn't have time to run them home, and your apartment was so convenient—"

"They're at my apartment?" I was confused. "But I locked my apartment—"

"Yes, I know." Ann frowned, exasperated. Apparently locking my door was bad manners.

"You found the key I keep under the doormat?"

She looked at me, dumbfounded. "Under the mat. I can't believe I didn't think to look under the mat."

So, she'd picked the lock to my apartment. I glanced at my watch.

"Garby, we need to talk..." I began again.

"Later," he said. I'm sure Miss Alexander isn't interested in us talking business with her here." He smiled warmly at her.

"I'm sure Miss Alexander has no intention of leaving until we do," I replied through gritted teeth. The comment went right over his head,

164

however, as he continued to stare at Ann.

"So, what are you doing next weekend?" Garby asked Ann sweetly.

"Well," she replied, "a mycology conference will be in town and I was thinking of going to some of their lectures. Saturday morning they'll be talking about varieties of molds...

Ann clearly had no intention of giving Garby any real information about herself, obviously, but she was capable of spinning fantastical lies without the least bit of forethought. Garby nodded with intense interest, so Ann continued. "Then the afternoon will be dedicated to fungi and how they can be made into meatless food products."

Garby looked absolutely fascinated, hanging on Ann's every word. I could feel my temper flare. I decided to interrupt this little tete-`a-tete before it went any further.

"Garby, did you kill Ricky Simms?"

That probably wasn't the smartest way to open the interview, but it worked. Garby looked at me, his mouth open and his face a sheet of white. Now we could have a conversation.

"I— What are you talking about?" Garby began.

"You know what I'm talking about. You've got the drive-by vehicle parked in your garage, undergoing a color metamorphosis."

Ann was staring at me. "So that's why you stopped in the alley last night."

I expected Garby to say something, anything, but he just sat there, taken completely by surprise.

"Who are you working for, Garby?"

Ann stood and took my arm. "Lane, can I talk to you?"

"Why?"

She dragged me across the room, stopping out of earshot of Garby. "Don't you think you should leave the interrogation to the police? I mean, they have the bright lights and the two-way mirrors and everything."

"Why are you still here?!" I snapped.

"So you're going to make this about me again?"

"Yes! I—"

She hushed me. "Listen, I think you're barking up the wrong tree with Garby."

"What? Why?"

She frowned at me. "Is Garby's address on your fax page?"

"Well...no," I confessed. "Isn't it on yours?"

"No. So it can't be Garby."

"It could be," I argued.

"Nope." She was firm.

"Why not?"

"It's the list."

"Wonderful. That explains everything. What does that mean?"

"The addresses for the drop-offs. Everyone in Barnes' ring rents from one of his properties he manages. It's Barnes' cover. David Case could run the drugs to the street dealers on his regular maintenance route that way."

"I figured that much out."

"Well, Garby doesn't rent and his address isn't on the list. He doesn't fit the profile."

"Except for one little detail. He has the truck."

"So? Tell me about the truck."

I sighed. I might as well. She was going to hear it when I talked to Garby anyway. "A red truck was spotted driving away from Ricky's body at the time he was killed. It had a smashed headlight. Herbert Garby is now in the process of changing the color of a truck meeting that same description. It's parked in his garage. His own daughter, Trina, claims it belongs to him."

"I think there's more to this."

I shrugged. "Fine. Let's talk to him."

As soon as we got to the table, Garby spoke. "Okay. I did it. You caught me. Why don't you just call the police?"

Ann and I looked at each other. Alarms were going off in my head. Ann was right. There was something very not right about this.

"Garby—" I began.

Garby interrupted. "I'm not going to give you an interview. I'm turning myself in. Call the police."

I know when someone is playing games with me, and I don't like it. "Garby, I'm not interested in your quick confession," I said sharply. "I've got ninety-five good reasons not to believe it. You start talking now, and your story had better match every detail of what I know."

Garby talked slowly, dry-mouthed. "I got the call in the evening— it sounded like a cell phone—to kill Ricky. They just said—"

"They who?"

"I don't know. He never gives me his name. He just sends me money when I do a job for him. He said Ricky'd seen too much, and he had to be 'taken care of.' I knew what that meant."

"Garby," I eyed him, "this sounds like a bad movie. It had better get more interesting than this."

Garby took a deep breath. "I got in my truck and drove around

Butchertown until I saw him. I drove up next to him and shot him several times, right in the chest. I wanted to be sure he was dead."

"What kind of gun did you use?" I asked.

"A .32."

I looked at Ann, silently confirming the caliber. "When you drove away—which direction did you go?"

He hesitated a moment. "East," he answered.

His answers were all on target, but his face was lying. A thought occurred to me. I told Ann and Garby to wait. Running out to my car, I pulled the school yearbook out from under a pile of file folders, and went back in to the table. I opened the yearbook to the class photo and, covering the names with my hand, turned the book toward Garby.

"Garby, you must have known Ricky pretty well if the mystery man counted on you to identify him on a dark street. Which of these students is Ricky?"

Garby's jaw clenched. The photo was very clear, but he stared at it without focusing on individual faces. Obviously he didn't know who he was looking for. I waited for him to guess. He had a one in fifty chance. He pointed to a black male. I turned the book around and looked. I didn't have to check the names.

"Nope. Sorry, Garby." I slammed the book shut.

Ann turned to me. "Very good. How did you figure that?"

"Trina said she hardly ever saw her dad, and Trina's mom had told me he was a very uninvolved parent." I looked at Garby. "Why the fake confession, Garby?"

"I did it! I told you! If you're not going to call the police, I'm leaving!"

"Right, right." Ann said sarcastically. She reached in her pocket and pulled out a piece of paper, sliding it over to me. "Here you go, babe," she said. "This is my half of the list."

I pulled out my fax page and we placed both pages flat on the table in front of us. Two pages of nameless addresses of all the people who worked for Barnes.

I was struggling with Garby's fake confession. Why had he lied? In order to protect someone? I read Ann's page carefully, from top to bottom. As much as I wanted it to happen, nothing leaped out at me.

Out of curiosity, Ann read over my half of the list, then hers again. She shook her head. "I don't recognize any of these addresses either— except of course for Ricky's and Trina's."

My blood chilled. I looked at Ann.

"Ann, I need your car keys."

"What?" She looked at me, surprised.

"I need the keys to your car. I need a fast car."

She pulled the keys out of her pocket. "What's going on?"

"Garby isn't our man. I think I've figured it out. But I need to get to my apartment right away." I handed her my keys so she could drive my car home.

"Lane, I wish you'd—" she began, but I was gone. I flew out the door of O'Malley's and jumped into Ann's white T-top. It roared to life with the turn of the key, the tires squealing as I tore out of the parking lot. I drove like a madwoman, speeding past cars and running red lights when I could. Minutes later, I pulled up to the curb in front of my building, leaped out of the car, and raced up the stairs to my apartment.

At my door, I froze, unsure of what I might find inside. I was hoping to find the two of them, Trina and her mother, seated on my sofa, watching television, safe and sound. But my imagination was running wild. I ran my hand under the mat and pulled out my apartment key. Inserting the key in the lock, I walked in. The door swung itself closed behind me, locking automatically.

The living room was empty and the apartment was silent, but Trina was supposed to be here. "Trina?" I called out, breaking the thick silence. My voice had a forced natural tone. No one answered. I walked cautiously, as if the air around me might shatter like glass. I glanced into my kitchen. It, too, was empty; only a half-finished glass of water on the counter indicated another presence in the apartment. I moved on to the bedroom.

The door had swung to without being latched. I took a deep breath and gently pushed it open. As it moved away from me, I heard the click of a pistol being cocked. I was once again staring into the barrel of Teresa Coleman's .32.

She was seated in the chair beside my bedroom window wearing a dirty jogging suit, her red hair matted. There was a small form in the bed next to her under the covers. I knew it had to be Trina; I just couldn't see her well enough to answer the question that was racing through my head. Teresa's face registered confusion. She couldn't decide whether or not to pull the trigger.

"Ms. Coleman, I'm Lane Montgomery," I said quickly. "This is my apartment. Ann Alexander told me she brought you here. I know what happened." I wanted to appear calm, but my voice gave me away. Teresa didn't lower the gun.

"I know you. I know you from somewhere," she said suspiciously. I had no intention, however, of reminding her just at this moment that I had been her exterminator; I was willing to let her grapple with that one on her own. I strained to see Trina, just to distinguish whether or not she was breathing.

"Trina," I said to her. "What's the matter with Trina?"

Teresa Coleman looked at me oddly. "She's sleeping. She's exhausted." As she spoke, Trina lifted a hand to her face in her sleep. A sound of relief caught in my throat. Teresa looked up at me sharply. With that one look, I knew she knew. Her voice was low so as not to wake her daughter, but angry. "What? You think I'd hurt my own child? What do you think I am? I'd do anything to protect my daughter. Anything. I wouldn't let nobody hurt my girl. I would steal, I would…" Her voice trailed off. "If you were a mother, you would know! But they lied. They called and said, 'Ricky and Trina got into somethin' they shouldn't have, but Ricky is who we really want. You take care of Ricky and Trina is safe. You do the job; we'll spare Trina. But they lied to me. They just waited for me to lead them to her. There's a blue van parked out back. The man sitting in it must have been following me. Now he's waiting for me to leave with Trina. He's going to kill us both. I know he will. I know him. He works for them." She was shaking. "You can see him out this window. He's got a gun. I saw it."

I leaned a little and looked. David Case was seated in the van, staring at my bedroom window. I was too far into the room for him to see me, but he must have spotted Teresa at my window earlier, because he knew which window to watch.

"You deal for Barnes," I stated, thinking of the drug paraphernalia I had discovered in her apartment, and her complaints about him as her apartment manager. "Your address was on a list of his dealers." Until a few minutes ago, back at the pub, I had always thought of it as Trina's address. But that's when I realized the connection. The address had never been referring to Trina. It had been referring to her mother.

She shrugged. "I don't know who I deal for. That guy outside in the van, the handyman at the apartment, brought me the drugs; I sold part, kept some for myself as payment. Seven, eight years now."

"How did you find Ricky?"

"That night they called, Ricky came and knocked right on my door, all out of breath and asking was Trina home yet. I said no, go home. He begged me to let him stay with me, but I couldn't. Finally, he left. I went out and got in the truck I'd borrowed from Herbert and followed him. When Ricky was well away from where anyone could see us, I pulled up and called out to him. He was staying along the fence and out of the light, but he recognized my truck and ran right up to me. When he got real close, I shot him. Over and over. I had to be sure he was dead, you know? It was for Trina's sake. I kept thinking about what they said about letting Trina live. I did it to save Trina's life. I just can't sleep anymore. I just keep seeing it over and over in my mind." She looked at the gun in her hands. "I told Herbert everything that happened. I begged him to help me! But Trina had run off. We had to find her so we could move far away from here—from the drugs, the police—"

"And Garby helped you because he still has feelings for you. In fact, he tried to say he killed Ricky in order to protect you."

"He's a silly, weak man. He can't protect us from them." She glanced out the window. "Nobody can protect us from them. If I'd been the kind of mother I should have been, I'd have got clean years ago. We'd have moved to a nicer place. None of this would've happened…"

Teresa looked back to me, rubbing the gun in her hands nervously. "They're going to kill Trina. And it's all my fault."

"Teresa—if you'll put the gun down, I'll call the police. They can help us. We can get Trina out of here."

"You do that," Teresa said, as if she'd given up. "You call the police. I killed that boy. I deserve to die. But Trina don't."

Thinking we had come to a kind of resolution, I stepped toward her, but she pointed the gun at me again. "You stay back," she demanded. "You just stay back." Then, almost silently, she began to sob. "Trina," she said in a grief-stricken whisper, "what has your mama done? What has your mama done?" Teresa looked up at me. "You explain to Trina everything I said. Tell her I said I was sorry."

Teresa stood, and as she rose she turned the pistol from me and brought it to her own head. It gave me the fraction of time that I needed. I bolted across the room. With my left hand I reached out to grasp the wrist of the hand with which Teresa held the gun, pushing it away from her head and into the air. Instinctively, she lashed out at me with her other fist, but I caught her arm and forced her backwards.

The next moment was surreal. There was a crash, and I thought the gun had gone off in the air, but I hadn't felt it kick and it hadn't sounded right. Then I was in a shower of glass as Teresa Coleman fell forward into my arms, a dead weight. I caught her and eased her to the floor. Blood was pouring from the base of her neck and she wasn't breathing right. I looked up. My bedroom window was shattered.

David Case had spotted his chance and shot her. Had the angle been different the same bullet would have drilled through me. Case wouldn't hesitate now to come into my apartment and finish his job.

I couldn't think—I was in a fog. I looked over at my bed and realized why my skull was splitting. Trina was awake and sitting upright in bed now, screaming, "You killed my mother! You killed my mother!" I grabbed Teresa's .32 and opened the chamber. There were two bullets inside. I shoved the gun into my belt and, shying from the window, grabbed Trina with both arms, pulling her off the bed. She was flailing her arms and legs at me, trying very hard to hurt me.

"Trina—Trina!" I shouted over her screams, "Your mother isn't dead, but she's hurt badly. Somebody fired a shot at her through the window—that's why there's glass everywhere—I need to get you out of here because you might get hurt, too."

She wasn't taking the time to listen; all of her energy was being spent in resisting me. In my mind I could see David Case running from his van to my apartment building, and I hadn't managed even to get Trina out of the bedroom yet. My heart was pounding. I had maybe a minute before Case made it to my door, probably less.

Everything was moving in slow motion. With my arms around Trina's waist, I dragged her to the door a foot at a time. All the while, she lashed at my face with her fists and kicked at my shins. I didn't have the hands to ward off the blows, and I couldn't risk loosening my grip on Trina's body. I was in a nightmare, pursued by a monster, my arms and legs made of lead—only the monster was real and making his way up my back stairs.

I had to force my brain to think. I wasn't sure if I had time to make it out of the apartment. I needed to hide the two of us, but there was no way for me to hide someone who was fighting me. How much time did I have before Case entered my apartment? Thirty seconds? Fifteen?

Not even fifteen. As I gave another pull on Trina's body and dragged her into the living room, there was a loud pounding against my front door and the crack of wood as the doorframe near the lock split. Of course, I hadn't deadbolted the door behind me because I'd believed the only danger to Trina and me might have been inside the apartment. There was another loud pounding noise as someone threw his body weight against the door. The doorframe cracked and split. One more blow with that kind of force would do it. Trina kicked and screamed in my arms.

As he pounded on the outside of the door one last time, I threw Trina to the floor, hard, and reached for the gun in my belt. Splintered wood flew everywhere as the door swung open toward me, masking the figure behind it. My heart stopped. I raised the gun with both hands and pulled back the hammer. Two small bullets. I hoped I knew what I was doing.

Chapter Thirteen

A dark figure appeared from behind the door. It was Garby. "Where's my daughter?!" he bellowed at me. Suddenly, the gun I held pointed at him registered in his mind and he stumbled backwards, instinctively raising an arm in front of his face. I lowered the gun.

"Dad!" Trina yelled, running to Garby.

"Garby, Teresa's been shot and she's hurt badly. Use my phone to call the police and an ambulance. I need to get Trina out of here. The man who shot Teresa will be coming after Trina right now." Trina was listening now. Her eyes widened.

"I'll get my daughter out of here!" Garby protested, his arms around Trina. He did have fatherly instincts, after all.

"Garby, I know the building. I know the exits. If I have to go another way, I can do it without running into a trap."

Garby pushed Trina to me gently. "You go with her," he said. Then he spoke to me. "Miss Alexander's at the front of the building with your car running. There was a man running around the side of the building when we pulled up, but when he saw us he went around to the back. If there's a back way he's probably coming up that way now. Be careful."

"You be careful. He may come here." I took Trina's hand and, checking the hallway, pulled her out the door with me, the gun in my right hand. At the top of the stairs, I held my breath, listening for any sounds below. Hearing nothing, I eased my way down the steps, trying to keep Trina behind the barrier of my body, and trying to see as far in front of me as possible.

The foyer was empty. I glanced out the window next to the building entrance. Ann saw me from my car, her expression changing at the sight of the gun in my hand.

Ann glanced around and waved at me to run for the car. I threw open the building door and bolted for the car, pulling Trina along behind me. Ann leaned over and pushed the passenger door open for us. As we were about to reach the car, I sensed movement out of the corner of my left eye. Without even turning to look, I pulled Trina from behind and nearly threw her into the front seat of the car, diving on top of her to shield her with my body.

"Drive! Drive! Drive!" I was yelling, but the car was already moving. Ann stepped on the gas with such force I would have been flung out of the car if I hadn't grabbed her seat belt. I heard the crack of a pistol from behind us, and a sharp ping as the bullet pierced the inside of the open car door. I drew my feet inside and managed to pull the door shut. Trina was crying quietly. I asked her if she was all right.

"That hurt me," she responded, not really complaining. I'm sure it had. I apologized automatically.

"He's running for his van," Ann said, looking in the rear view mirror. She smacked my steering wheel. "I wish we were in my car," she groaned.

"You and me both," I responded. "Trina, keep your head down."

Ann raced to the corner and made a right. I sat up and looked back. Case's van was making the corner in front of my building.

"He's pulling out," I informed Ann. "He's just half a block behind—" My words were cut off as Ann whipped it to the left. I actually fell to the floor.

"Sorry," Ann mumbled. "Put on your seat belt."

I tried not to grumble because Ann was just doing what she had to do, but my adrenaline was up. I picked up Trina, who had rolled to my side of the car, helped her into the backseat and watched as she belted herself in. Then I belted myself in and locked the door. I heard police sirens in the distance.

"That figures," I said. "Now they arrive!"

"Great!" Ann said cheerfully. "The cavalry's here! Let's go meet them!" She whipped my car into a left them at the corner and circled the block until we were headed back to my apartment. I glanced into my sideview mirror. The van was making the last corner behind us.

"Step on it, Ann," I advised.

"This is it, sweetie," she replied. "This is the best your car will do." I suddenly felt sick.

The van gained on us as we approached my apartment. At a distance, I could tell we were too late. The police car and an ambulance had pulled in front of the building, lights flashing, but abandoned; everyone had gone inside. We wouldn't have time to make it from our car into the building with Case right behind us; he would shoot us down on the street. Ann had to race right past.

"Is my mom gonna be okay?" Trina asked softly.

"I think so, Trina," I answered. "That's why the ambulance is there. They're helping her right now." In my heart, however, I wasn't as hopeful.

"We can't outrun Case," Ann said. "The car's not fast enough."

"Then head for a police station," I said.

"Where's the nearest one?" she asked.

"I don't have a clue," I admitted. "Head for one you know." I pulled out my cell phone and punched in 911.

Ann made a sharp left. I could have sworn the tires lifted off the ground. The force of the turn hurled me into the passenger side window and knocked my phone onto the floor. Ann followed this with a quick right and then another left.

I looked behind us, then felt around on the floor for my phone. "Ann, I haven't seen him the last three turns. You may have lost him," I said.

"Let's hope so," she replied. "Let's cut through this alley—he won't think of looking for us down here."

She made a right before I could say anything. We were now on a little one-way alley, with no room to turn around, and brick or fence on either side for nearly a block ahead of us. I could feel the sweat break out on my brow.

"I don't know if this was the best place to—" I began.

"I've been in this alley before," she snapped, defensive. "I just forgot it was too narrow to U-turn."

I grasped my cell phone and pressed the connect button for 911. Ann sped the car toward the exit at the other end. The phone began ringing on the other end of the line.

I held my breath and watched the rearview mirror while I waited for an answer. "What's the name of this alleyway?" I asked Ann.

"I don't think it has a name," she said.

"Sure it does," I said. "But what is it? It sounds like Fizer or Kaiser or...or..."

My attention was diverted by a large dark shape entering the alley from the opposite end. It was Case's van. It seemed to pause, then began driving toward us from a block away. Ann slowed to a stop.

"911." Someone answered on the other end of the line.

"Ann... Ann... Ann..." was all that was coming out of my mouth. Case recognized us and the van picked up speed. Within seconds he'd be right on top of us, slaughtering us like mice in a bucket.

Ann took a breath and spoke steadily. "If I threw this thing into reverse, we couldn't outrun him, could we?"

"No," I replied simply.

"911," the voice repeated on the other end of the phone. I looked over at Ann. Her face was tense with concentration. She was working on a solution. I put the phone back to my ear. "Yes. This is Lane Montgomery. I'm in a car with two other people in an alleyway between—"

Ann was mumbling something under her breath. Then suddenly, calmly, as if she'd come to a decision, she stomped on the accelerator.

The force of the acceleration flung me back against the seat. A moment passed before the significance of what was happening registered. "Ann!" I tried to speak calmly, but I was terrified. "I don't know what you think you're doing. There isn't room to drive around the van. This is no time for a game of 'chicken!' We can ram him all we want, but this little car's going to lose against that van every time!"

Ann ignored me; our car and the van charged toward each other down the little alleyway like two knights in a jousting match. If her purpose was to scare him, it wasn't working. Case didn't flinch at our speed; he knew who was bigger. I began to wonder if the stress of dying a passive death was just too much for Ann to handle. I decided to try again.

"Ann, you know—" My throat was so tight from the tension it was hard to speak, but I had to try to talk some sense into her. "If you don't kill us, we might have a chance. I do have a gun. And it's got two bullets left in it."

Ann laughed. She actually laughed. Anger surged up in me. Case's van was bearing down on us at a terrible pace. I threw the cell phone onto the floor and, in the unlikely event I survived the impact, reached for the gun.

"Ann!" I was shouting now. "You're going to kill us! Stop the car! What do you think you're going to do? Go under the van? Ann! Stop!" I looked through the windshield. The van was seconds away, looming large, gigantic in front of us, as if it weren't coming closer and closer but instead growing to an inhuman size.

I'd already spoken the last words I would ever speak. I put my hands in front of my face, ducking my head to my knees. There was a sickening lurch as my body was thrown violently to the left and then an earsplitting sound, as if the driver's side of my car was being peeled away.

But I wasn't dead yet. And this wasn't possible.

I was confused. Maybe I was dead. In the back, Trina cautiously began to sit up in her seat. I looked up slowly, but I didn't know where I was. We were in a different alley.

"What...where? Ann?" was all I could get out. She was beaming.

"Close, huh?" she said.

"What did you do?!" I demanded.

"We're in the little alley that runs perpendicular to the alley we were in. It's not a real road, they just use it for trash collection. But that's why I had to drive so fast. If Case had passed it before we had, we'd be dead now. But I reached it so close to him that he didn't have time to make the turn at his speed. He went on down the alley."

I looked over the hood of my car. We had made the right turn into this little side street from the alley so fast she had skidded my car into the building. A piece of my front bumper was now sticking up above where my left headlight used to be, and my hood resembled an accordion.

"Aw, Ann! You killed my car!" I whined loudly.

"Lane! I saved your life!"

"Man!" Trina whooped. "You're a cool driver, Ann!"

"Shut up, Trina," I complained. "It's not your car." Trina laughed at me.

"Hang on," Ann advised. "Case knows where we're coming out."

We emerged from the alley and Ann took a quick left. I checked my sideview mirror. A block behind us, the van was making a left onto the street. "He's picked us up again," I said.

"Beautiful," Ann said sarcastically. "Look ahead of us. Traffic."

A wall of cars was gathering in front of us at a red light. Already we were too enclosed by traffic for Ann to change lanes. In my side view mirror, I watched as the van crept to a stop several cars behind us, one lane over. I spoke to Ann.

"If he gets out of the car, I'm going to run with Trina. I have a hunch Case could probably take care of us and disappear before anyone realized why this car wasn't moving."

"We can't keep trying to outrun him, Lane," Ann replied. "Try the cell phone again."

I reached for the cell phone, but Ann interrupted me. "He's getting out of his van!" she said. I looked up. The driver's door had opened. "I'm going," I said to Ann, reaching back for Trina's safety belt.

"Wait," she put an arm in front of me. "The light's changed."

The cars in front of us began to ease forward. Ann kept checking for breaks in traffic, but was only able to move one lane to the right before we were once again boxed in by cars. The van had also moved one lane to the right, perhaps a car-length closer to us than before.

"He's catching up to us," Ann said, her eyes on the rear view mirror.

"The gun!" I announced. "What happened to the gun?!"

I looked around the car. Everything had become disheveled since Ann's wicked right minutes ago. Ann and Trina began searching. I leaned over and ran my hand underneath the seat.

Suddenly I realized that no one was watching the van. I looked into my sideview mirror to see the van door open and Case walking toward us between the lanes of traffic. His hand was thrust into his pocket, concealing something which caused his jacket to bulge. I didn't have to guess what it was.

"Forget the gun, I'm gone," I said to Ann. If Case was going to kill us, it would be in broad daylight in front of all these people, not hidden inside the car. I released myself from the seat belt, jumped out quickly and pulled open the back door. Taking Trina's hand, I pulled her out of the car so that she hit the pavement running. I shot a glance behind me. Case was following quickly, but seemed reluctant to run, probably because it would attract too much attention.

Holding tightly to Trina's hand, I weaved between the cars. As I came to cars with their windows down I quickly begged the drivers to call the police. I got no response other than people began rolling up their windows as I approached. The light changed and the traffic eased forward. Drivers leaned on their horns at us. I looked for Case, but couldn't see him anywhere. I didn't like that.

I had made it about a block up the street, but now cars began to whiz past. I decided to get out of the street, because if Case didn't get us, one of these vehicles would. Hanging on to Trina, I watched carefully for a break in the traffic and made a dash to the sidewalk.

A wall of traffic began forming in the street again as the light changed back to red. I still could not find Case. I was frightened. I didn't know which way to run. I hadn't heard horns blowing at Case like they had at us. Why?

Carefully, I scanned the cars up and down the street. A hand touched my shoulder. I whipped around to stare into the face of a thin, balding man wearing glasses. He looked shocked by my reaction.

"Excuse me," he asked, flustered. "Do you know what time it is?"

"No," I answered sharply. I gripped Trina's hand and continued walking quickly down the street, looking for a door or an office that looked like it was occupied. At one end of the block was a long warehouse building, at the other end was a large parking lot filled with tractor-trailers and surrounded by a tall fence topped by barbed wire. The traffic began moving again. Case was here somewhere, watching us, but I couldn't find him.

I was starting to panic. Silently, Trina kept up with me, her shorter legs working twice as hard as mine. Was Case anticipating my movements, I wondered? Should I switch directions and go back up the street, or was that walking right into his hands?

I stopped again, holding Trina's hand tightly in mine. Traffic was whizzing by now, and there was no sign of anyone walking in the street. I heard the strange roar of an engine, accompanied by car horns blaring. I looked. A block away, the blue van climbed the curb to the sidewalk and turned to face us. Case had gone back to his van. The engine revved twice, then the van came barreling down the sidewalk towards us.

With traffic moving so fast, I was afraid to run back into the street. I started running away from the van, dragging Trina behind me. Trina began screaming. Quickly, I veered toward a building and tried a door, but it was locked.

It was too late to try another. I could hear the roar of the van behind us. I lifted Trina up in one motion and dove back into the traffic. Cars steered everywhere to avoid us, blowing their horns, but I continued a cautious, steady pace with Trina across the six lanes. Halfway across, vehicles all around us slowed and stopped, creating a wall of cars that protected us from Case's van. I heard a screech as Case threw on the brakes. The slam of a door told me that Case had left the van again and was following us on foot. I was sure he had his gun with him, too. Trina began crying quietly in my arms. I couldn't keep up this pace with her weight, and she really couldn't run fast enough. Case on foot could move a lot faster than I could with a child. I began to look ahead of us for a place to hide Trina. Perhaps then I could fake Case into following me away from her. It was the only thing I could think of.

I set Trina down quickly and we continued our slalom through the last two lanes of traffic. As we reached the sidewalk on the other side, a horn sounded behind us, followed by a screech of tires. I looked behind me. A station wagon had barely missed hitting Case, and he had turned to look. This was the moment I needed. I pulled Trina around the corner of a building into an alley. It wouldn't take Case long to realize that this was the only place we could have disappeared into, but it might give me the precious seconds I needed to hide Trina.

I flew down the alley, dragging Trina behind me. She had grown tired now, and began to stumble. I held tightly to her hand.

Within seconds, we reached a dumpster. I picked her up to help her into it. "Lane?" she questioned breathlessly. Her eyes were wide. She couldn't believe I was going to put her in a dumpster full of garbage.

"Just do it, Trina," I said firmly. "And listen to me. Whatever you hear out here, don't make a sound—not a sound—until I or Ann come to get you, or the sanitation company comes to collect you. Do you understand?"

She managed a weak smile, nodded, and then inhaled deeply, holding her breath as if I was about to immerse her in water. I lifted her to the edge and she jumped in. Now it was up to me to distract Case.

I ran for the end of the alleyway, which was lined by a tall wooden fence. Trash cans stood in a row just to this side of it. I leaped onto the cans and gripped the top of the fence. The tricky part of this was that I had to wait for Case to see me. I turned and looked behind me. Right on cue, Case rounded the corner. I gave him a second to see if he would notice the dumpster, but he spotted me first instead. I turned and looked beyond the fence, as if I had already lowered Trina to the other side. "Run, Trina, run!" I said in a stage whisper, waving to an imaginary person. I turned and looked toward Case again. He began running toward me, right past the dumpster without a glance.

I turned to leap the fence, but as I did, the garbage can tilted beneath me and gave way. I fell, hard, to the pavement. There wasn't time to try again.

Just as I knew he would, Case slowed, reached into his pocket and pulled out the gun. I rolled to all fours. In slow motion, Case began lifting his gun. I was trapped. There was no need for him to hurry.

Case's gun was almost to eye level. I dove for cover behind the trash cans as the gun exploded and wood splintered away from the fence behind me. Case began walking toward me, leveling his sight on me again. There was nowhere for me to go.

There was a sudden roar at the entrance to the alley. Case was distracted from me; his eyes grew wide. Turning in time to see the grill of my car bearing down on him, he raised his pistol, but before he had time to get off a shot, the car hit him and he went up and over the hood, the gun flying from his hand. Ann steered wildly as she braked to avoid hitting me. She swiped the building to the left of me instead, creating a terrible crunching sound of metal and breaking glass.

There was a still moment of silence, as if time had stopped. I felt weak and couldn't breathe. Then the sound of metal grating against metal groaned from my car as Ann forced the door open and got out.

She was fine. I cautiously approached Case, concerned that he might cause us more problems. He was alive, but out cold. People were leaning out of the office windows above us. Ann ran up alongside me, not a scratch on her. "Lane?" she asked.

"He's not dead," I answered quickly. "But I think you broke his legs." I indicated the odd turn of his knee and foot. Ann shook her head. She was looking a little pale. "You did the right thing, Ann," I assured her.

Ann looked up at me then, her eyes welling with tears. Wordlessly, she threw herself into my arms, holding me tightly, oblivious to the crowds of people above us who were now watching, open-jawed, from windows in the floors above us. I looked up. "Someone call an ambulance," I shouted.

"Where's Trina?" Ann asked. I grasped Ann's arm and jogged back to the dumpster. I called to Trina and she appeared at the rim of the dumpster. She jumped from the dumpster into my arms, smelling like spoiled food.

"I threw up in there," she said.

"That's okay," I comforted her, brushing my hand across her hair. She hugged me tightly.

The ambulance arrived a minute later. The police showed up immediately after and Ann and I both answered their questions. When the TV news crews began appearing, Ann and I exchanged glances. "I can't believe it!" she said. "The story's broken! We've got to get to our papers!"

The police finished talking with me and I jogged to my crumpled car to retrieve my camera case. When I returned, Ann was with Trina, talking to a police officer. Ann glanced over at me and smiled discreetly. Once again, I was struck by how beautiful she was.

I wasn't the only one. A police officer, who hadn't taken his eyes off her since he arrived, intercepted Ann as she started toward me. She chatted with him briefly, made an excuse to leave, then walked over to me. Her back to the officer, she mumbled, "They want to take us both to the station for more questioning."

I glanced at my watch, then at the TV cameras. "If they take us in for questioning," I muttered, "we won't make deadline!"

"I know. What are we going to do?"

I glanced around at the media crowd and saw a familiar blond head. I looked back at Ann. "I've got an idea. The guy over there, on the right, standing next to the cameraman. That's Dirk Rutgers. He's a buddy of mine. I think he can help us."

Ann looked back at me. "Better give it a shot."

I skipped over to Dirk and explained our situation. "What do you want me to do?" he asked.

"Just run interference for us," I asked, nodding toward his cameraman.

Dirk grinned, pleased to be able to help out. "Okay, you've got it. Good luck!"

I took Ann's arm and walked over to the police officer. "We'll be right back," I said. "But we want to have a word with Trina before they take her to her parents."

He nodded, frowning at us, then brushed impatiently at his uniform as if to remind us of his position. He was certainly impressed with his own authority, I thought, even if we weren't. We walked quickly over to the police car where Trina sat with the door open, her legs still short enough that they dangled from the seat.

I knelt down by the car. "Trina, we're going to have to take off. They're going to take you to your mom and dad at the hospital, and the police are going to want to talk to you some more after that. But we're really glad you're okay. You're quite a courageous kid, you know that?"

Trina jumped forward and hugged my neck, then turned and hugged Ann. "You know what? You guys are the coolest—really. I'm glad you guys are the ones that found me."

I smiled at Trina. She didn't understand just how important it had been that we were the ones to find her. "We're glad we were the ones that found you, too, Trina."

"You know…" She faltered. "You know, I've never known anyone like you guys. I was wondering…do you think, like maybe if I get my grades up and stuff, I could be a reporter, too, someday?"

Ann reached out and rubbed Trina's head playfully. "Hey, girl! Of course you could! Why, you've already got experience!"

"Well, Trina," I said, "we've got deadlines. But we'll be in touch. I promise."

Trina wriggled back into the police car. Ann shut the door and we turned around. The police officer was still watching us.

"He obviously hasn't forgotten us," I said under my breath.

"Nope," she replied. "I hope whatever deal you've got going with the blond TV guy works."

Together, we casually started to walk away from the scene. The officer picked up on that quickly and swung around to intercept us. "Ladies!" he called us down. "Right this way to the car." He indicated a police car parked in the alley.

"Mmm…just a second," I argued. Ann and I slowed our pace but didn't stop walking. "We just want to run across the street to the ladies' real quick…"

The officer trotted along beside us. "If you don't mind waiting, you could do that at the station. Ladies…ladies…"

C'mon, Dirk, I was thinking. C'mon. Where are you? Ann and I kept walking. The officer was growing irritated.

"Sir… Officer! Sir!"

It was Dirk. I stopped so the officer would too, turning toward Dirk and his cameraman. The officer looked confused.

"Sir, if you don't mind, I need you to answer a few questions." Dirk thrust a microphone into the officer's face.

The officer tried to wave it away. "Hey, I'm not the person you need to talk to. You need to go back over to the building and speak to Officer Walsh. He—"

Dirk signaled the cameraman and the light over his camera blinked on. I turned to the officer and silently mouthed the words, "We're going to the ladies'."

As Ann and I turned to go, the officer looked back and forth between Dirk and us frantically. Dirk held him by the arm and stated with a commanding tone, "We're rolling, sir," then began firing questions at him. Defeated, the officer faced the camera and submitted to the interrogation. When I glanced back to be sure it was working, Dirk winked at me. I grinned back at him.

I turned back to Ann. "It's working, it's working," I mumbled. "Head for that hotel across the street."

Ann shook her head and grinned. "People are so funny," she said under her breath. "It's just a camera, not a chain! All that officer has to do is walk away, and yet we both know he won't!"

I glanced back once more to see what was happening. The officer was still standing in front of the camera, but was staring right at us. He motioned to Dirk to wait on the interview and then said something into his radio. "Uh-oh, Ann," I turned back, but I couldn't help grinning. "I think he's on to us."

To our right, an older, heavier police officer motioned an acknowledgement to the first officer and started walking toward us. We had just made the hotel steps.

I took Ann's arm. "Time to pick it up a little, babe," I whispered, but couldn't help laughing under my breath.

"Okay, okay," Ann was laughing, too. "But we can't look like we're running!" We skipped up the steps as fast as we possibly could without looking evasive.

The second officer was right behind us now, at the bottom of the hotel steps and gaining. We went through the revolving door together, and the moment we were through the doors and out of his sight, we broke into a run in the lobby. Seeing a sign, we made a left and walked down a long hall to the ladies' room. Ann started to go in.

"No, Ann," I said. "They know that's where we were going."

"We can go out the window," she countered.

"You've forgotten we just came up a flight of steps," I whispered. "I don't think we can make it with broken ankles. Here..." I opened the laundry room door. "In here."

She glanced behind her and ran for the laundry room. I shut the door and locked it from the inside. A dim light shone from a small window above us.

Within minutes, footsteps came down the hallway. There was a knocking sound on the ladies' room door, and a male voice called out, "Hello! Hello! Ladies?" A pause. "Hello? Hello?" Another moment. Then, "I'm coming in!"

In seconds he was back out in the hall again. We heard the sandpaper sound of his radio. "You were right! They're skipping out on us!"

I looked at Ann and grinned. She grinned back. The officer's footsteps approached the laundry room door, and I found myself holding my breath. He paused in front of our door, then took hold of and shook the handle.

Ann suddenly found this very funny. She looked over at me, then realized that was a mistake. She turned her head and casually put a hand over her mouth. Then, right outside the door, the officer sneezed. Ann nearly guffawed. He paused and blew his nose and I looked over at Ann, afraid she was going to give us away. She was trembling with suppressed laughter, but wasn't making a sound. We heard the officer as he turned and walked about halfway down the hall before getting on his radio again. He was saying something about hanging around in the hotel for a while to watch for us.

"That's not good," Ann whispered to me, her smile disappearing. She tapped her watch to indicate the passing time.

"Do you have your cell phone?" I said under my breath. "We could call our papers."

Ann shook her head. "It was in my car. Where's yours?"

"I looked for it in what was left of my car. But I didn't find it."

The officer's footsteps echoed back up to us from the end of the hall. Apparently he had chosen to move to where he could watch the lobby as well. Ann began to look a little frantic. "How are we going to know when he leaves?" she said.

I made my way around tables of folded sheets and towels to the back of the room, then hopped up onto the counter at the small window. Looking out, I could see the steps leading up to the hotel, as well as a couple of the TV news trucks. "We'll see him leave from here," I said.

"It had better be soon," Ann quipped.

"I hear you," I answered. "One of the news vans is pulling out already."

A tense, silent minute passed while I watched and Ann paced. "You know what really gets me?" Ann finally broke the silence. "Gerald Barnes. That crook. It's not right." She turned toward me, and I glanced down at her. "I wanted him to pay for this, Lane. And we don't have a thing on him—I mean, nothing that will stick." Ann's frustration was coming through in her tone. "Case, Ricky, Trina, Franklin—they were all just players, wittingly or unwittingly. But this was Barnes' game. And the only information I have on him would be just enough to get my paper sued."

"Don't worry about it, Ann—it'll be all right." I turned back to look out the window.

"I can't help it. It's not right."

"It's all right, Ann."

"No, it's not."

"Ann." I said with intention. "I said it's all right."

She looked at me, realizing. "You got him! You pinned something on Barnes!"

I nodded, but kept an eye out the window. "Yes—earlier today. At the building where Barnes works. I called the police. They came and looked at what I had found. Then I had to negotiate with them how and when I could print it. That's why I was late for my meeting with Trina's father."

"I don't believe it—how did you get something on him?" She didn't expect me to explain how. She shook her head. "You got him. What do you know! You're a ringer, girl. Has anyone ever told you that? You're a ringer."

"Thanks," I said, "but unfortunately I haven't been to the office since then. Nobody at the paper knows what I have. If I don't get to the paper before deadline, they're not going to have the story."

Ann came back to where I was sitting and leaned against the counter. She glanced up at me, her eyes dark, then looked away. "You know, I thought I'd lost you back there. When I came around that corner and Case was raising his gun..."

I looked down at her and put my hand on her shoulder. "It's okay, Ann." I said. "It turned out okay." I looked back out the window.

"Yes, I know," she said. "But it makes you think. It makes you think about what's really important to you—"

From the window, I saw a heavyset figure in blue emerge from the building. "Ann." I squinted. "Ann! There's the officer! He's leaving!"

"He's leaving?!" Ann couldn't conceal the excitement in her voice.

I slid down off the counter and came face to face with Ann. "We've got to go."

"B-but…" Ann stuttered. "There are some things I wanted to tell you—"

"Look at your watch. It's ten till six."

Ann looked at her wrist and her face lost its color. "Ten till six?" she repeated. "Ten till six?" She looked up at me, wide-eyed. "But that's ten minutes to deadline!"

I nodded.

"We can make it!" she almost shouted. "We can still make deadline! C'mon!" Ann lunged across the room, flung open the door to the hall, and left me behind in the dark.

"Hey!" I yelled, "hey, Ann! Wait!" I ran after her. I was halfway down the hotel hallway when I skidded to a stop. I turned, ran back to the laundry room, pulled open the door, reached inside for my camera case, turned again, then ran my fastest trying to catch up to her. As I exited the hallway, I could see her flying out the back lobby doors to the street. I picked up speed and hit the doors ten seconds behind her, just in time to see her shoe disappear behind the door of a bright orange cab as it tore away from the curb.

I shouted after it, but the cab sailed away. Stomping furiously, I called Ann a few choice names, then waited two minutes for the next cab. It passed me by. So did the next two. After seven minutes, I ran to a payphone on the street and tried to flag down cabs while I dialed the paper.

"Patrice, this is an emergency. Put me through to Rosemary." I was going to kill Ann. Next time I saw her, I wouldn't be responsible for what happened.

"Sure, Lane," she said. "Just a second." I could hear Patrice shuffling through papers, looking for her phone extension list. At last she punched in the numbers, and Rosemary's line began ringing.

Seven…eight…nine rings. "Pick me back up, Patrice," I started saying out loud to myself. After the eleventh ring, Patrice picked back up.

"She's not in her office, Lane," Patrice said.

"Is her secretary in?" I waved wildly at another cab as it flew right past me.

"I doubt it. It's after six," Patrice explained.

"Yeah. Boy, do I know it's after six. Ring Harry's number for me, will you?"

"Sure. Is there anything I can do?"

"Just ring Harry's number!"

"Gosh, Lane, don't get snappy. I'll ring it." There was another pause as she went down the list, mumbling numbers, looking for Harry's extension. Then I heard Harry's line ringing. Three...four... He picked up.

"Bridgeman here."

"Oh—Harry—you're there!"

"Montgomery!! Where are you?! We've been calling all over the place for you! Your story broke! We needed you there to cover it!"

"I was there, Harry! I very nearly was the story!"

"Are you all right? Have you been hurt?"

"I'm fine, Harry."

Harry exploded. "Then why aren't you here?!!"

"I've got the story, Harry! I've got the whole thing! Just hold the presses!"

"I can't hold the presses. The cameras were there; we can't justify holding up the run. Besides, it's not big enough."

"It is big enough, Harry. The TV news has Noah Franklin's killer being caught after a car chase this afternoon. But I have the whole story. Franklin was murdered because he discovered he was being used by a drug ring. And Ricky Simms was killed because he saw the men who murdered Franklin. And the head of the ring is Gerald Barnes!"

"Are you sure about that?"

"Yes! I found evidence that implicates him in Noah Franklin's murder."

"Good grief, Montgomery. If you needed more time, why didn't you call us before?"

"I'm sorry, Harry, I wasn't able to call."

"I'll try to track down Rosemary—"

"Better go straight to Walter. This is more his area."

"I don't know, Lane—"

"Just try. We've got to get the story to print, because the *Metropolitan* has got it for sure."

"How do you know that?"

"S-Sources," I stuttered.

"I'll go look for Walter. You. Get in here right now!"

I didn't bother to say goodbye. At that moment, a cab rounded the corner not ten yards from me and headed my direction. I threw the phone down and ran into the middle of the street. The cab slammed on its brakes, the driver cursing at me until he realized I was a fare.

I wrote my article in the cab on scrap paper out of my camera case. When the cab stopped in front of the paper, I threw money at the driver and, without waiting for change, hightailed it up to my office. Harry met me at my office door.

"Lane—"

I could see it on his face. "Don't tell me, Harry."

He shook his head. "They're already running it."

I grabbed his shoulders. "No, Harry, make them stop!"

"I can't make them stop."

"But the *Metropolitan* has it!"

"We have it too, they said."

"What? How can we have the story?!"

"We don't have what you have, or what the *Metropolitan* must have, but we covered it."

"What are you talking about?"

The way Harry hesitated, I knew this was going to hurt. "We sent Tiffany down to write something up."

I exploded. "Tiffany? Tiffany, the intern?! Tiffany, the 'I'd-rather-go-to-the-Gay-Rights-Parade-than-the-Circus' Tiffany? Harry!"

"We had to send her, Lane. We spent too long trying to track you down. We had to send somebody!"

"And she wrote the article?"

"Yeah. It's small. She read the police sheets, called the station—"

"She wrote it from the sheets!" I slapped my forehead. "Harry, Harry. Make them stop the presses—"

"Nobody does that. This is real life—"

"But this is a scoop! This is a blockbuster!"

"As far as the paper is concerned, we've got the story. Tiffany gave it to them. We can print your article in the afternoon edition."

"The afternoon edition! We won't be the story then! We'll be the story after the story—"

"That will be fine."

"I'll go talk to Walter myself." I started to leave, but Harry caught my arm.

"Lane, it's too late."

"But I've got it, Harry! Gerald Barnes is the head of a huge drug ring in Louisville and was directly involved in the deaths of Noah

187

Franklin and Ricky Simms."

The click of high heels rounded the corner and Rosemary entered the room, stopping and crossing her arms. "Are you still ranting about Gerald Barnes? Because if you're implicating Gerald Barnes in something, you're going to pass it by Legal first."

"Rosemary," I ran over to her, "make them stop the presses!"

Rosemary looked at Harry, then back at me. "Good grief, Lane. This isn't the movies. People don't do that."

"But I've got the whole story. This is front page!"

Rosemary sighed. "This is not front page, Lane. This is just—"

"I know." I glared at her. "Just another inner-city killing."

Rosemary looked at Harry. "Harry, I'm glad you can handle her. I can't stand the ego." She turned to go.

I caught her arm. "But, you've got to stop the presses."

She smirked. "Lane—we don't stop the presses just so you can have your name on the front page again—"

"Get Walter. Go get him. I'll show you what I've got, then he can decide."

"What have you got?"

"Pictures."

"So?"

"Not just any pictures. I've got Gerald Barnes walking Noah Franklin to his death."

Rosemary and Harry both looked at me like I'd lost my mind. Finally, Harry spoke.

"Lane, what are you telling us? That's not possible. Noah Franklin was murdered before you even started on this story."

"I know."

"Where are these pictures?"

"Right here in my camera."

"That's impossible."

"It's not impossible. I've got them. I worked it out with the police already. Call the Louisville Police Department. If they have Barnes in custody by now, we can print them. And go get Walter."

Rosemary and Harry stared at each other. I grabbed my camera case and ran for the darkroom. Behind me, I could hear Rosemary on the phone trying to track down Walter.

Half an hour later I walked into Rosemary's office. Harry and Walter were there with Rosemary. I stopped and threw the photos onto the desk in front of her. Rosemary's eyes widened. "Oh, my God," she said. "Somebody get the LPD on the phone."

Chapter Fourteen

They didn't stop the presses for me, of course. They ran my photos and stories in the afternoon edition. That was a weird day anyway. Everyone at the paper got really nuts when I set off the smoke detector in my office. It wasn't my fault, though.

I was burning a copy of the morning edition of the *Metropolitan Inquirer*, the one with the exclusive interview with Trina Garby and the byline of Ann Alexander. I needed a container to burn the newspaper in, and the pot that I kept my dead plant in seemed like a good choice. Unfortunately, the paper caught the dead plant on fire and that sort of got out of control. Then after they brought the fire extinguisher in, I couldn't get the smoke alarm to turn off until I stood on my desk and knocked it off the ceiling with my stapler. Cheap smoke detectors.

My photos did create a rather big stir, however, even for the afternoon edition. You see, the morning I called Trina Garby's dad at five a.m., I was puzzling over how Barnes had gotten Noah Franklin to the cellar of Ricky's apartment building. Then I remembered that the building where Barnes' rented office space—the building where I had shot pictures of Ann that afternoon—was a high security building. I had spotted the security cameras in Barnes' office that day. When I walked into the lobby the morning before my meeting with Trina's dad, I was checking the walls for video cameras. I saw them everywhere, so that's why I'd talked to the security guy. He dug out the tapes for me from the night of Noah Franklin's murder, and we spent an hour or so fast-forwarding through them until, lo and behold, I spotted Gerald Barnes himself escorting Noah Franklin from the building.

Franklin's expression was so strained I asked the security officer for the tapes from other cameras, which had different views. Sure enough, in one angle that wouldn't have been seen by the security officer at his desk, Big Fat Gerald Barnes was clearly holding a pistol to Franklin's side.

The security officer and I called the police and then, with my camera, I took pictures of the TV screen with the video on pause—pictures

189

that included the security camera's image of the date and time of the video, less than one hour before Noah Franklin was murdered. When the police arrived, they gave me permission to print the photos once they had Barnes in custody. Those were the photos I had tossed on Rosemary's desk, when I missed the deadline.

Teresa Coleman didn't survive her wounds. Herbert Garby, however surprisingly, seems to be a really good father to Trina. He did care about his daughter after all; apparently the complicated emotions he felt for Teresa had kept him at a distance. I've already been in touch with Trina once since school started. She has joined the staff of her school paper.

The *Daily* ran my photos and articles about the drug ring and the murders as a package, with my profiles of Ricky, Lamont, and Trina on the inside. I titled the profiles "Three Stories from the City." I hadn't gotten the good-kid-in-the-city story I'd wanted in Ricky, of course, but I pointed out that despite Ricky's drug involvement, he had lost his life while trying to protect his friend, Trina. The good-kid-in-the-city story went to Lamont, who had dared to put himself at risk by steering me to David Case. Lamont had the brains and the courage to go places in his life. I hoped that my article about him might somehow help boost him toward his goals.

Two days after the story broke, as I was down on my hands and knees trying to pick the glass out of my bedroom carpet, my landlady stopped by. For some reason she implied I might be posing a risk to the other tenants and asked me to move out. She said I could leave my things here until the end of the month, but she thought it would be better if I stayed somewhere else. I started to call my grandmother to see if I could live with her for a few days. Then, I realized, maybe it was time to call home.

I picked up the phone and punched in the numbers. Dad answered.

"Hi, it's me," I said.

"Who is this?" He was teasing, but there was an edge of sarcasm to his voice.

"Dad, c'mon…"

"Gee, the voice sounds familiar—"

"Dad!" I was starting to get angry. He hadn't called me either. I decided to cut to the chase. "I was wondering if I could move back in for a few days."

There was an almost stunned silence on the other end. I knew what was coming. It was bad enough having a gay daughter, but to

190

have her living in the same house with you? No way.

"That would be great!" His enthusiasm was genuine. "I'll tell your mother! But why?"

For a moment I was speechless. The cold, clenched fist in my chest began to warm. "I had a little incident at my apartment—a little crisis associated with my career, I guess you would call it—and my landlady is throwing me out. And I... I need a place to stay until I can find an apartment that doesn't ask for references."

There was a pause, and then he began to laugh—a deep, warm, infectious laugh. Soon I was laughing, too. It will just be for a week or so. I'm hoping it will be a good thing. Maybe we'll start talking like old times again. At least my grandmother will be proud of me for trying. The biggest challenge will be keeping the conversation away from politics and religion.

My car was totaled. The money the insurance agency gave me might buy me a good ten-speed. Since I haven't bought the bike yet, I'm trying to do investigative reporting on the bus schedule. Ann seems to be doing well, though. Apparently there were rumors that an Indianapolis paper was trying to snatch her up, so to give her an incentive to stay, her paper presented her with a new car.

I did hear from Ann. She dropped by the evening of the day our stories came out—right after I set my office on fire. Stopping just outside my door, she frowned. "Have you been toasting marshmallows in here?" she asked.

She was wearing a dark tailored pinstripe pantsuit with heels. The jacket was one of those that is worn without a blouse underneath, and the collar plunged right down to here without looking the least bit cheap or even inappropriate for the office. I don't know how she pulls it off. I took a breath. "Just a little accident. It was nothing."

She walked on into my office and leaned her lithe body against the doorframe. "I thought I'd take you to dinner. We can celebrate."

I was still furious that she'd beaten me to the cab and made her morning edition. I stepped around my desk to face her, my arms crossed. "I don't think so."

"Then I'll kidnap you. I'll take you to dinner and force-feed you lobster. Then if you enjoy it, it won't be your fault."

I couldn't help smiling, but snuffed it out quickly. "Look Ann—"

"You've heard, haven't you?" She stepped closer, her hands in her pockets.

"What?"

"You should turn on the radio. Or the TV. Every station in the city is talking about the reporter from the *Louisville Daily* who dug up the evidence that brought down a drug ring."

"Really?" I asked.

"Lane, the photos were sensational!" she said. "You don't have a paper left in the racks anywhere in the city!"

"Yeah, but," I couldn't help it. "You beat me to the story."

"Yes," she agreed. "But you got Barnes! Not me. That's what everyone's talking about! And they've got a search warrant for David Case's apartment. You and I both know the bullet that killed Noah Franklin will match David Case's gun."

"Yeah, I guess so." My spirits were starting to lift.

She was standing closer to me now. She reached down and took my hands. "So let's celebrate! Go to dinner with me! Let's have a date!"

I was smiling despite myself, but I shook my head. "Ann—"

She frowned. "I know what you're afraid of, Lane. I know, because..." she hesitated, "...I'll admit it. I'm afraid of it, too." Ann watched my face carefully as she spoke. "You're afraid that if you let me get too close to you, you're going to lose your competitive edge. That's it, isn't it? Because you live for the front page." She looked me steadily in the eyes. "Well? I'm right, aren't I?"

I didn't answer.

She shook her head. "I'm just asking you to dinner, Lane. I'm not asking you to give up your career. So, what do you say? Italian? Or lobster?"

I started to argue, but she leaned forward and met my argument with a warm, lingering kiss.

"Then tomorrow," she whispered in my ear reassuringly, "we can be mortal enemies again."

I smiled. I could do dinner tonight. Tomorrow, however, would be a whole new game.